MONTANA
Mavericks:

Welcome to Whitehorn, Montana—
the home of bold men and daring women.
A place where rich tales of passion
and adventure are unfolding under the Big Sky.
Seems that this charming little town has some mighty
big secrets. And everybody's talking about...

Baby Jennifer: Ruthlessly kidnapped from her new family, this adorable child hasn't had an easy life. Now neither do her parents...

Sterling and Jessica McCallum: The happiness they find as man and wife—and the joy they discover as parents—is destroyed with the disappearance of their daughter. Now they place their faith in...

Clint Calloway: This veteran lawman never would have dreamed that trailing a kidnapper would mean unlocking his own past. And he certainly couldn't have anticipated his feelings toward his beautiful new partner...

Dakota Winston: No matter how Clint feels about rookies—or women—she isn't about to shy away from the biggest case to hit Whitehorn. She's hot on the trail for answers. And she has her suspicions about a certain little librarian...

Mary Jo Kincaid: She is on the verge of securing her fortune when a tiny little hitch fouls her plans. Her secrets aren't so safe anymore—including her connection to a man who has spent his life wreathed in mystery....

Rafe Rawlings: After a lifetime as "Wolf Boy," this rugged detective is about to learn the truth ab...
are better left hidden—som...

Lexine Baxter: The town bac...
the skies above Montana. O...

RACHEL LEE

wrote her first play in the third grade for a school assembly, and by the age of twelve she was hooked on writing. She's lived all over the United States, and now resides in Florida.

Having held jobs as a security officer, real estate agent and optician, she uses these, as well as her natural flair for creativity, to write stories that are undeniably romantic.

Rachel Lee has garnered numerous industry awards. In 1991 she earned the *Romantic Times* Award for Best Series Romance and in 1993 she won the *Romantic Times* Reviewer's Choice Award for Best Romantic Suspense, as well as landing a Romance Writers of America RITA Award nomination.

Rachel Lee

Cowboy Cop

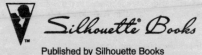

Published by Silhouette Books

America's Publisher of Contemporary Romance

Special thanks and acknowledgment to Rachel Lee
for her contribution to the MONTANA MAVERICKS series.

For Cris

SILHOUETTE BOOKS

ISBN 0-373-61734-8

COWBOY COP

One

"We have to *work* together. You don't have to *like* me."

Clint Calloway didn't even glance up when Dakota Winston spoke. His attention remained fixed on the small piles of matchsticks in front of him, and on the street below his window. She might have been talking to a deaf man.

"Look, Clint, it's apparent you don't like having me for your partner," she continued earnestly. "I guess I can understand that. You're an experienced detective and I'm just a rookie." A *female* rookie. The unspoken adjective, seemed to vibrate in the air.

He still didn't respond, just reached out with one blunt fingertip to move a matchstick across the blotter on his desk, placing it in another group. Dakota had been watching him do that periodically since they had started working together two days ago. She couldn't imagine what he was doing with those matchsticks, and when she asked, he wouldn't answer. All she knew for certain was that the end of each of them had been painted a different color. It was clear to her that they represented something, but he wasn't going to enlighten her. That was just another of the man's frustrating characteristics, and he had quite a few of them.

The matchstick, tipped in red, joined a different pile. Then Clint turned his head a fraction of an inch and studied the street to his left. His cubicle was in a corner of the police station and had two windows, the one in front of him overlooking Center Avenue, the other overlooking

Coyote Path. Dakota figured that absolutely nothing on this corner of Whitehorn, Montana, escaped Clint Calloway's attention. Not that too terribly much seemed to happen down there. Leaning forward a little, she looked over his shoulder at the dress shop, the beauty salon, the sagging McManus Hotel and the Dogie Diner. Other shops and vacant storefronts were visible, stretching along both streets for a block or two, until the residential areas began. Nothing out there to hold anyone's attention for long.

"Look," she said to Clint's back, "I'm a fast learner. Just tell me what you want me to do and I'll do it. If I mess up, I want to hear that, too. I really want to be a good cop."

Not even that drew a response. Her sense of frustration was overwhelming, but there didn't seem to be a thing she could do about it. If this man didn't speak a single word to her throughout the time they were paired, she'd just have to live with it. She had too much to prove and was too new at this business to make a stink about anything a respected veteran detective might do. If she complained, she'd be labeled a pain in the neck, never mind that it was Clint who was being the pain.

So she bit back any further words and tried to find another way to handle this. The only thing she could come up with was to shut her mouth and try to be the best damn cop this guy had ever worked with. It was a tall order for a rookie, and she knew it, but he sure wasn't leaving her any other alternatives.

The seconds dragged by. He moved another matchstick. Then, slowly, he turned his head a little and asked, "Are you through?"

Her cheeks heated. "Yes."

"Then let's get some things clear here. I don't like you. I'm not *going* to like you. You can work your butt off trying to be a good cop, but you aren't going to make it. Women shouldn't be cops. They get too tangled up in their feelings and mess things up. This job calls for a cool head, not emotional reactions to everything.''

''I—''

He cut her off ruthlessly. ''I've been listening to your drivel, now you can listen to mine. What I think about women cops doesn't matter. Fact is, I got saddled with you because you're a rookie and need supervision and I have to put up with it or get fired. So I'm stuck with you and you're stuck with me. Just keep your mouth shut, do what I tell you and stay out of my way.''

Anger blossomed inside her, but it was tempered by the fact that she had already suspected these were his feelings. Getting them out in the open this way merely saved her from having to wonder about it. He was a male chauvinist. Fine. He wasn't the first she'd met and he wouldn't be the last. If his objection to her was simply that she was a woman, she could handle it, and prove him wrong in the process. She certainly wasn't going to slink away with her tail tucked between her legs.

''Great,'' she managed to say steadily. ''I prefer to know where I stand.''

''Now you know.'' His voice was deep and as rough as gravel, which suited his appearance. Built solidly, he looked tough, invincible, like the kind of guy you'd want beside you in a fight. She'd heard he'd earned that toughness as a kid on the wrong side of the tracks. She could only imagine what that must have been like for him, but she was willing to excuse some rough edges as a result of it.

His gray-green eyes were stormy as they raked over her, and she found herself thinking that he had the raw, ragged good looks of a successful alley cat. There were faint scars on his knuckles, mementos of any number of fistfights, she supposed, and his nose had an interesting little bend in it, probably from contact with someone's fist. An old scar bisected one of his dark eyebrows, giving him a satiric appearance.

The look he gave her was distinctly male, that of a man measuring a woman and evaluating her sexual attributes. Dakota had received plenty of those looks in her life and had learned to ignore them, but this time she felt an almost overwhelming urge to fold her arms across her breasts. Instead she pressed her fingertips into the sides of her thighs and resisted the urge to clench her hands into fists. Act relaxed, she told herself. Don't let this guy know he can get to you.

Evidently it worked. His gray-green eyes became hooded and he looked toward his desk. He pointed to a stack of thick manila folders. "These are our open cases. Start reading."

"I thought we were supposed to be looking for Jennifer McCallum's kidnapper."

He made an impatient sound. "The kid was kidnapped a week ago. We haven't a damn thing to go on. No ransom demand has been made, and nobody saw a thing. Rule of thumb is that after forty-eight hours the trail is ice and the kid's chances are slim. If we're going to accomplish anything at all now, we have to use our brains, Ms. Winston. If you have one, familiarize it with the case."

"Why you son of a—" She caught herself and bit the word off, glaring at him.

"If you can't stand the heat, get back in the kitchen." He pointed again to the stack of files. "Start reading all the unsolved cases. You'll be no damn good to me if you're not ready to work on any of them when opportunities arise."

He swiveled his chair back to face his desk, pointedly dismissing her. Dakota clamped down on her anger, her teeth clenched so tightly that her jaw ached. Keeping her movements deliberate so as not to reveal the depth of her anger, she picked up the stack of files and carried them to her desk. Two days with Detective Clint Calloway and she was ready to commit murder. She wondered what she'd be ready to do in another couple of days. Wipe out the entire station?

But at her own desk, away from the source of her anger, she calmed down swiftly and began to think. She couldn't keep on getting this upset by his provocation or she was going to seriously mess up...which was probably what he was hoping for. Once she messed up, he'd be justified in asking that she be assigned to someone else.

And while that might be a whole lot more comfortable, the bottom line was that she didn't want to mess up, and she wanted to work with Clint Calloway. He had a reputation for being a maverick, a not quite by-the-book and almost psychically talented investigator. That meant he knew tricks she wanted to learn, that he had a way of viewing problems that could be really useful for her to know. Skills that could someday set her apart the way Clint Calloway was set apart. She always was driven to be the best at anything she attempted.

So she had to hang on to her temper and endure whatever hazing he gave her. She had to prove to everyone that she had what it took, sort of a trial by fire. She'd expected some of this, of course. Women cops weren't rare by any means these days, but they still weren't entirely welcome, and would probably never be welcomed at all by some policemen. She'd suffered from some of that attitude at the academy, and even a little of it in college when her classmates in criminal justice had learned of her desire to join law enforcement. She'd certainly suffered from it during her two years with the Miles City force. Clint Calloway was just a more blatant expression of an outdated attitude. She could handle it. She could handle *him*.

Reaching out, she snagged the first file and began to read about the abduction of a three-year-old child named Jennifer.

Sometimes, thought Clint Calloway, he was positively sure that the gods hated him. There could be absolutely no other reason why he had found himself saddled with both an unsolvable kidnapping and a female partner within the short space of a week.

The "Baby Jennifer" kidnapping—as everyone in Whitehorn was referring to it—ought to be enough karma for one man. He shouldn't be forced to sit here, staring out a window at the quiet street below, wondering what awful fate had befallen a little girl with a cherub's face. He shouldn't have to sit here and bear the weight of responsibility for finding her when he hadn't a clue as to what had happened to her.

The whole damn thing was gnawing at his guts with a persistence that was keeping him up most of the night. Terrible things happened to sweet little girls in this awful world, and well he knew it. The scariest thing was that there had been no ransom demand. The kidnapping had followed so fast on the heels of the discovery that Jennifer was the illegitimate child of rich old Jeremiah Kincaid that it was impossible to believe she had been taken for any other reason. But no ransom had been demanded, no attempt had been made to contact the child's distraught adoptive parents.

And then, to make the kidnapping even more horrible— as if it weren't already just about the most horrible thing that could be—the police had been told by an attorney that Baby Jennifer wouldn't have inherited a dime. Jeremiah's estate had long since been settled in probate, and left at his direction to his son Dugin. "After-discovered heirs," as the lawyer had described the little girl, had no claim at this late date. Clint himself was one of those "after-discovered heirs" of Jeremiah Kincaid, and the news had given him a blessed sense of relief. Bad enough to find out that his unknown father had been someone he had loathed all his life, without finding himself the recipient of any of the old man's wealth. Bad enough to have to live down all the looks and all the speculation *again*. Seemed like he'd been doing that his entire life.

But little Jennifer was another problem, and the lack of inheritance raised some thorny questions about her fate. If someone *had* kidnapped her, thinking she stood to inherit, why hadn't he or she—they—demanded any money? Had they found out the little girl had no claim? The possibility made Clint's stomach knot, because then Jennifer would be useless to them, and they might well have killed her.

For at least the hundredth time in the past week, he wished Jeremiah Kincaid were still alive so he could get his hands around the old reprobate's throat. Somebody should have castrated that man fifty years ago.

But nobody had, so little Jennifer McCallum had been kidnapped. At least Clint was presuming that to be the motivation. Somebody with a grudge against Jennifer's adoptive parents might have conceived of this, too. Her father, Sterling McCallum, being a police officer and a damn fine detective, certainly had his share of enemies. But a revenge motive seemed farfetched compared to greed. If someone had wanted revenge on McCallum, shooting him would have made more sense than this.

But then who said a bad guy had to make sense?

Clint looked down at the matchsticks on the desk before him, but saw no useful pattern in them. It wasn't the first time he'd had the feeling that something more than met the eye was going on in this county, but so far he hadn't a single fact to substantiate it.

His big mistake, he found himself thinking, was wanting to be a detective. He should have stayed in uniform. At least then he'd had the satisfaction of a quick solution to most of the problems he had encountered. Now…now cases dragged on for months or years, and some never got solved.

And then there was Dakota Winston. Yep, the gods must hate him. Had she been anyone else, he'd have been glad to spend time with her. She was a beautiful young woman, with a delicate appearance that made an enticing contrast to her straightforward manner. All feminine without any of the affectations that drove him nuts, she had dark hair and blue eyes, the bluest, most attention-grabbing eyes he'd ever seen. She was probably a great date and a fantastic lay…but he absolutely did not want her for a partner.

In the first place, she hadn't been a cop all that long and she'd only hired on in Whitehorn two months before her promotion to detective. Clint had a sneaking suspicion that her family's influence had had something to do with her quick promotion. The Montana Winstons, he had learned long ago, weren't afraid to buy what they wanted. Oh, the sheriff, Judd Hensley, wasn't a man who could be bought, but he *was* a politician, and politicians had a slightly different view of things than career cops did. Still, Clint didn't hold Judd responsible, except for not putting his foot down about it. The promotion committee that made the decision to make Dakota Winston a detective took the full blame for this one, but Judd *could* have flatly refused to approved the placement. Which he hadn't.

So Clint was saddled with a relatively inexperienced

partner, and he honestly couldn't decide which was going to be worse—the fact that she was a woman or the fact that she was inexperienced. Either one was a liability.

He was aware that his attitude wasn't politically correct, but he didn't give a damn. Women looked at things differently. An investigator had to be objective, and women tended to be too damn emotional. Emotion could blind you to important clues or slow you down, two serious handicaps.

Then there was the question of why a woman became a cop, anyway. Some of them wanted to be men, and to his way of thinking they were less trouble than the others. The others were just cop crazy—drawn to the badge and the gun not so much for themselves, but because they wanted to be surrounded by men who wore a badge and a gun.

He figured Dakota Winston had to be one of the latter group, because there was sure nothing about her that suggested she was a tomboy. Nope, she had to be cop crazy; no other explanation sufficed. A woman with her background and money didn't *need* to work this hard to make a living, so she was probably drawn to the men. Hell, every cop knew that some women were just turned on by the uniform. You didn't have to pass out very many speeding tickets to discover that.

That assessment, while seeming so obvious to him, left him feeling uneasy. It didn't fit Dakota, somehow.

Nor did it matter, he told himself harshly a couple of minutes later, when no other explanation for the woman surfaced. It didn't matter why she was a cop or what she thought she could get out of it. All that mattered was that he was saddled with her until she screwed up or hell froze over. Either one couldn't happen soon enough.

Clint's landlady, Mrs. Preston, was waiting in the yard for him when he got home that evening. Something about the way the eighty-year-old woman's arms were folded told him she was angry about something. He almost smiled as memory carried him back twenty-five years to a time when she had been chasing him around the yard with a broom, trying to keep him out of her apple trees. More than once she'd folded her arms just that way and scowled at him, telling him that he was going to come to no good.

Well, he'd turned out better than anyone had expected, and now, instead of chasing him out of her yard, she was waiting impatiently for his return. He pulled up the driveway and parked beside her car. By the time he'd turned off the ignition and climbed out, she had almost reached him.

"Something wrong?" he asked.

"Just come take a look out back, Clint." She shook her head. "I thought you were bad, trying to steal those apples, but I'm sure that never in all your days would you have done something like this!"

"Kids?" he asked as he followed her frail figure around to the back of the white clapboard house.

"Must be. Who else would do that?" She waved dramatically with one bony hand, and Clint stopped dead in his tracks.

There were nearly two dozen apple trees in the backyard orchard, trees that only a few weeks ago had been covered in delicate white blooms. Yesterday Clint had walked under them with Mrs. Preston, admiring the tiny green apples that grew in healthy profusion. Now it appeared that many of the tiny fruits were littering the ground, as if boys had used them in a game of war.

He muttered an oath, ignoring her disapproving cluck. Having lived with her for several years now, he knew just how much time and money she put into those trees in order to keep them healthy and productive. And each year she turned those apples into many delicious things that she shared with her neighbors, everything from green-apple pie to applesauce and apple jelly. Hell, even when he'd been ten and she'd often had to chase him out of her orchard, she had just as often treated him to a baked apple or a piece of pie.

"You're right," he heard himself say. "All I ever wanted was to snatch a few to eat. This is—" He broke off and shook his head.

"Nasty," she said sharply. "Just plain and simple nasty. No reason on earth to do this except to make an old lady mad."

"When did it happen?" he asked Mrs. Preston.

"It must have been this morning, when I was over to the church helping Molly Rafferty clean the parish hall for the wedding Saturday. Do you know, that nice Mary Jo Kincaid was there, too, helping out. Poor woman, with all she's been through I can't imagine how she can still find it in her to be helping others. 'Course, I suppose it helps to keep busy since her husband died...." She trailed off and shook her head. "That family's cursed, don't you think?"

"Seems like it the past few years, doesn't it?" Not that he cared. The Kincaid clan could burn in hell, where most of 'em belonged. He supposed the clan included him now, like it or not, but that was a piece of news he hadn't yet dealt with. And maybe he never would. It was a hell of a thing to discover your unknown father hadn't been dead while you were growing up. Hadn't even been on the far side of the planet. Instead he'd been a couple of miles up the road and had simply ignored you for thirty-odd years. At this late date it didn't even pay to get angry, so Clint brushed the thought aside like an annoying gnat, the way he'd been brushing it aside since the first shock had passed.

"Well, I don't know how much I can do about this,

Martha," he told Mrs. Preston. "It must've been kids probably using the apples as ammunition. I can keep my ear to the ground and see if anyone brags about it, but otherwise I doubt we'll find the culprits."

She nodded in understanding, her head trembling slightly on the delicate stalk of her neck. "I didn't think there was much you could do, but I needed to complain about it, anyway. Guess I'll have to buy most of my apples this year. Well, it won't be the first time."

He watched her walk back to the house and wondered how a kid could think a prank like this was amusing. Victimizing an elderly woman this way was sheer meanness, and if he found out who had done it, the culprit was going to hear from him. Clint spent a few more minutes in the orchard looking for clues, but found nothing. The ground was heavily mulched and it hadn't rained recently, so there wasn't even a good footprint to be found.

Turning, he headed back to the old bunkhouse he was renting from Martha Preston. Her place was on the outskirts of town. Once a huge ranch, the property had dwindled to a few acres as the family sold it off. Within sight were the Crazy Mountains, looking dark as the day began to fade.

Up and down the road other homes stood on lots an acre or two in size. Many of them were trailers, intended to be only temporary until their owners could construct a house. Many kids lived nearby, and plenty more closer to town. Clint had been one of them, growing up a half mile from here, near the railroad station. On summer afternoons he'd gotten up to his share of mischief, some of it here.

But for all that folks around here had believed he was destined for prison, he'd never once pulled a prank as vicious as this one. Whoever had ruined the apple crop might as well have broken into the house and taken some of Martha Preston's most prized possessions. Though Clint hadn't known it when he'd been a kid trying to swipe some of the fruit, these apple trees were the woman's pride and joy. Temperatures sometimes dropped beneath forty below zero, cold enough to kill the trees, but she burned smudge pots to protect them. Other times the snow would come after the trees blossomed—all too often in this place where summer was sometimes interrupted by sudden bursts of winter. All that care and love over the years had made those trees almost as important to Martha as her children, now scattered all over the state.

The sun sank behind Crazy Peak, casting the world into the abrupt twilight of the mountains. Clint unlocked the door of the bunkhouse and stepped inside, into a rough-hewn world where he could be completely private.

It was hard to explain to someone who hadn't grown up as he had just how much that privacy could mean. He'd been asked numerous times over the years, usually by women, if he wasn't lonely. But he wasn't. Loneliness was a state of mind, and not one he had time for. As a kid, he'd have given almost anything to be alone sometimes. His mother had never quite managed to make enough money to provide a place of their own, so they had always lived in someone else's house or apartment, usually made to feel unwelcome and grudgingly granted a spot on the floor somewhere. Clint had had no place to be alone, no place sacred to himself. His meager possessions had always been vulnerable to prying eyes, and he'd learned early that if he ever treasured anything, someone else's child would claim it. Clint wouldn't be able to complain or protest, because he and his mom might get thrown out onto the street. So he had had nothing.

But here in this rustic bunkhouse he could be utterly and blessedly alone. If he wanted to leave yesterday's clothes lying around on the floor, he could, without worrying that he might lose the roof over his head. Here he could have secrets, and possessions that were touched by no hands but his own. Never again would he allow his privacy to be violated by anyone.

He changed swiftly out of the gray suit he'd worn that day and into battered jeans, a white Western shirt so old it had become as soft as silk and his custom-made cowboy boots. Now he was home.

In the small kitchen, where he'd tiled the counters and refinished the floor, he heated up some chili in the microwave. While it cooked, he prepared a tossed salad, making the inevitable comparison to his childhood, when meals had been scanty and poorly balanced…when he'd had one at all. He'd never had a salad until he was in the army. Now he couldn't imagine a meal without one. Yep, he'd come a long way.

While he ate, he tried to read a news magazine, but kept losing his focus. He couldn't stop thinking about Jennifer's kidnapping. He'd seen the little girl once or twice around town or with Sterling, her father. She'd been pretty, lively and full of laughter, and it made his gut twist to think someone might steal that laughter from her. Bad things shouldn't happen to kids. He knew from bitter experience that they did, but that didn't make it acceptable.

Finally he gave up pretending to read, rinsed his dishes and headed for his desk in a corner of the front room. There he often put in as much time and effort as he did during the day, working on cases that wouldn't let go of him. The kidnapping was one of them. For the last week he'd sat here night after night, trying to see some rhyme or reason in what little they knew, any clue that might help him figure out where the child was.

Turning on the desk lamp, he looked down at the little piles of matchsticks he had left there last night, when he'd been too tired to stare at them any longer. Still no pattern leapt out of them, and for an instant Clint felt an urge to sweep them all aside in anger.

Instead he flipped the light switch and reached for his jacket. He was not going to sit around here tonight brooding. Not again.

Moments later he was heading back into town.

Dakota Winston realized too late that she had made a mistake. Coming over to the Sundowner Saloon with some of the uniforms had seemed like a politic thing to do. Unfortunately, a bunch of them had just walked out, and she was now stuck in a dark booth with two men she didn't particularly like who had already had a few beers too many. She'd been a cop long enough to know she was in a potentially dangerous situation.

A quick scan of the room didn't reassure her. There were only two other women present, and they didn't look like churchgoing types. The men who filled the place were getting louder and more boisterous as the beer and whiskey went down.

"I need to be going now," she told Hank Rostow and Phil Loomis.

"Aw, what's the hurry?" Rostow complained from across the table. Loomis, who was sitting beside her and had her hemmed in, didn't move an inch.

"No hurry," she said, as pleasantly as she could manage when her skin was beginning to crawl. "I just have to meet a friend."

"A guy friend," Rostow said.

"Yeah. A guy friend." She smiled and turned to Loomis. "Can you let me out, Phil?"

"Not so fast," Rostow said. "It's not often we get to have beer with a pretty lady." Phil didn't even look at her.

"It won't be often at all if you make me late for my date." Dakota tried to say it with a laugh, but something in Rostow's expression made her think he was aware of her anxiety and was enjoying it. Her scalp began to prickle.

"What do you need a date for? You got the two of us. We're better than anybody else, ain't we, Phil?"

"Yeah."

"I'm sure you are," Dakota answered, keeping her smile firmly in place. Despite the constriction of the booth, she half stood. "But I need to go anyway. I keep my promises."

"She keeps her promises." Rostow mimicked her unpleasantly. "Lady's got too big for her britches now she's a detective, Phil. Too good for the flatfoots."

"Probably can't remember what it was like to have a nightstick," Loomis answered.

"Probably can't," Rostow agreed.

Loomis eased a bit closer on the bench. "You remember what a nightstick feels like?" he asked, his eyes drifting up and down over her body in an almost possessive way.

"I remember what it sounds like when one cracks against a skull," Dakota answered, immediately regretting her quick tongue. "Look, I really gotta go." Her mind was working at lightning speed, trying to determine the fastest way out of here. If she threatened these guys in any way, they might decide to teach her a lesson. If she didn't leave quickly, though, they'd take it as a come-on. "Let me out, Phil." If he didn't right this instant, she was going to climb over the table.

Phil didn't budge. She opened her mouth to try one last time, because fleeing across the table would probably constitute an irresistible provocation to these guys. But just then a familiar, rough voice intervened.

"Damn it, Dakota," said Clint Calloway, "when you say you're going to meet me, I expect you to be on time!"

There was no one else on earth she'd have been less happy to see just then, but the Fates weren't paying attention. Clint Calloway was riding to her rescue even though she'd have given almost anything to be able to tell him to get lost.

But she had enough sense not to do that. Escape had been offered, and she grabbed it. "Sorry. I got…tied up." She eased to the side and Phil moved swiftly out of the booth, setting her free.

Clint nodded to the two men who had just been tormenting her. "See you guys around." Then he motioned toward the door and followed Dakota out of the saloon.

"Damn it, woman," he growled as soon as they were outside, "what the hell do you think you're doing going into a saloon with a couple of cretins like that?"

She turned to face him, already fighting mad, but he took her arm and kept walking briskly down the street. "I didn't go to the saloon with those two idiots," she said sharply. "A bunch of uniforms invited me to join them, but then everybody left and I got stuck with those two. They wouldn't let me leave."

"You're a damn fool. No woman in her right mind goes into a saloon like that!"

"Why not? Are you telling me that men can't be expected to behave like civilized human beings?"

His grip on her elbow tightened until it was almost painful, and he spoke from between gritted teeth. "I thought you had some experience as a uniformed cop!"

"I do!"

"Then don't tell me you don't know what can happen when a bunch of men have too much to drink!"

She did know, and it made her excuses seem all the

weaker. Still, she wasn't going to let Clint act as judge and jury on an indictment of foolishness without defending herself. "I went out to have a beer with my co-workers. Co-workers who are cops. They should know better."

They were around the corner now, and he stopped, blowing out a long, exasperated breath. Turning, he stared down at her with narrowed eyes. "I imagine you became a cop because you have all kinds of idealistic notions about helping people."

"That's why most people become cops."

"But not all." He leaned toward her. "Some people become cops because they get high on the power. Because they can carry a gun and order people around. Because they can make people afraid of them. Rostow and Loomis belong to that category. The line between either of them and a criminal is a damn fine one consisting of a single fact—they haven't been caught yet." He straightened and shook his head. "God deliver me from infants and rookies."

Dakota wanted to clobber him. The man was incredibly arrogant and intolerably patronizing. "Do you get off on ordering people around?"

As soon as she'd opened her mouth, she wanted to cut off her tongue. She wasn't easily intimidated—if she were, she wouldn't have survived this long as a cop. But it struck her even as she rebelled against his domination and patronization that it was never wise to rile a tiger. Clint Calloway didn't look like a man who would quickly forgive and forget, nor was it going to help their partnership if she kept annoying him.

He stared down at her now, his gaze narrowing even more. She wondered in the fleeting instant before he spoke if he was capable of resorting to violence, and knew that he probably was. A chill trickled down her spine.

"Are you always this stupid, Winston?" An instant later he stalked away down the dark street, leaving her alone with the night.

TWO

Dakota stared at Clint's retreating back, feeling as if she had just been kicked by a mule. Maybe she *had* spoken incautiously, but that certainly didn't excuse *him*. Was she going to stand here and let him get away with that?

She tore after him. He certainly must have heard her coming, but he didn't even glance back. When she caught up to him, she wanted to grab his arm and make him face her, but at the last second common sense took over and stopped her. Instead she forced herself to fall into step beside him and speak to his hard profile.

"I'm not stupid, Calloway."

"You couldn't prove it by me."

"Damn it!" Frustration caused her to halt and spin to face him. Some part of her was astonished when he paused, too. "I'm not stupid! Why don't you just give me a chance?"

"A chance to what? Compound your idiocy? You shouldn't have been in that bar alone with those guys. You should know better! Instead of saying you miscalculated, you argued with me about it! Then... Oh, hell, never mind."

He turned and resumed his angry march up the street.

Dakota trotted along beside him, disturbed by the feeling that they were talking at cross purposes. Perhaps she could have phrased her arguments differently. Perhaps he could have been less accusatory in his comments. In any case, things couldn't be left like this. They had to work together.

"I'm sorry," she said. "I guess I did sound as if I were arguing with you about going into the saloon. I wasn't, not really. You're right, it wasn't a safe place for me to be on my own, and I miscalculated when I trusted to the fact that they were all cops. The reason I got so hot was the way you talked to me. I don't like to be talked to as if I'm a fool."

"Then don't act like one," he said gruffly.

He was the most maddening, infuriating, arrogant s.o.b. it had ever been her misfortune to work with, she decided as she walked beside him. It was a wonder someone hadn't murdered him years ago. Certainly no wonder that he'd apparently never married. Seething inwardly, she forced herself not to say something that would cause more strife with this man. Finally, she managed to speak calmly. "I'm not acting like a fool. There's a world of difference between making a mistake and acting like a fool."

"Provoking me isn't smart."

She made an exasperated sound. "Damn it, Calloway, you riled me! You can't expect me to stand there and take it like a tongue-tied lamb!"

"You're a cop, aren't you? You gonna get riled like that whenever some crook gives you a hard time?"

She wanted to sink into the sidewalk. She wanted to kill him. She wanted to… Oh, hell, he was right, and that made her more furious than anything else he had said. She *was* a cop, and couldn't afford to get angry over remarks of any kind, let alone remarks as relatively innocuous as his. "This was different," she heard herself say.

"Different from what? Trying to arrest a perp? You mean it's okay to get riled with your partner? Sorry, Winston, it won't wash. You either have self-control or you don't. There's no middle ground."

"That's not true. People are freer in their reactions with close associates than they are with total strangers."

"I wouldn't have thought we were much past being total strangers."

There had to be some way to get around this, she thought miserably. Some way to get past his bad impression of her. But nothing immediately occurred to her. She wished she had bitten off her own tongue before she'd gotten sharp with him. He had come to her aid, and she should have had the common sense to just agree with his little lecture instead of arguing with him.

She wasn't ordinarily easy to rile, not that Clint would believe it now. A sigh escaped her as she continued to walk beside him. She had no idea where they were heading, nor did she particularly care. The only thing that really mattered was finding some way to salvage their partnership from this mess, because they were going to be walking together for a while. Possibly a long while.

She smothered another sigh and racked her brain for some way to ease the situation. Still nothing occurred to her, and she was just about to give up when Clint spoke.

"I've been thinking about the kidnapping."

In a flash, she forgot everything else. "Did you find something new?"

He shook his head. "There's nothing new to find. Somebody walked into the library in the middle of the afternoon and enticed a little girl away from the preschool story hour. What I can't understand is why no one noticed."

"Especially the person giving the story hour."

"Mary Jo Kincaid." He nodded his head, not so much in agreement as in acknowledgment.

"Well, she did have a lot of preschoolers on her hands. Fifteen or twenty, didn't she say?"

"Something like that. No, I'm not surprised she might have briefly lost track of some of the kids. It'd be really easy for one of the children to wander away from the story-telling group. What I can't understand is why nobody saw her being taken. Kids that age don't generally go happily with strangers, and besides, the McCallums have already given her the 'stranger' warnings."

"So somebody must have enticed her somehow."

"Seems like it. Even so, somebody at that damn library should have noticed something. It's not as if this kid weren't already well known. I think everyone in the county has heard that she's Kincaid's by-blow, and nearly everyone knows the McCallums. I can name three people who were there at the time of the abduction who *should* have noticed someone walking off with the kid. No one did."

"Which means they got her out surreptitiously."

Again he nodded. "It doesn't help a whole lot."

"Did you check all the ways out of there?"

He glanced down at her, but his face was unreadable in the dark. His voice, however, conveyed sarcasm. "It never occurred to me."

"Sorry."

"Didn't you read the damn file?"

"Of course I did. All that was legible. Someone needs to give you handwriting lessons, Calloway. Most of your notes haven't been typed up yet, and I couldn't make out a lot of it."

"You have some mouth, Winston."

"It's not the only one around here."

He shook his head and made a snorting sound. She couldn't tell if it was in anger or amusement. Anger, she decided. He seemed like an angry person.

"Yeah, I checked all the possible ways out of the library," he said. "I walked every one of them, trying to imagine what I'd do if I wanted to sneak a kid out of there."

"Nothing helpful?"

"Nope."

"Maybe I ought to check it out, too." As soon as she spoke, Dakota knew he wasn't going to like what she'd said. She was correct.

"You think I'm an idiot, Winston? You think your eyes are better than mine?"

"No, actually I don't. I'm just suggesting that maybe I should be as familiar with the setup as you are." It sounded good, but the truth was she didn't believe anybody, even the almighty Clint Calloway, was too good to occasionally miss something.

"Yeah," he said after a moment. "Guess it wouldn't hurt. We'll check it out in the morning."

Something happy bubbled up inside her, and she felt as if she had just won a major victory. Wisely, she reminded herself not to let it go to her head. Clint was still the same cantankerous male chauvinist he had been ten minutes ago. Maybe he was just throwing some kind of sop to her to shut her up? No. She refused to look at it that way. No point in imagining the worst.

"Thanks," she said.

"Don't thank me," he said roughly. "No law says you can't check it out on your own. I just want to be sure you don't miss something."

In two seconds flat he had her steaming mad at him. Again. "Damn it, Calloway, didn't you ever learn common courtesy?"

"Nope. My mother was too busy drinking, and I was too busy scrounging for food."

The words were hardly out before he clamped his teeth together with an audible snap. Turning abruptly, he strode rapidly away down a dark alley. He was furious at himself for telling her that, she realized. Furious for having revealed so much. An instant later she was running after him.

"Clint. Clint, wait!"

He didn't pause, just kept walking swiftly on long legs. Even when she caught up to him she had to nearly run to keep up with his pace.

"Look," she said, her breath choppy, "I'm sorry. I had no call to say what I said. Well, I did, but I shouldn't have said it anyway. Sometimes my temper gets the best of me."

Boy, this alley was dark, she found herself thinking as she continued to trot beside Clint, who was ignoring her as if she didn't exist. Businesses backed onto it, and their lights were out for the night. Even the street light at the end of the block.

Dakota wondered if Clint had noticed it at exactly the same moment, for he halted so suddenly she almost bumped into him.

"What?"

"Shh!"

It was evident even in the dim light that he was staring intensely off to the right. Rising on tiptoe, she tried to train her gaze in the same direction, wondering what he saw in the shadows beyond the sagging board fence that lined the alley. In the silence, as they waited, her heartbeat drummed loudly in her ears.

From the distance came a muffled sound of laughter, probably as someone opened the saloon door. The night wind was growing chillier, and Dakota shivered a little in her light jacket. A piece of paper skittered down the alleyway with a soft, scraping sound.

Clint tensed even more; she could feel it even though

she wasn't close enough to touch him. He must have heard or seen something. Squinting, she stared into the shadows and tried to see if anything was moving.

There was another scraping sound, of something not too heavy being dragged over the ground. She glanced up and saw Clint looking down at her. When their eyes met, he nodded, indicating with a gesture that he was moving down the alleyway and wanted her to stay here.

She nodded in turn, understanding that he wanted both ends of the alley blocked before they let whoever was in that yard become aware of them. Of course, she told herself as she watched Clint's lithe shadow slink down the alley, it might only be a cat.

But she didn't for a minute believe it. She'd been spooked by animals before on dark, lonely patrols. This hadn't sounded like an animal. It had sounded surreptitious. Stealthy. As if someone were aware that he was no longer alone.

Another sound, hardly more than a whisper on the night air, reached her. She couldn't tell what caused it; it was too faint. Nor could she see anything in the yard from which it seemed to have come. Except now, because she was staring so intently, all the shadows seemed to be moving—dark, shifting shapes, here and then gone when she moved her eyes just a little.

Blinking hard, she turned her attention down the alley and tried to pick out Clint's form. There he was, his hand a white blur as he motioned that he was going in.

Damn him! He'd left her up here, where the fence blocked her entry to where they suspected someone was lurking. Left her where she could hardly be of any use! Heck, if someone came running out of that yard down where Clint had entered, she wouldn't be able to see clearly enough to know who it was.

Turning, she scanned the alleyway on either side, looking for another place someone could easily escape from the fenced back lots. There were plenty of gates in the wood fences, but all appeared to be bolted shut.

Except for the one Clint had just passed through. That made her scalp prickle even more.

Moving swiftly but as quietly as she could, she hurried to the point where Clint had disappeared. A quick glance told the story: the padlock on this gate had been broken and dangled uselessly from the hasp. Someone was in there, and it was dollars to doughnuts they were up to no good. Why had Clint gone in alone?

The answer stared her in the face: he didn't trust her. Not even when he knew she'd been a patrol officer for two years now. He didn't believe her capable of performing the most routine of police tasks.

Damn him!

Reaching under her jacket, she pulled her 9 mm automatic from her belt holster and peered cautiously around the fence into the yard.

She couldn't see Clint now, nor could she hear anything to let her know where he was. Moving cautiously, she slipped around the corner of the gate and into the yard.

A big trash bin, nearly as tall as Dakota, blocked her view of everything to the right. Easing forward, she poked her head around the corner and saw that the yard was empty except for a pile of lumber against the fence.

The back door of the business stood wide open to the night, and inside was darkness. Clint had gone in there.

She hesitated a moment, biting her lower lip. He could get into serious trouble in that building. But if the perp came running out the back, she'd be in a better position to stop him if she waited here.

As she weighed her options, she wanted to castigate Clint

for his folly. He shouldn't have plunged ahead without talking it over with her. He should have taken the necessary sixty seconds to organize this. Instead he had dismissed her assistance, because she was a female. Boiling in oil was too good for that man!

But he was in there and she was his partner, and she had to do what she could to cover his back. Holding her pistol in both hands, she moved quietly across the yard, taking care to avoid any darker shadow that might be an obstacle. When she reached the back of the building, she began to ease her way along it to the open door.

And still she heard nothing at all. If someone was in there, he must know he'd been discovered. God, she hoped the noise had been made by a cat.

Silently, she slipped through the door and stood to one side, staring into the darkness.

It was like looking into a barrel of pitch. There was no light that she could see, no shapes or shadows to give anything substance. It looked as if one misstep would send her over the edge into an abyss of night.

Clint couldn't possibly be moving around in here. Not even with dark adaptation was there enough light to find your way around a strange place filled with obstacles. So where was he? What if he'd been hurt? What if someone had clobbered him the instant he'd set foot in here? Damn it, why had he left her all the way up the alley when she should have been here to help?

A sudden sound from within the building sent her heart climbing into her throat. It was a stealthy sound, as if someone were trying very hard to be quiet. If only she could see...

Just then a hand covered her mouth and an arm wrapped around her throat from behind. In a moment of blind panic, she lifted her gun, even though she knew it would do no good. Throw it into the darkness, some objective voice in her mind shouted. Throw the gun into the darkness before he wrestles it away from you!

"Damn it," someone whispered roughly in her ear as she struggled. "Didn't I signal you to stay in the alley?"

Clint! It was Clint. Relief poured through her, and she sagged. He didn't let go of her, but continued to whisper harshly in her ear.

"I could have killed you. Damn it, stay put! There's someone over there and I don't want you in the crossfire!"

She managed a nod, and he let go of her, leaving her to slump against the wall. Over the pounding of her heart, she heard a faint noise as he moved away from her. If the perp came this way, he'd be heading for the door and she could stop him. Beyond that, she'd gotten the message.

Stay put. It went against her grain to do nothing, but this time she followed directions, because to do otherwise would be truly foolhardy. It was too dark in here to see anything.

All of a sudden there was a crashing noise, as if a pile of tin buckets or bowls had fallen over, followed by the hammering of running feet. They were headed straight toward the door. Dakota readied herself, moving until she was only inches from the door frame. If the suspect came barreling through, she would stop him by the simple expedient of stepping in front of him...if she had to.

"Freeze!" Clint shouted. "Police!"

The footsteps hesitated, then resumed their sprint toward the door.

"I'll shoot," Clint warned.

Dakota stepped into the doorway, leveling her gun into the darkness. "Police!" she shouted. "Halt or I'll shoot!"

"Oh, God!" cried a frightened voice. Moments later, a

blur of pale white came to a halt in front of Dakota. "Don't shoot, lady. God, don't shoot!"

"Down on your knees," she commanded hoarsely. "Hands up where I can see them."

Rapid footsteps joined them, and she made out Clint in what little light came through the door. As the suspect knelt, Clint grabbed his wrists one at a time and cuffed them.

"What the hell were you doing in there?" Clint demanded.

"I know my rights, man." Now that there was no gun pointing at him, the youth could pretend bravery. "I don't have to tell you anything."

"I haven't arrested you yet, dirtwad. But you're under arrest now." Clint had been patting him down as he spoke and now hauled him to his feet. "Let's get this guy to the station."

The next couple of hours passed swiftly as the suspect, a fifteen-year-old named Roy Candela, was booked and the business owner was called in to verify damage.

"Well, punk," Clint said harshly to the young man after the owner had departed, "you're in for a little dose of reality now."

"Reality?" The kid laughed harshly. "What do you know about reality, man? Reality is a few rich guys have it all and the rest of us got nothing, not even enough to eat."

"Get a job."

"Right." The kid leaned forward, his dark eyes burning. "You need decent clothes to get a job, hotshot. Not dirty jeans with holes in the knees. You need to be able to take a bath sometimes…pretty damn hard to do when they shut off the water. You need—"

Clint suddenly leaned across the table, until his eyes were level with Roy's and their noses were only a few inches apart. "I know all about it, punk. I've been there. The only difference between you and me is that I didn't buy the self-pity gig. Quit making excuses and find a solution. There're places in this town where they'll find you clothes and give you a bath and a meal and help you look for work."

"I don't want no charity!"

"No? You want five to ten for burglary, right? Then you can sit on your can all day in a cell and feel sorry for yourself permanently. And when you get out, you can feel sorry for yourself even more because even though they give you clean clothes, you can't find work because you're an ex-con. So you go out and pull another job, with a gun this time, and you're up the river for twenty years. Charity for the rest of your life, courtesy of the State of Montana...but that's okay because they forced it on you, right? Get real, jerk. Self-pity is a dead end."

Roy looked away. Ten or twelve seconds passed before he spoke. "That guy who was just in here? Mr. Hotshot Businessman? He turned me down for a job today. Said I wasn't good enough to sweep his floors."

"He said that?" Dakota was aghast. "He actually said that?"

Clint sent her a withering look. "That's what dummy here *heard*, Winston. Not what LeClerc said. Was it, punk? Tell us what he really said."

Dark eyes glared at them. "He said he didn't think I'd show up every day. I told him I would, but he said he had other applicants with better backgrounds. Same thing, isn't it?"

"Damn near," Dakota answered, glaring at Clint.

He ignored her as if she hadn't spoken. "That's no reason to steal from the man."

"I didn't steal anything." Roy smirked. "Not a damn thing, cop."

"But he meant to," Clint told Dakota when the boy was taken off to a holding cell. "He'll get off with a slap on the wrist. I hope he gets the point."

"He's so angry. Were you like that?"

Gray-green eyes leveled at her. "What the hell difference does it make? Poverty breeds anger, especially when it's next door to relative affluence. Now I have a few words for you, *Ms.* Detective."

Dakota stiffened, sensing she was about to get another tongue-lashing. Did this man never have anything pleasant to say?

"I signaled you to stay in the alley. You disobeyed me. Worse, you came into the building when I believed you were still out there. I could have shot you, Winston. I could have thought you were another burglar and I might have hurt you. Killed you. Damn it, woman, you have to follow orders!"

"You went into that building alone without having any idea what the threat was!" she protested. "I was worried! You should have had backup!"

"If I need backup I'm capable of asking for it! Do you have any idea how many cops get shot by their partners in situations just like this one? You had your gun drawn. What were you going to shoot at—the first shadow that moved? Next time I tell you to stay put, stay put! I can't be worrying that you'll go off half-cocked and get in the middle of the situation without me knowing it."

"Then maybe you shouldn't tell me to stay out of the way. Maybe you ought to consider that you'd be safer with your back covered!"

"I might be if I knew what you would and wouldn't do. But I don't know that about you, Winston. I don't know how well you keep your head in a tense situation, and after tonight I'm inclined to think you don't keep your head at all. Damn it, even a green rookie ought to know better than to pull that kind of a stunt. God, when I saw you come through that door—" He broke off sharply and shook his head before continuing. "You're lucky I don't have an itchy trigger finger. I drew a bead on you before I recognized you."

Even through her anger she felt a chilly trickle of fear. She had a swift, clear image of herself silhouetted in the doorway.

"So tell me, Winston, are you going to follow orders from now on and stay where you're supposed to? If I ever get into another one of these situations, I don't need to be wondering if I'm aiming at the perp or at you."

She nodded slowly, biting back all the angry words that still wanted to escape. This man knew nothing about winning friends and cooperation. It seemed that even when he was right he had a tactless, annoying way of presenting his points. Right now she would rather have walked through a snake pit than admit out loud that he *was* right. But he was right, and innate honesty forced her to acknowledge it.

He nodded, his gaze intent, almost unnerving. Then he looked away, as if dismissing the whole thing. "I guess that takes care of *this* evening. You can write the arrest report. Good night."

She could write the arrest report. An hour later she was still seething, and tired of being angry at Clint Calloway. But leaving her to write this report was treating her like a secretary. Let the woman do the typing.

But not really, she told herself as she stared at the computer screen. Not really. Writing reports was a miserable job that nobody wanted to do, and consequently that task quite often got left to the junior partner.

Maybe, she told herself, Clint wasn't the only problem in their partnership. Maybe she was being too bristly about minor things. Yes, the man was a male chauvinist, but did she have to look for that in everything he said? Why take umbrage at being left to write the report when she would have left it to her partner if *she* were the senior person? There'd been nothing sexist in that. Nothing at all.

And he'd also been right about what had happened tonight. She'd been smarting from his earlier lecture about being in the saloon, and had filtered what occurred in the alley through that set of emotions. She had felt he was leaving her out because she was a woman, and then had pole-vaulted herself into a tricky situation, acting out of concern for his safety and in defiance of his order, because she had concluded his order was ridiculous.

Not true. Well, maybe he had told her to stay in the alley because she was a woman, or because he didn't know her well enough yet to take a chance on her in a potentially dangerous showdown. Regardless of *his* reasons in leaving her where she was, going in after him had been foolhardy. He was right; he could have mistaken her for a criminal. He had no reason to suspect she might even enter the building, since he had told her to stay outside.

In short, she had behaved like a rookie, even though she knew better. She had allowed her judgment to be clouded by her feelings and her attitudes. And when she thought about that, Dakota wanted to dig a hole and crawl into it.

Tomorrow, she promised herself. Tomorrow she was going to begin the day with a positive attitude and hang on to it if it killed her. She hadn't worked herself nearly to death just so she could blow up her career because some guy made her angry. No way! She'd keep her cool, be pleasant and show him she was just as good at this job as any male would be.

The determination stayed with her all the way home and right up until she climbed into bed, beneath the quilt her mother had pieced together years ago. Right up until she closed her eyes and all she could see was Clint Calloway.

It would, she thought dismally, be a whole lot easier to remain cheerful and pleasant if she didn't care so much. The trouble was she had been attracted to Clint from the moment she had joined the department. She *wanted* his good opinion. And that made it awfully hard to keep calm when he was yelling at her.

For an instant—a brief, almost undetectable instant right before sleep claimed her—she felt a tear prickle at the back of her eye. It had been a hard day, and something told her tomorrow was only going to get harder.

Three

"Okay, you ready?"

Dakota nodded in answer to Clint's question and picked up her navy blue purse from the desk, slinging it over her shoulder. This morning she had worn a navy blue slack suit in an effort to look as businesslike as she could. Clint wore faded jeans, a sports jacket and an open-throated Western shirt. He crammed a tan cowboy hat on his head, and together they walked out of the station into the brilliant light of a cool June morning.

To the west, up the main street, the Crazy Mountains were visible, almost blue in the early light. The air smelled clean, spiced faintly with sage and newly mowed grass.

In keeping with her resolution, she had come in early this morning and reviewed the kidnapping file so that she wouldn't be ignorant of any details when they went over to the library. The paucity of information still appalled her. She absolutely hated to think that a little girl could disappear and not one soul have any idea what had happened to her. Jennifer McCallum had vanished from the library preschool story hour as if she had been plucked out by an invisible hand...and no one had seen the vanishing act.

The child was well known at the library, according to the file. She had come regularly to story hour, while her mother had volunteered with a literacy project that was running at the same time. Jessica McCallum had finished tutoring her pupil and came to the activity room to pick up her daughter, only to find her gone, and no one there except Mary Jo Kincaid, who led the story hour. Mary Jo couldn't remember having seen little Jennifer leaving...which wasn't surprising in a continually shifting crowd of three- and four-year-olds.

"Do you know Mary Jo Kincaid?" Dakota asked as they drove up Center Avenue to the library. The town park was bright with the green glory of spring, and flowers bloomed in neat beds throughout it.

"I've talked to her a few times in the course of business. I don't know her."

"It must be funny to realize she's related to you by marriage."

Clint turned sharply into a parking slot and hit the brakes so hard that Dakota's seat belt locked and her teeth rattled. "Clint, what—"

He switched off the ignition with a flick of his wrist and turned to glare at her. "Let's get something straight here. Jeremiah Kincaid may have deposited his genes with my mother, but that doesn't make me feel like a Kincaid. As far as I'm concerned, that old bastard and his weak-kneed son were no kin of mine."

"But you stand to inherit—"

He shook his head fiercely. "Damn it, didn't you read Jennifer's file? Neither that kid nor I stand to inherit a single dime, and it doesn't matter how much proof there is that old Jeremiah was our biological father. He left his estate to Dugin, and once the will was probated it was too late for anyone to change anything. Even if I wanted to sue for some of that money, I couldn't now. Not that I'd want to. I don't want a thing from any Kincaid."

Ignoring his glare, Dakota cocked her head to one side, absorbing what he'd said. "That information must have been in those handwritten notes I couldn't decipher. Everyone thinks you and Jennifer stand to inherit."

"Doesn't matter what everyone thinks. We don't. Not even a lawsuit could change that fact."

"But somebody thinks it could."

He sighed and ran his hand over his face, letting go of his anger. "That's my guess about why she was kidnapped, yes. And if the perp has figured out that she won't inherit anything, and therefore there's no ransom money...well, I don't give a plugged nickel for the kid's chances."

"Is that why you haven't announced it publicly? That she won't inherit?"

He nodded. "I'm keeping it under my hat for now. I don't want to do *anything* that might jeopardize that little girl."

It was then, for the first time, that it occurred to Dakota that Clint might have had a conflict of interest in this case if he and the little girl both stood to inherit. Someone could have reasonably suspected that it might be to his advantage *not* to find Jennifer. It was a measure of Clint's reputation for honesty that the notion hadn't occurred to her right off.

They were climbing the steps to the library side-by-side when Clint suddenly swore under his breath. She glanced up at him, then followed his gaze. Coming down the steps toward them in a swirl of printed skirts was Winona Cobbs, the local psychic. Her hand was lifted, and she was hurrying.

"Clint! Clint, didn't you get my messages?"

Dakota could understand why Clint looked so pained. Even though she had been in Whitehorn a relatively short time, she had heard that when Winona had a vision, she could be as dogged as a bull terrier about it.

The small, round woman reached them, panting breathlessly and flushed from her exertion. "Did you get my message, Clint? Of course you did. You're just ignoring me again.'' She waggled her finger at him, but her scowl wasn't at all convincing. "I know you're working on the kidnapping case.''

"That's no secret, Winona."

"Then you ought to be going after every clue. Leaving no stone unturned.''

Clint suddenly chuckled softly, astonishing Dakota as much as if he'd suddenly turned green. Good heavens, he was attractive when he looked amused.

"Winona," he said, "I've got the greatest respect for your talents, but they're not evidence. I need *evidence*.''

"I know that!" She waved a dismissive hand and turned her smile on Dakota. "You're Dakota, aren't you? Be patient, dear. Some people are willfully blind, but this time the person in question is too smart to stay that way.''

Dakota felt her cheeks heat ever so slightly and hoped no one would notice. She had no idea why she should feel embarrassed, except that it was extremely unsettling to think someone could see into your mind. Not that she had anything to hide…

But Winona was already turning back to Clint. "I'm working on it, dear," she told him. "All I really know right now is that the little girl is alive. Very much alive.''

Dakota felt her heart leap and suspected Clint was just as relieved by the news as she, albeit unwilling to admit the fact. "Can you see her?" she asked.

Winona nodded. "Cute little thing. She's being kept by a family. They didn't have anything to do with the kidnapping. They think they're doing a favor for someone.''

"Where? Do you know where?"

Winona shook her head. "Dear, if I knew that I would have camped in front of the police station until this stubborn man saw me. No, I haven't any idea where she is. Not too far away, but not too close."

Clint snorted.

"I know." Winona sighed. "Useless. But I wanted you to know not to let up. Jennifer is safe for the moment and very much alive. I know that so often that isn't the case when a child is gone this long, and I had to tell you so you'll keep looking." Her gaze seemed to turn inward, then she nodded again. "Yes, she's all right at the moment. A woman with two faces…" Her voice trailed off as she stared into the distance.

Dakota felt the back of her neck prickle with uneasiness as she wondered what Winona was seeing and how she managed to do it. She glanced at Clint and saw that he was watching the woman intently, waiting patiently for whatever she had to say. For some reason that surprised her.

Finally Winona sighed and shook her head. "I'm sorry. A woman with two faces…I can't figure it out. I've been seeing her face for so long now, but I can't see clearly enough.…" Again she shook her head, looking disheartened. "I can't. Well, I'll keep trying."

"You do that, Winona," Clint said. "You do that. And I wasn't really avoiding you, you know. There are a couple of things I want to talk to you about, but not just now. I have some other details to handle first, and then I'll want to hear every impression you have about a couple of other matters."

Winona beamed at him, then said farewell.

Dakota turned to watch her waddle down the steps. "Do you believe her?" she asked Clint.

"About Jennifer being alive? It's better than the alternative."

Which was no answer at all, Dakota thought. No answer at all.

The library was cool inside, and like so many libraries of its era, it seemed dim as they stepped in from the brilliant morning light outside. They paused a few moments, allowing their eyes to adapt.

"Detectives." A woman's pleasant voice greeted them. Turning, Dakota recognized Mary Jo Kincaid. She'd never exchanged more than a couple of words with the woman, but she was inclined to have a great deal of respect for her. Despite all the misfortune Mary Jo had recently suffered, she still volunteered at the library, making the preschool story hour possible. "Is there something we can do for you this morning?"

Clint's face suddenly blossomed in a warm, wide smile. Dakota wanted to grind her teeth with…frustration, she told herself. Frustration because this man refused to treat her with basic decency, yet drag a pretty blonde across his path and he couldn't be sweet enough. Yes, she felt frustrated. Not jealous. She had nothing to be jealous about.

"We just wanted to take another look around, Mary Jo. Do you mind?"

"Of course not! I've been thinking about that day the way you told me to, Clint, but I'm afraid I haven't been able to come up with any new information."

She looked so earnest and concerned, Dakota thought. Genuinely sweet and caring. It was hard to feel anything but liking for Mary Jo Kincaid, even if she was an attractive blonde. Dakota's mother had always wanted her to bleach her hair—"It'd go so well with your blue eyes, honey"— and Dakota had always stubbornly refused. Still, sometimes she felt that dark hair was a decided disadvantage where men were concerned. Every one of them seemed to be a sucker for blondes. Clint was apparently no exception.

"Don't worry about it," he said sincerely.

"Well, I do! I feel responsible! That little girl was here

for *my* story hour. If I'd just been more alert..." Her voice trailed off as she looked away and blinked rapidly. Dakota wanted to reach out and give her a reassuring pat on the shoulder, but refrained.

"Nobody can be *that* alert," Clint said.

After a moment, Mary Jo nodded. "Well, you'll see what it was like if you stay for a little while. The day-care center is bringing up a group for a story. It'll give you some idea what was going on that day."

"Thanks. We'll just wander around for a while...if you don't mind."

"Go ahead. I'm sure the librarian won't mind." She was all-smiles again and motioned for them to go ahead.

"Brave woman," Dakota remarked. "Losing her husband so recently, and now this...."

Clint shook his head. "She wasn't too happy with Dugin Kincaid. Or at least he complained that she wasn't."

"When did he say that?"

"More than once at the saloon." Clint glanced down at her and looked almost amused. "There are some advantages to being a male cop, Winston."

"Yeah, you get to hear all the dirt in the saloon." She made an irritated sound. "So what was wrong with the marriage?"

"Seems sweet little Mary Jo was an ice princess."

For some inexplicable reason, that cheered Dakota considerably. But then Clint utterly ruined her mood by adding casually, "Of course, that may have been because Dugin didn't know how to love a woman."

And of course, Dakota thought sourly, *Clint* would know how. Or at least he would think he did.

There were far more exits from the library than Dakota would have imagined—four fire exits were just the obvious ones. There were also service doors leading to the basement and to a loading dock in back. There was also a small, almost hidden door beside the chimney that, surprisingly, led to an enclosed staircase that led up to the offices on the third floor.

"Now I never would have expected this," Dakota said as they emerged into a short, windowless hallway upstairs.

"Interesting, isn't it? And it doesn't open onto any of the public rooms, only straight into one office...an office that isn't being used."

"This is probably how she was taken out then."

"I'd be inclined to think so. The question I haven't been able to get a satisfactory answer to is whether anyone searched up here. No one seems to remember. They may have overlooked this part of the building entirely because the office was thought to be locked."

"It's not the most obvious exit in the world," Dakota said.

"No, but it's not a secret, either," Clint answered. "I did a little checking around town last week. Everybody and his mother knows about this exit. It's used as part of the haunted-house thing for Halloween."

"I missed that."

"You didn't grow up here."

No, she hadn't. Her family, wealthy from mining concerns, lived in beautiful Missoula. Being new here gave her both advantages and disadvantages as a cop. This time it was a disadvantage; anyone else in town apparently would have known about this exit.

The office the stairway led to had once been the head librarian's, Clint told her as he led the way into the musty room. In a bygone era, a librarian had sat up here in his pleasant, third-floor eyrie and had supervised his young assistants.

File cabinets, dusty with disuse, still lined the walls, and an old wooden desk, massive and ornately carved, had probably never been moved from its position in the very center of the room. A tall, dirty window let in sunlight and offered a view of the park. Boxes, all neatly taped, had been stacked against the walls.

"The Halloween stuff is stored up here," Clint remarked. "I checked the boxes." Idly, he touched one atop a nearby stack. "Somebody's already been up here to tape them shut again."

"Very efficient." Dakota turned around slowly, looking for anything that seemed out of place. Because something was very definitely out of place, only she couldn't put her finger on it. "Why doesn't anyone use this room anymore?"

"Because it's two flights up...and because it feels isolated. I guess there was some talk in the past that it was haunted."

Well, it *did* feel isolated, Dakota thought, turning around again. Sounds from below were almost nonexistent, and even street noises didn't seem to penetrate. "Is there anything else on this floor?"

"Some storage rooms. Come on, I'll show you."

There were rooms filled with boxes, old furnishings, filing cabinets. "I'm surprised nobody wants to use this space!"

"There are offices on the second floor, and I guess that's all the room anyone needs." He shrugged. "Don't ask me. I don't organize this place."

Nor did it really matter, she thought. Why these rooms were used for one thing and not another held little relevance to their investigation, except that the lack of traffic up here had made it an ideal place to hide a little girl until she could be taken out of the library. "I'll bet she was held up here."

"Crossed my mind," Clint agreed. "It's a perfect hiding place, and the best way to make sure no one on the street happened to see anything, either."

"They'd have to keep her quiet." Dakota didn't want to think about the ways that could be accomplished. Any one of them would be awful and potentially dangerous for a child not quite four. "From the time she arrived here, did anyone particularly notice her? I mean, we're *sure* she got here?"

"What are you suggesting? That Jessica McCallum lied about bringing her daughter to the story hour?"

Boy, that made him bristle, she noticed. Did he have a thing for Sterling McCallum's wife? That could make for some interesting job tensions. It could also make for some tension in this investigation. "I'm just trying to pin down the time frame. I can't read your handwriting, remember?"

His mouth drew into a tight line. "Yes, she got here. Mary Jo recalls her being in the group and asking for a black crayon to draw with. Evidently she has the kids draw pictures while she reads to them. Anyway, she gave Jennifer a jumbo black crayon. After that she's not sure whether she noticed Jennifer again. Apparently nobody noticed anything until Jessica started to look for her. Then they tore the place apart and even searched the park and nearby businesses, thinking she might have wandered out."

"But there was no sign of her."

"Not a thing. And when I had them open up this office for me, there was no sign of her here, either. It seems the likeliest way to smuggle a child out of this place, but it could have happened any number of ways."

"I guess someone might just have walked out with her," Dakota agreed with a shake of her head. "It doesn't seem likely, though. Too much chance that someone would see and remember. Apparently nobody saw a thing, or remembers a thing."

"Evidently not."

They returned to the abandoned office with its private entrance and stood there again, looking for the least little thing they might have missed.

It was then that Dakota realized what was wrong. "Clint? Clint, when you came up here last week, was the floor swept?"

"What?" He looked at her as if she'd lost her mind.

"I'm serious. This room is never used, right? Look at how thick the dust is on top of the file cabinets. When you came in here the first time, there should have been footprints in the dust on the floor if anyone had been in here before you. I don't see how you could have missed them if there were. But this floor has been swept clean. The desk, too. We need to find out if some janitor regularly cleans this room."

She turned to look up at him. "Do you remember?"

He started to shake his head, then stopped. "It was clean. I'm sure it was clean, because I would have noticed if there was a whole lot of dust around."

She could tell when their eyes met that they both understood the possible significance of that fact.

"I'll go downstairs and ask about cleaning," he told her. "You keep looking around here."

But it was so obvious it almost leapt up to bite them, Dakota thought as she wandered through the storage rooms. Dust was layered on everything, including the floors in the other rooms. Someone had swept out the one room only, probably because dust had made footprints obvious. The person hadn't bothered with the other rooms because they hadn't been disturbed.

This would tend to confirm their suspicion that little Jennifer had been hidden here and carried out under cover of darkness. Not that this was evidence. Not that it seemed to help much at all.

But you never knew how some little bit of information might become important eventually. Working any case was like working a big jigsaw puzzle. And if you worked at it long enough, some obscure little piece would suddenly fill in an important hole somewhere.

What broom would have been used to sweep the floor? There must be one up here somewhere, and it must be in plain sight, unless the person who used it knew the library well enough to know where to look for one.

Dakota began to wander through the various rooms looking for a broom, trying to construct a scenario in her mind. Someone had lured or carried the little girl up here and had hidden her in the office. The hue and cry had been raised within…oh, a half hour or so. Initially, the ground floor would have been searched, then the second floor, which could be reached by a public staircase. But the staircase leading from the second floor to this one was closed off by a door, and it was unlikely a little girl would have wandered up those stairs on her own.

So perhaps no one had searched up here immediately? Dakota made a note to ask if the initial search had even covered the third floor. Say it hadn't. Say it had first moved out to the surrounding park, businesses and streets. The library would have been all but abandoned then. Someone could have come up here to sweep the floor so that when the search expanded to include this level, the tracks wouldn't be visible.

An hour or so might have passed before the search, with police assistance, returned to the library. At that point the third floor would have been opened and explored, Dakota imagined, perhaps still without going into the locked room.

Had anyone checked to see if the room had still been locked? She made another note to ask about that.

And little Jennifer…where had little Jennifer been? In a taped-up book box, perhaps, bound and gagged and even drugged? The mere thought made Dakota angry, and she paused in her survey of the rooms to allow herself a moment to deal with her emotions.

Either the child had been removed before anyone noticed her absence—at a point when no one would have paid any particular attention to someone carrying a small child—or she had been held up here until the search had moved elsewhere and night had fallen. Those were the only two options, and the swept floor of the locked room sure seemed to indicate that the child had been held. Held until late night, perhaps, when no one would be watching. Held, perhaps, for several days…? No, too risky. Held until she could be removed under cover of darkness.

Nowhere did Dakota come across a broom, so she returned to the office where she believed the child had been held. Someone had searched all these boxes, Clint had said. Of course they had. They'd have been looking for a body, out of concern that the child had been murdered. No body had been found.

Maybe Jennifer had been removed from here in one of these book boxes. They were small, but not too small for a curled-up three-year-old to fit into. A box of books being carried out of the library would hardly excite suspicion, even in broad daylight.

That made even more sense than that the little girl had been concealed up here. Someone had brought her up here, knocked her out—with ether, perhaps? Or a sleeping pill slipped into juice?—and then had stuffed her into a book box, which had been removed at the first opportunity. Safer than leaving the child up here, when it was obvious that every nook and crannie of the building would be searched when she was discovered missing.

A sleeping child in a taped-up book box would be overlooked in the initial search. Perhaps even in subsequent searches. Several boxes being moved in or out would not even be remarked on.

Dakota made a note to inquire whether any boxes had been moved in or out of the library that day.

The initial search would have skipped this room, she decided, even when they didn't find the little girl anywhere else and came back in to search again. This room had been locked, and the initial assumption was that the girl had wandered off. No one would think she could possibly be behind a locked door. At what point had they decided there had been foul play and then checked this room?

She made another addition to her growing list of questions. Clint had probably thought of all this stuff, she told herself. He'd been an investigator for years and probably missed very little...except for a swept floor. Just like a man not to notice that.

She almost smiled, and found her thoughts wandering away from the case to the brief glimpse she had had of a smiling Clint Calloway. That smile was enough to send any woman's heart into a tizzy. Maybe it was a good thing he preferred to scowl.

She heard Clint's footsteps coming down the corridor. Moments later he appeared in the doorway. "We need to go talk to Wilbur Tamison," he said. "He's the janitor. Nobody downstairs has any idea when he last swept or cleaned up here."

Wilbur Tamison lived in an apartment above the Ladyland Boutique, a place that catered to the ranchers' wives' desire for the silky, soft and feminine. Demand wasn't huge, but Ladyland held on. A narrow stairway behind a street-level door led up to a dark hallway illuminated by a single yellow bulb and what light managed to pass through a filthy window at the far end.

His place, however, was an amazing contrast. Through tall, spotless windows overlooking Center Avenue, sunlight poured in to illuminate a spacious, three-room apartment that had been recently painted. Houseplants filled the corners, and brightly upholstered furniture invited them to sit. Wilbur himself was almost completely deaf, with hearing aids in both ears. His wide smile revealed a few missing teeth.

"Measles," he told Dakota in a high-pitched voice. "My mother had measles when she was carrying me. Never could hear right."

But he'd learned to talk anyway, and talk pretty well. Dakota wondered what this man might have accomplished if he'd had hearing. Or if he had been born in a later time when he wouldn't have been shunted aside because of his disability.

She wondered even more when he ushered them into his kitchen and dining area and offered them coffee. Through the open bedroom door she could see shelves full of books lining the walls.

"I love to read," Wilbur said when he saw the direction of her gaze. "Read everything in the library, so I had to start buying my own."

The coffee was rich and strong. Wilbur shook his head when the discussion turned to the kidnapping.

"Terrible thing. Never would have thought such could happen here. Poor little girl. Why would anybody want to hurt a child?"

"Beats me," Clint said. "If I live to be as old as Methuselah, I'll never understand why anyone would harm a child. But we need to ask you a couple of questions about the library, Wilbur.''

"Sure thing.'' He smiled. "Janitors know just about everything.''

"I imagine you do. Do you happen to remember the last time you swept the third floor?''

"The storage rooms, you mean?'' He sat back in his chair and narrowed his eyes. "It'll be three, four months now. Nobody goes up there, and I only think about it when I have to carry something up.'' He shook his head again. "Gets a mite dusty.''

"So you didn't sweep up there last week?''

"Naw. I'd 'a remembered if'n I had.''

"If somebody wanted to sweep up there,'' Dakota asked, "would they have to carry a broom up from below?''

Wilbur shook his head. "There's a janitor's closet on each floor. Somebody at some time or other was thinking about old backs. Naw, you wouldn't have to carry nothin' up there. It's all there in the closet.'' He patted the key ring that hung at his waist. "Got the keys right here.''

"The janitor's closets lock?''

"Yup.''

"Does anyone else have the keys?''

Wilbur thought awhile. "I don't know. I 'spect somebody does, but I don't know.''

Dakota felt excitement rising within her. This could be important. "Where would we find the closet?'' she asked Wilbur. "I don't remember any locked doors up there.''

Wilbur suddenly grinned. "It's hidden. I'll take you there and show you.''

"Thanks, Wilbur,'' Clint said, "but it's not necessary. I was there Thursday when we searched the closet. I know where it is.'' The look he gave Dakota was almost baleful. "I don't miss much. There's a master key that fits every lock in the library, including the janitor's closets. Three of them hang on a wall in the librarian's office. Anybody could have gotten to them.''

"But not everybody would know how to find the closet," she argued. "Not if it's hidden the way Wilbur says."

One corner of Clint's mouth lifted. "Every boy in the damn county knows about it. Sorry, Winston, you've narrowed the field to a few thousand suspects...and we pretty much had that many to begin with."

Just like that, she was mad again. This man made her angry with frightening ease. Saying not another word, except to thank Wilbur for the coffee, Dakota stomped down the stairs ahead of Clint Calloway, wondering how many more times today he was going to make her want to pop her cork.

"I have a great idea," she said, turning to glare at him when they were out on the street again. "Let's go back to the office and you *read* your notes to me. That way I won't keep duplicating your efforts."

For a moment she thought he was going to snap right back at her. Then he relaxed visibly and shrugged. "Look, you didn't duplicate my effort. We found out that it was probably the perp who swept the floor. I hadn't even noticed that."

"Mighty big of you to say so."

"I think so." Then he stunned her by flashing one of his devastating smiles. "Come on, we need to go check for prints on the broom and door. Then let's get some coffee at the café, and you can tell me what makes a debutante want to be a cop."

Four

What makes a debutante want to be a cop?

There were a lot of ways that question could have been asked without being offensive, but Clint had asked it in the most offensive way possible. Dakota never for a minute doubted that he'd done so on purpose.

That was the reason, the *only* reason, she didn't let him see how his words annoyed her. She knew exactly what kind of woman he was thinking of—heck, she had a couple of them for cousins—but she wasn't at all like that. She was, however, sick to death of people making assumptions based on her family background.

They went to the Hip Hop Café for their coffee, settling into a booth amidst an eclectic assortment of brightly colored used furniture. Somehow Melissa Avery North, the café's owner, had managed to turn ragtag odds and ends into a cheerful, charming environment.

Looking at Clint over the rim of a steaming mug of coffee, Dakota realized that she might be able to control her anger at his insinuation, but she wasn't going to let it pass unchallenged. "You're a cop, Calloway. I thought you'd be more perceptive."

He arched a sardonic brow. "More perceptive than what, Winston?"

"More perceptive than to classify me as a debutante."

"Are you claiming you don't belong to the Missoula Winstons?"

"No, I'm saying I'm not the kind of person you're making me out to be. I'm saying that I'm damn sick and tired of people leaping to conclusions about my character and intelligence based on the fact that my parents are rich!"

"So *you* aren't rich, too? Spare me, Winston. That kind of thing tends to run in families, like weight problems, hair color and poverty."

Now, she thought, they were getting to the root of it. "The fact that my father is wealthy doesn't excuse me from the responsibility of leading a productive life."

His eyebrow flew upward, as if he were about to make some kind of sarcastic response to her vehemence, but he surprised her by saying nothing.

After a moment, Dakota felt herself flush. It would have been a good point to fall silent herself and let go of the subject, but somehow Clint's opinion was important to her. Embarrassed, she plunged on.

"My father always said that the good Lord never put a soul here just to spend money and waste time. He works hard in his business. My mother volunteers forty hours a week in charities and convalescent homes. And yes, she gets her hands dirty and her heart broken doing it. She's *not* simply on committees. My brother is a tropical-diseases specialist at the Center for Disease Control in Atlanta. My younger sister is in nursing school. Believe me, we weren't raised to be decorative."

His expression never changed as he lifted his mug to his mouth. "So you're a cop because of social conscience?"

She felt herself flush again. "Only partly."

"What's the other part?"

"The excitement."

The harshness of his expression dissolved as he broke into a hearty laugh. "The excitement? Good God, woman, it's the boredom that'll kill you!"

"So it seems sometimes," she admitted with a sheepish smile. He had the most wonderful laugh, she found herself thinking. It was a dangerous train of thought. "It's an important job."

"It is," he agreed, his laugh dying. "Too important to play at."

Just that quickly, he infuriated her again. She didn't need it spelled out to understand what he was implying. Her brain scrambled madly for a suitably cutting response, but failed to come up with one before he started speaking again.

"Have you read all the files I gave you?"

"Yes." Beneath the table her hands clenched into tight fists as she tried to hammer down her anger and clear her head for thinking. "Some of those cases are pretty old."

"And unsolved. I don't like unsolved crimes. Especially murder."

"The Avery murder case is probably too old to solve. The man disappeared some thirty years ago, didn't he? He was probably murdered at the time he disappeared, and I'm inclined to agree with the supposition that Lexine Baxter killed him."

"Why?" His gray-green eyes were sharp, intent.

"Given that they already tried to pin it on Ethan Walker, and he was acquitted, that makes her the most likely suspect. Especially since she disappeared, too. Come on, you know that most murders are committed by family members or friends. She probably wanted him to marry her, and he refused because he was already married to—" She broke off sharply, remembering suddenly that the woman who owned this café was the dead man's daughter. "Because he was already married," she continued quietly. "Maybe she was even pregnant."

"And maybe they were both murdered out there. Did you think of that?"

She hadn't. "No, but that's not very likely."

"Likely or not, it's a possibility, and no cop can afford to ignore a possibility. The problem, Winston, is that statistics are useless in individual cases. Without any other evidence, we have to assume that anyone could have killed that man. And there is even a possibility that Lexine Baxter was killed along with him."

She wished he'd stop calling her by her last name. "Winston" was her dad. "Did anybody ever report her missing?"

Clint shook his head. "Her aunt asked some questions, but she wasn't from around here. There wasn't anyone else who cared, from what I gather. Her father was dead, and she was garnering quite a reputation as a tramp. I suspect folks were glad to have her gone. But then, nobody reported Charles Avery missing, either. Everyone just assumed he ran off with Lexine."

"But he was dead."

"Exactly." One corner of his mouth lifted. "Which is why we shouldn't make assumptions. Although in this case I'm inclined to agree with you. Lexine is probably our perp."

"The report mentioned that the FBI anthropologist had found some hairs."

"Tracy Roper Hensley."

"Judd's wife? She's Tracy Roper, the forensic anthropologist?"

"The same."

Dakota almost smiled as she remembered her latest glimpse of the sheriff's wife. The renowned anthropologist had been busy soothing a crying infant and calling something over her shoulder to Judd about ribs for dinner.

"Anyway," Clint said, "she found a few hairs. Some short brown ones, probably Avery's, and a single long blond one, dark at the root. A lot of the evidence was stolen, though.''

"By the Indian who attacked her?''

"Whoa!'' Clint held up a hand. "Damn it, Dakota, slow down. You're leaping to conclusions. A detective has to *think*.''

Her cheeks burned yet again, and she looked down at her coffee. "Sorry.''

"By a *person* who was garbed as something reminiscent of a Hopi kachina figure—but not precisely, mind you. Tracy has a good background in anthropology, and she was disturbed by what she called a 'hodgepodge' of Indian regalia. Anyway, yes, that person stole all the evidence Tracy had collected that day.''

"That would seem to indicate that someone around here has a vested interest in preventing this case from being solved.''

"Bingo.'' He sat back in the booth and took a long sip of his coffee. "Still think the case is too old to solve?''

"Maybe not.'' Then she shook her head. "But after all this time, there's not enough evidence. How would we even know where to begin to look for more?''

"I was thinking more along the lines of smoking out the perp.''

Excitement zinged through her. *This* was the kind of police work she had always dreamed of doing. "How would we do that?''

"Well, I've been giving it some thought, but the likeliest thing is to make it seem that the investigation is gathering steam again. After all, it was Tracy's work on the DB—dead body—that brought it to a head last time. We could just go out there and poke around some more.''

"Wouldn't we need permission from tribal authorities?''

"Yeah, but that's not impossible, given what's already

happened out there. I'm pretty sure we could get permission.''

"If the sheriff agrees.''

"Judd'll agree. He's never liked the idea of not catching the person who tried to hurt Tracy.''

The Hopi-type figure, Dakota recalled from the reports, had threatened Tracy with skinning knives, and might actually have tried to kill Judd by knocking him over the edge of a cliff, though that couldn't be proven. Plenty of reason to catch this person if there was any way to do so. Whoever it was seemed to have no conscience. She nodded her agreement.

"Then there's the case of that guy who was murdered at Dugin Kincaid's wedding to Mary Jo. It bothers the hell out of me that Floyd Oakley was knifed under the ribs with a carving knife and we have no idea who may have done it.''

"That was…strange,'' Dakota agreed, summoning the case to mind. "It looked like a professional hit, the report said.''

"And it's been half dismissed as a case of a stranger who came to town with his own trouble hard on his heels. Crime connections that caught up with him.''

"But that doesn't explain what he was doing on the Kincaid ranch. On the day of the wedding.''

"Well, old Jeremiah wasn't so clean that that part bothers me overmuch. When you've got that kind of money, you're apt to have had a few shady dealings.''

Dakota bristled instinctively, but kept her mouth shut. This man came from the most awful poverty, and it was hardly surprising that he had no love for wealthy people, considering what Jeremiah had done to him. "I agree that Jeremiah Kincaid wasn't the most decent human being,

Clint, but that doesn't prove he was involved in any crime.''

"Of course it doesn't. I'm just saying it isn't beyond the realm of possibility. Oakley was a con man with a string of convictions behind him. Somebody apparently wanted to get even for something. That doesn't trouble me. The troubling aspect was that he was on Kincaid property…a strange place for a stranger to be.''

"Maybe we ought to look into Oakley's record a little more closely and see if we can find out who some of his associates were. Maybe somebody who was implicated in one of his crimes came after him.''

"And might lead us directly to the Kincaid connection. Yeah. I like that. You check it out, Winston.''

She pulled her notebook out of her shoulder bag and scribbled a reminder.

"And then there's the Homer Gilmore kidnapping.''

Dakota's head shot up. "Good grief, Clint, the man said he was abducted by aliens. Even *I* know that, and it happened before my arrival in Whitehorn. Everybody was still talking about it when I got here. You don't seriously want to chase flying saucers!''

"Do you believe in aliens?''

Dakota shifted uncomfortably, unsure whether that gleam in his green eyes was mockery. "Anything's possible,'' she said stubbornly. "He's certainly not the only person to think he was abducted by little men.''

"His description doesn't fit the usual one, Winston. Go read it again. Now that a little time has passed, I'm thinking about questioning him again. Matters may seem a little different to him now that the fright has worn off some. Besides, it's another weird occurrence around the Kincaid place.''

"Next you'll be claiming that Jeremiah's and Dugin's

deaths weren't accidental." The barn fire in which Dugin Kincaid had received injuries that had later proved fatal had been one of the first cases she had worked on after joining the department, before she had been promoted to detective. Arson had been suspected, but the pile of oily rags in the tackroom had laid that to rest. While she had been helping with the investigation, though, she had heard all about how Jeremiah had drowned after a fall in the shower. The Kincaids, local folks were beginning to think, were under some kind of curse.

Which was, she admitted, what Clint was suggesting, sans the supernatural overtones. Something was happening on Kincaid land. Something more than a single crime. There had been two accidental deaths, one murder, an abandoned baby, Homer's abduction by aliens....

She let her gaze wander past Clint to the window overlooking the street. The day was the kind Montana produced with perfection—sunny, dry, breezy. Overhead the endless sky would be colored a blue so deep you felt you could fall into it. Until later this afternoon, it wouldn't be marred by a single cloud. What was she doing inside on a day like this?

She returned her attention to her partner. "Let's see if we can get permission to check out where the Avery body was found." The trek through the woods on the reservation would give her a chance to sort through the links Clint had just drawn by implication. A chance to ponder why so many strange things should be happening to one family.

And at least the Avery murder wasn't part of it.

Sheriff Judd Hensley heard Clint out doubtfully. "Sterling and I, not to mention the FBI, did our damnedest to get to the bottom of that two years ago. We thought it

was Ethan Walker, but he was acquitted, and he can't be
tried again.''

"If it wasn't Walker, it had to be someone else.''

Judd regarded him thoughtfully with narrowed eyes.
"Very likely. Have you come across something?''

"Nothing I could go to court with. Just call it a hunch.''

Judd pursed his lips, looking from Clint to Dakota and
back again. "What do you think you can accomplish?''

"If the person who attacked Tracy and stole the evidence
bags is still around, maybe we can smoke him out again.
Reopening the investigation might put the fear of God into
him.''

"And get him to come after you the way he came after
Tracy?'' Judd nodded slowly. "It might work. I'd sure like
to see the so-and-so behind bars. But I don't want either of
you taking stupid risks. This could be dangerous.''

"It could be, but we'll be on the alert.''

Judd looked at Dakota. "How do you feel about that?''

She was surprised that he asked her, and it made her a
little uneasy. Shouldn't it be assumed she was in agreement
with her partner, unless she said otherwise? What had Clint
been saying about her? "I'm with Clint.''

"Okay then. I'll see about getting you permission to get
onto the reservation. When you go, you might take Rafe
Rawlings with you. He spent a lot of time out there helping
Tracy, and he'd be the best one to show you exactly where
everything was found.''

Clint nodded, but Dakota had the distinct feeling he
wasn't planning to take the advice. She filed that away for
now, wanting to see where he would go from here.

"Now,'' he said when they were pulling away from the
curb in their unmarked truck, "I want to go out to the
Gilmore place and see if we can rustle up Homer.''

"Isn't he kind of hard to find? I mean, he might be

almost anywhere in those hills and canyons, prospecting. How do you even know he'll be at home?''

"I don't. In fact, I don't expect him to be. He seems to be real busy lately. Something about sapphires and an old mine. Homer's been prospecting as long as anyone can remember. Once in a while he even finds something of value.''

"He must be awfully sure there's something out there, to spend so much time at it.''

"There are plenty of tall tales about mines and such in those mountains.'' He nodded his head toward the Crazy Mountains. They looked dark and brooding this afternoon, beneath a cobalt sky and cottony puffs of cloud. "Sometimes I wonder if every bunch of mountains has tales about lost mines.''

"Wouldn't surprise me. What kind of mine was lost hereabouts?''

"A sapphire mine. Not much for most people to get excited about, but now there's talk of some new medical tool that uses sapphires, and the price of the gems is supposed to go through the roof. Of course, if somebody finds a large enough sapphire mine, the price just might bottom out. You never know.''

Dakota felt herself smiling. "Are you a pessimist or what, Calloway?''

"Just realistic. You ever hear how the Guggenheims caused the silver market to crash back in the 1890s? All they did was open a bunch of South American mines and overload the market. Just because they got mad at the other mine owners. Anyway, the medical need for sapphires is probably limited. There will be a sharp, temporary rise in price until immediate demand is met, and then it'll taper off. If somebody were to find a so-called mother lode, they might depress even the initial price rise.''

Dakota looked at him with surprise and respect. It was probably stupid of her, but she just hadn't imagined that Clint would be interested in such matters. In fact, she realized uncomfortably, she had assumed he had no interest in anything except police work and making her miserable. "They probably need a very specific type of sapphire for medicine," she suggested. "A particular color or clarity...something that isn't easily come by."

"Probably. That's how it usually goes. Anyway, the mine is just a tall tale. They have corundum deposits near Helena and do some sapphire mining there. It's possible we have some of the same here, but I keep wondering how Homer could have missed it if we do. The man's been scouring the area for a lifetime."

"Why should it be easy to find? I imagine it would be possible to drill within a few feet of a lode and miss it entirely."

"You know how gold is panned from streams? That's generally how gold veins are discovered. It's the same with sapphires. They show up in alluvial deposits. Somebody would have found something in one of the streambeds or floodplains by now, I would think."

"Maybe someone has."

He glanced at her sharply. "What do you mean?"

"Well, if your suspicion is right that something strange is happening on Kincaid land, maybe it has something to do with sapphires."

"Well, I'll be damned," he murmured. "I must have had my head up my..." He trailed off.

By this she gathered that he was impressed with her reasoning. Better still, when he turned to look at her, she saw the glimmer of real respect in his eyes.

He looked back at the road and nodded. "It couldn't be Homer. He was kidnapped."

"He *says* he was kidnapped," Dakota reminded him.

At that, Clint chuckled quietly. "Wait till you meet him. He's a feisty old geezer, but there's no way on God's earth he'd be capable of murder."

"Not even in self-defense?"

"Fred Oakley wasn't killed in self-defense. There was no sign of a struggle. Nope, the man wasn't expecting what he got. That means Oakley was taken unawares, somehow, and that's a long way from self-defense."

Dakota leaned her head back against the seat and watched the spring countryside roll by. Wildflowers dotted the roadside, and cattle grazed peacefully with deer on tender buds and new shoots. "That still leaves the problem of the abduction," she said presently. "If somebody wanted to keep Homer from finding something out there, why stage an alien abduction? Why not just kill him?"

"That's one of the things I want to talk to him about. If we go over every detail of what he can remember about the experience, we may be able to find a clue as to what this 'alien' was really up to."

But Homer wasn't at home, which didn't especially surprise either of them. Dakota watched with amused curiosity as Clint left a message for him tacked to the front door.

"How often does he check here?" she asked.

"It varies. I'm not going to hold my breath. Whenever he happens to come by here, he'll read the note and come into town to see us."

"Cooperative, huh?"

"Not exactly." He flashed her a smile. "He never checks until he's ready to come into town anyway."

On the way back to town, Dakota found herself thinking about Judd Hensley, and the fact that he was married to a leading forensic anthropologist. This seemed like such an out-of-the-way place to find someone of Tracy Roper's stature. "Did Tracy and Judd meet on the Avery murder case?"

"Nope. They were married to each other years ago, but broke up after their son died. They got back together after the Avery remains were discovered. Guess Charles Avery did a second lick of good in his life."

"What was the first?"

"Fathering Melissa. She's a good woman."

She sensed that phrase meant something important to Clint, and wished she could come right out and ask him. Instead, she opted to tease him. "Sweet on Melissa, Clint?"

He scowled at her. "I'm not sweet on anybody."

"Why not?" The question escaped her before she could prevent it.

"Because I don't let my brain be ruled by my hormones. And I never will."

Later that evening, while she cooked dinner for herself, Dakota thought about what Clint had said. It disturbed her that he equated "being sweet" on someone to being ruled by his hormones. Did he really reduce male-female relationships to a matter of ordinary sexual urges? Did he really believe that was all there was to it?

Of course, considering the way he had been raised... She caught herself sharply, putting a halt to that line of speculation. She didn't really know anything about how he had been raised, other than that he'd been abjectly poor. His mother could very well have been a woman of high principles, not the slut she was imagining. Perhaps Clint simply felt that no woman could ever be as good as his sainted mother.

Hardly. Nope, that rang about as true as a wooden nickel. Clint Calloway was more than a male chauvinist; he sometimes appeared to be an out-and-out misogynist. He was a tough nut to crack...although today she had once or twice felt she was edging upward in his estimation.

Leaning her hip against the counter, she idly stirred the sautéing mushrooms and wondered what Clint's story was. Something had to have seriously soured him on women. A failed love affair, perhaps. Whatever had happened to him, Dakota had the distinct impression it wasn't going to be easy for her to change his mind about women in general, or about herself in particular.

And that intrigued her.

The fact was, growing into womanhood in a wealthy family had taught her that most men were easily won. Dab on a little makeup, put on a strapless gown and Dakota Winston was a knockout. She had learned very early that a smile and a few sweet words could tame the most difficult of men. Now, sitting at her breakfast bar and eating her dinner of steak, mushrooms and salad, she decided that life had spoiled her.

A winning smile hadn't helped her that night at the saloon. It sure wasn't going to help her with Clint. If one thing was apparent now, it was that Clint Calloway might allow himself to come to respect her professional performance, but he was going to refuse to see her as anything but a nuisance on a personal level. In fact, he'd make a point of it, because he wouldn't want anyone to mistakenly think that he was succumbing to his "hormones."

There had been cops she'd worked with in Miles City who hadn't wanted to seem like they were soft on her, so they'd given her a tough time. She'd handled it and had eventually won acceptance. Upon arriving here in White-horn, she'd anticipated facing the same thing, but she hadn't counted on Clint Calloway. So far he hadn't given her as much static as her first partner in Miles City had, but she also felt he was going to be that much harder to win over.

Settling into bed that night, she decided that being a cop wasn't what she had expected it to be. Not at all. Instead of rescuing the world from terrible criminals, she seemed to spend an extraordinary amount of time dealing with interpersonal relations. Quarreling neighbors, abusive spouses, abusive parents, obstreperous drunks, recalcitrant witnesses...misogynistic partners.

Maybe it was time to consider a career change. Yeah, to something where she didn't have to deal with people at all. She grinned into the darkness. Computers. Computers sounded like just the trick...except that she kept seeing Clint on the keyboard....

The next thing she knew, her alarm clock was ringing and it was time to rise and face another day.

Five

"We've got permission to go to the reservation and check out the site where Avery's body was found."

Clint greeted Dakota with the news first thing on a bright, warm morning nearly two weeks later. After so many days without a break on the kidnapping case, it was a relief to have something to do at last.

Sterling McCallum, the child's father, was back at work. Other than an occasional question about progress, he didn't bother them about developments, but he worked in the office and it was impossible to forget that he must be continually sitting on the edge of his seat. Oh, he kept busy on a variety of cases, but Dakota could never forget that he was waiting for some word about his daughter.

Nor, she gathered, could Clint forget. Each morning and night he stopped at Sterling's desk to tell him there had been no news.

Everybody had worked on the case right after the child disappeared, but as the days passed and the trail grew colder, there was less and less hope, and less and less to do. Now only Clint and Dakota were handling it. The most heartwrenching thing she had ever heard was something Jessica McCallum had said just last night, when told there was still no news.

"I need to *know*," she had cried in an anguished voice. "Oh, God, I need to *know*."

The same need was plain in Sterling's eyes. The wondering was intolerable.

So it would be a real relief to get out of the office and spend a few hours in the woods at the old murder site. "Are we going to get Rafe Rawlings to show us the way?"

Clint hesitated. "I guess so," he said finally. "It'd save time."

"Why are you so reluctant?"

"I'm not reluctant. I just had to think about it."

"Why?"

He turned to scowl at her. "Sometimes you remind me of a six-year-old with all your questions. I'm just debating how much noise I want to make today. The more of us who go out there to look around, the faster word will get out that we're looking into the Avery case again. I'm not sure I'm ready for that."

She ignored his insult and pursued the issue. One thing for sure, Clint knew how to test her self-control. "Why not? Isn't that the whole point of this exercise?"

He released an exasperated breath. "Timing, Watson. Timing is everything."

Frustrated and annoyed though she was with him, she almost laughed when he called her Watson. Better to be likened to Dr. Watson of Sherlock Holmes fame than some of the other things he'd probably compared her to in the privacy of his own mind. "Okay, Sherlock. What timing? We want to see if we can flush out a murderer. Why does it matter when?"

He turned his back to her and pushed a couple of those mysterious matchsticks around on his desk. "It's a hunch," he said finally. "Just a hunch."

"A hunch about what?" Her frustration growing by leaps and bounds, she plopped into the chair beside his desk and tried to read his stony face. "Are you turning psychic on me?"

He scowled at her. "Haven't you ever had a hunch?"

"Actually, yes. What I want to know is what hunch you've had, what it's about, but talking to you is like trying to pull teeth from someone whose jaws are wired shut!"

He looked startled for a moment, then burst into laughter. "Okay," he said, still chuckling. "Okay. It's hard to explain. I feel like there's this invisible applecart, and all I can see is an apple here and an apple there, but none of the rest of it. So if I pluck the wrong apple..."

"Everything will tumble down." Dakota tilted her head, never taking her eyes from him. "But what makes you think this Avery case is one of those apples? The murder happened so long ago...." She trailed off, shaking her head. "Are you proposing some kind of conspiracy theory? That Avery's death is linked to other crimes?"

He hesitated perceptibly, then sighed. "I don't know. I just have an uneasy, edgy feeling. Humor me."

"Sure." For now. But she couldn't imagine what applecart they could upset by investigating an almost thiry-year-old murder, unless somehow Avery's death was linked to more recent events. At the present time, there was certainly no evidence to indicate that Avery's murder had been anything but an isolated act of anger or passion.

The only reason, in fact, that she could see to dig it up all over again—especially now that Ethan Walker had been acquitted—was that both Judd and Tracy Hensley had been attacked out there. Half the county probably still thought that Walker was responsible. Personally, Dakota didn't think so. The man's only failings were that he was gruff and reclusive, but even that was softening since his marriage to Kate Randall. He didn't strike Dakota as a murderer at all. Certainly not as the kind of man who would attack a woman.

She caught herself and smiled inwardly as she realized how much of the local gossip she'd managed to pick up in her short time in Whitehorn. Of course, knowing Lily Mae Wheeler helped. That woman knew everything about everyone and loved nothing better than to tell it all. Having a cup of coffee with her at the Hip Hop Café was guaranteed to bring forth of flood of local trivia.

And as a cop, Dakota knew how important that could be.

She watched Clint finger one of those small heaps of matchsticks on his desk, but bit back the urge to ask yet again what they were for. No way was she going to give him the satisfaction of once again ignoring her question. "So we go out to the res this afternoon?"

"I'm thinking about dropping in on Homer again first."

"That's right, it's been almost two weeks, hasn't it?"

"A little more." He glanced down at his matchsticks, then shoved his chair back from his desk and went to stand at the window. Over the tops of the buildings, the Crazy Mountains seemed to loom.

"Is it unusual for him not to come into town for so long?"

"Well, that depends. Lately he's been hanging around at Kane's a lot more getting to know his daughter and granddaughter but...well, in the past it wasn't unusual for him to wander up into the hills and forget the rest of the world until his supplies ran out. I stayed with him for a while when I was a kid and ran away from home—such as it was. Two weeks isn't unheard of." He shook his head, emphasizing.

"Did you go off into the hills with him when you were a teenager?"

"Yeah. I did once. You know, people underestimate Homer. They always have, because he's odd and looks eccentric. Bottom line is he's as sharp as a tack, and anybody who forgets that for long is going to regret it."

"Everybody says he's loco. Crazy as cracked glass."

Clint turned to face her, shaking his head sharply. "He's not that crazy. Things sometimes get tangled up in his mind, but not so much that he loses touch with reality completely. I wouldn't waste my time questioning him if he were loony."

Twenty minutes later they were headed out to the Gilmore place yet again. Dakota was of the opinion that this was probably a waste of time, but after only a couple of weeks, she was still trying to be the perfect partner on this job and said nothing. Whether Homer Gilmore was really crazy was probably moot anyway, she thought. Whatever had happened to him late last summer had confused him, leaving him with sketchy memories of aliens. She doubted his memory had improved with time; no one's did.

"How long did you stay with Homer when you were a kid?" she asked Clint. His profile was sharply etched against the spring pasture they were driving past, and she wondered errantly how those perfectly chiseled lips would feel against hers. The thought flitted gently across her mind like a soft summer breeze, hardly noticeable except that it left her feeling vaguely dissatisfied.

"Not long."

"You had to go home?"

He shook his head impatiently. "You just don't get it, do you? I didn't *have* a home. My mother wouldn't have noticed if I'd never come back."

"But you did." Obviously, because he hadn't stayed with Homer.

"I had to." He shifted on the seat.

"Why?"

"None of your damn business."

She bristled. "Why not? Homer was a friend of yours from childhood—"

"I didn't say that," he interrupted harshly. "I stayed with him. Briefly. He wasn't a friend."

She opened her mouth to question him further, but thought better of it. He didn't count Homer a friend. Why not? Homer had apparently treated him with a kindness that had been rare in his childhood. Why hadn't they become friends?

The answer that came to her was sad. So very sad. Homer and Clint hadn't become friends because Clint didn't permit it. Clint didn't let anyone inside his walls.

The Gilmore place was once again deserted. This time Clint slipped a note into the crack between the door and its frame, and then once again they were heading back to town empty-handed.

"Let's stop at my place and grab a tuna sandwich," he said. "Then I guess we'll see when we can get Rawlings to take us out to the res."

The invitation to a tuna sandwich at his place warmed her. He must be coming to think of her as a partner at last or he never would have offered. And at last she was going to get a peek at the dragon's lair. As far as she could ascertain, everyone in town knew where Clint Calloway lived, but no one had ever crossed his threshold. Not that she had been trying to learn everything she could about her partner.

"You've decided to have Rafe take us out there?"

He nodded. "You know him?"

"I've talked to him any number of times." Rafe Rawlings was with the police department. As a baby, he'd been abandoned in the woods, and some folks still called him "Wolf Boy." Though probably not to his face, she thought. "But he's generally on city patrol. What was he doing out on the res investigating that murder?"

"He was helping Tracy with her explorations, I guess."

"Was he around the day she was attacked?"

"No."

No help there, obviously. "Anybody could have put on a hodgepodge of ceremonial regalia to conceal their identity." Dakota mused idly.

"Old Jeremiah Kincaid collected the stuff."

The statement fell into the midst of their conversation and left silence in its wake. For several seconds, Dakota could hardly grasp what Clint was saying, it came from so far out in left field. Slowly she turned her head to look at him. "Surely you're not suggesting Jeremiah Kincaid attacked Tracy!"

Clint shook his head sharply. "The old man was dead long before that. No, I was just making a comment. It's one place I know of outside of a museum where you could find all that stuff easily. And I've already checked with Sara Dean who's in charge of the Whitehorn Museum. She says nothing is missing."

"Other people around here might collect the stuff."

"Could be."

But he didn't think so, she realized. He was convinced that Jeremiah Kincaid's collection was somehow related to the attack on Tracy Roper Hensley. "Dugin?" She had heard of the Kincaid heir, who had died just recently, in fact.

"He was too much of a wimp."

"Can you be sure of that?"

Clint turned, his gray-green eyes boring into her. "Anything's possible, but I grew up around here, remember? Dugin would be at the bottom of my list.''

"Then one of the hired hands?''

He shook his head again. ''I doubt any of them have been around long enough to have an interest in preventing Avery's murderer from being discovered. No, it had to be someone who was around here thirty years ago.''

"Well, that rules out Mary Jo Kincaid," Dakota said facetiously. She expected Clint to snort or make some other derogatory sound, but he didn't. ''Oh, come on! You can't possibly think—'' She broke of sharply. "Clint, don't be ridiculous!''

''It's possible,'' he said flatly. "And as long as it's possible, I won't rule anyone out completely.''

"But that's absurd! The woman only moved here a few years ago. What could she possibly have to do with a murder that happened nearly thirty years ago?''

''Probably nothing. But 'probably' is a long way from 'absolutely.' I agree it's not likely that she had anything to do with Avery's murder, but she had access to ceremonial regalia. And she might be involved with someone who *is* connected to the murder. Someone who might be using her without her knowledge.''

Dakota nodded slowly, seeing where he was headed. "That's possible.''

''Of course it is. Use your head, Winston. It's not just there to hold your hair up.''

''Why don't you quit being such an obnoxious jerk, Calloway?'' As soon as she'd spoken, she wished she could recall the words. Her intended plan of action had been to keep her cool at all times and give him no excuse to criticize her in any way. Getting into a heated argument with him would give him an excuse to tell everyone she was a bitch to work with. Given that Clint had been around for a long time and was highly respected, she was sure he would be believed. This was not the way to win friends and influence people in the Blue Lake County Sheriff's Department.

"So you think I'm an obnoxious jerk, eh?" He wheeled off the road into Martha Preston's driveway and pulled up in front of the bunkhouse that was his home.

"You can be," she heard herself say. Her heart hammered uneasily, but she decided not to back down. There was just so much a person could be expected to take, she decided. Just so much. So what if he told everybody she was a pain in the butt?

He didn't bother to reply, leaving her to feel foolish the way she always did when she said something angry to someone who remained disinterested—as if she had behaved childishly. Swallowing her frustration, she smoothed her expression and followed him into his house, determined not to let him see that she was still annoyed. The man probably enjoyed annoying her, and she wasn't going to give him the satisfaction.

"Make yourself comfortable," he said, with a wave in the general direction of a couch and easy chair that looked as if they'd been purchased from Winona Cobbs's Stop 'N' Swap. Colonial style and maple, the furniture had cream-colored upholstery with large brown cabbage roses on it. It looked homey, comfortable and battered, and not at all like something the man making lunch would have chosen if he'd had other choices.

In the corner was a large, scarred oak desk that might once have belonged to a bank executive. On it were stacks of books, stacks of papers, a green blotter and the ubiquitous piles of color-tipped matchsticks, just like those on his desk at work. Apparently he, too, brought his job home with him.

Several bookcases groaned beneath a collection of hard-cover mysteries and law books. Dakota wondered if he had gone to law school or just read for his own pleasure.

The television was a small one that looked about as old as she was. It was a good guess he didn't turn it on very often. The stereo was a different matter, however. Everything was new, expensive and well cared for. His CD collection proved to be extensive and varied, ranging from country to classic.

Surprising, she thought, and turned to find him watching her. Her cheeks flushed immediately, even though she had nothing to be embarrassed about. She hadn't looked at anything that wasn't in plain sight, after all.

"Lunch is ready," he said, his own face revealing nothing.

They ate at a small dinette table with a chipped but clean plastic top. Everything was clean, she realized. This was not the usual bachelor pad.

"You've made it nice in here," she remarked. "Homey." And it was. It felt like a place where you could put up your feet and relax.

His mouth tightened in what might have been a scowl or a smile. Either way, she sensed this wasn't a topic of conversation he was comfortable with. But then, why should he be? From all reports she had heard, his relations with women were limited to brief flings. She doubted he'd ever invited one of them into this sanctum.

But eating in stony silence wasn't her style, either. She'd been raised to believe meals were social occasions, a time to share pleasant conversation. Sitting there and saying nothing was impossible for her.

"I wanted to thank you for not telling everyone in the department about my family."

He lifted a dark eyebrow. "Why would I bother? It's hardly the top of the day's news."

"Well, I'm still grateful. It's hard enough being a woman cop without having everyone think you're a spoiled rich kid on top of it. And I'm not, you know."

He shrugged disinterestedly, then took another bite of his sandwich. Apparently, Dakota thought frustratedly, this man couldn't converse on any subject except police work. And she'd be damned if she was going to spend her lunch hour talking about their cases.

"Have you ever been married, Clint?"

Now that got his attention, she saw with satisfaction. His jaw tightened and he stopped chewing. Slowly, his gray-green eyes lifted to her face. They were as hard as slate as they met hers, reflecting nothing but an old hurt.

"Women are a pain in the butt," he said flatly. "Why in hell would I marry one?"

She bristled instantly. "*Most* women are as decent, hard-working and honest as any man!"

"Like you, I suppose." He sounded almost weary.

"I'm nothing special," she said firmly. "I do the best job I can, and I keep my promises. Most of the people I know do the same."

"Which just goes to show how unfit you are to be a cop."

"What?" Stunned by this frontal assault, she gaped at him.

"Most people *don't* keep their promises. Hell, if everyone kept his word and did what he said he was going to, we wouldn't need lawyers, never mind cops. But most people don't keep their promises. They're out for what they can get and to hell with everyone else."

"That's true of some people, certainly—"

"The problem with you, Miss Winston, is that silver

spoon you were born with. You don't know anything about the seamier side of people because your money protected you. You're just a wide-eyed debutante who thinks the world is her oyster, and that's why you're never going to be a good cop.''

Furious, she jumped up from her chair and glared at him, her hands knotted into fists. ''You're a real bastard, Calloway. I'm a damn fine cop! I didn't make detective after only two years as a patrolman because I was lousy at what I do!''

He rose, too, scowling right back at her. She was struck suddenly by his size, by the coiled power in him, but she refused to back down. She hadn't made good as a cop by backing down from men who were larger than she was. And deep inside her, at the very back of her mind, grew the conviction that he was using anger and scorn to avoid something else.

''You go through life like a perennial Pollyanna,'' he growled. ''Looking for the good in everyone! A cop can't do that, Winston. A cop has to assume the worst about everyone in order to get the job done!''

''I don't—''

''You *do!* Poor Mary Jo Kincaid, all those losses and big, mean Clint Calloway won't rule out the devastated widow as a suspect in a string of weird happenings around the Kincaid land. What does that say about you, Winston? A cop doesn't rule out anybody without a damn good reason, and being a recently bereaved widow isn't a reason!''

Breathing rapidly, Dakota continued to glare at him, even as she admitted inwardly that he was right. Whether Mary Jo Kincaid could have anything to do with any of the incidents they were investigating was something that had to be determined through investigation, not assumed because she was petite, sweet and widowed.

And that was when a horrible suspicion uncoiled in her, something so awful she couldn't believe it had even occurred to her. So shocked was Dakota by it that she blurted it out before she realized what she was doing. "Well, you've certainly got a reason to want to nail a murder on her."

"What do you mean?"

"If you could prove she murdered Jeremiah or Dugin Kincaid, you'd stand to inherit after all, wouldn't you? Just as you'd inherit if you could get her executed for the murder of Floyd Oakley because you'd be the only remaining heir."

Six

It was suddenly so silent in the bunkhouse that the sound of the water heater clicking on seemed loud. Dakota was at least as horrified as Clint by her suggestion, and she stared at him, stunned, watching the emotions chase across his hard features—first shock, then disbelief and finally fury.

"How dare you!" he growled. "How dare you suggest that I'd use my position for personal gain! That I'd try to get an innocent women convicted just so I could get some money!"

Some imp must have taken possession of her mouth, because as much as she wanted to recall her rash suggestions, she instead stood by them. "*You* were the one who told me never to dismiss a suspect. *You* were the one who just sat here and essentially told me that nobody should be trusted. Why should I trust *you?*"

For an instant she thought he was going to hit her; the urge was written plainly on his face. Then, slowly, as if letting go muscle by muscle, he relaxed. "That's right," he said roughly. "Don't trust anybody." Abruptly he turned away to the sink, where he filled a glass with water.

"I didn't mean I don't trust you," Dakota said as her anger began to fade. Because she did still trust him. In spite of the terrible suspicion that had wormed its way into her brain, she still felt she could trust him as her partner.

He turned and faced her, leaning back against the edge

of the sink as he smiled cynically. "That's exactly what you meant," he said. "You just accused me of being willing to frame an innocent person."

"I did no such thing!"

"Sorry, doll, that's exactly what you said."

"It was not! I just meant it would be to your advantage if you could pin a murder on Mary Jo Kincaid."

"Same difference, if you ask me."

"It is *not* the same thing at all!" Her temper was firing up again, and for some reason she couldn't quite explain, Dakota felt it was necessary to make this man understand that there was a difference between what she had said and what he had understood her to say. To her it was a crucial difference. "What I meant was that it might be possible that your refusal to eliminate Mary Jo from the list of suspects could be motivated by something personal. I did *not* say you were trying to frame her, or that you would even consider such a thing."

"Just that I'd investigate her in hopes of turning something up that would bring all that money my way." Before she could respond, he shook his head and moved swiftly toward her. "Let me give you a few lessons, Winston. First, never tell a suspect that you're on to him. If I were the kind of person you just suggested I am, I might be tempted to get *you* out of the way before you caused me any trouble."

She gasped as he seized her by the shoulders and scowled down at her. His grip didn't hurt at all, but that didn't matter. She felt threatened and trapped, and her instinct was to fight free. She quelled it, instead lifting her chin and staring right back at him, refusing to let him know he frightened her.

His eyes narrowed a little and he leaned even closer. "Number two, don't ever tell a man you trust him."

"Why not?" She could hardly breathe. His presence was overpowering, dark. He seemed to surround her, closing out everything except him.

"Because a man might be tempted to take advantage of that trust."

She just had time to catch her breath before his mouth swooped down and covered hers in a searing kiss. She felt a moment's panic, followed by a dazed sense of disbelief that he could want to kiss her under these circumstances. And then everything drifted away on the exquisite awareness of the heat of his mouth and the hardness of his body pressing against hers.

She had been kissed before, many times. A shortage of boyfriends had never been one of her problems. But this was the first time she had been kissed by a man like Clint Calloway, a man who was sure of what to do with his lips, where to place his hands, just how tightly to hold her against him. A man who knew with just the pressure of his arms around her how to make her feel secure and safe...and desirable.

It was impossible to think. In the first flash of sensation, Dakota forgot all about why he was doing this, or what it could mean to their working relationship. Questions that would be important later were meaningless now. Now all that mattered was the texture of his jeans beneath her hands as she placed them on his hips, the rough prickle of beard stubble against her skin, the warmth of lips that were astonishingly soft.

Something inside her seemed to release, a deep internal letting go that left her soft and pliant against him. She wanted these moments to go on forever, wanted never to lose the wondrous feeling of strong arms around her, of a powerful body sheltering her.

His mouth was mobile, caressing hers with gentle movements that grew slowly harder as he drew her deeper into the kiss. Her head sank backward as she silently begged for more and yet more of these magical touches. When she felt the moist heat of his tongue tracing her lips, it seemed the most natural thing in the world to open and take him inside her.

There was nothing threatening in the invasion, nothing overpowering. Instead there was a gentle penetration, a coaxing, teasing exploration of the humid cavern of her mouth. Almost before she realized it, her own tongue joined the dance, stroking gently along his.

She had always thought of kisses as perfunctory things, messy sometimes, usually uncomfortable. Never had she understood why people considered them erotic—until Clint Calloway showed her that a kiss could be the doorway to sensation. A small blossom of passion began to unfurl deep within her.

Then, abruptly, he stepped away, leaving her cold, alone and somehow wounded. She shuddered, wrapping her arms tightly around herself, feeling as if she were teetering on a cold, windy precipice. "Why did you do that?" she asked, her voice almost unrecognizable.

He swore, a quiet but savage sound. "How old are you, Winston? Damn, they shouldn't let you out without a keeper!"

Humiliation washed through her in hot waves. Never in her life had she wanted so badly to flee as she did right then, but she forced herself to stand her ground. Running wouldn't help a thing. She had to work with this man.

She closed her eyes for a few moments to gather her resources. Muscle by muscle she forced herself to relax, until she stood with her arms at her sides. Pretend nothing happened, she told herself. Pretend it was all an hallucination. "Okay," she said aloud, her eyes snapping open, "let's go find out when Rafe can take us to the res."

Dakota didn't know Rafe Rawlings all that well, but she liked the young police officer, with his slightly shaggy hair and his warm personality tempered with reserve. Rafe was married to the public defender, which Dakota thought must give some interesting twists to their dinner conversations.

He was on duty, but they tracked him down at the intersection of Cascade and Kinsey, where he was writing a traffic ticket for a guy in a battered, dusty 1956 Ford pickup. "Just remember, Hank," Dakota heard him say good-naturedly, "a stop sign means 'stop,' not 'put the pedal to the metal.'" Hank laughed, signed the ticket and drove off with a friendly wave.

Rafe turned to look at Dakota and Clint, his smile fading a little. "What's up?"

Clint answered him. "We'd like to know when you could clear a couple of hours to take us out to the res and show us where Charles Avery's body was discovered."

"It's really not my beat. The sheriff could show you the place as well as I could."

"But you were out there more often helping Tracy," Clint replied. "I'd like you to tell us everything you saw, everything you suspect. You've got a clearer picture than Judd does."

Rafe tilted his head a little and regarded Clint steadily. "What do you want to dig all this up for? Walker was acquitted, and there weren't any other suspects, except maybe Lexine Baxter, and she was gone just about when I was born."

"But someone attacked both Tracy and Judd when they were out there."

Rafe nodded thoughtfully and settled both his hands on

his hips. "There is that," he agreed. "Bothers me to think
the culprit is still running loose. I suppose you don't want
to risk getting Tracy involved in it again."

"I'd rather not. She's got a child to worry about."

"Judd'd raise Cain anyway if you tried to." He smiled
again. "Sure, I'll take you out there. Plan on going early
Friday morning."

"Great. See you then."

The men shook hands, and Rafe nodded to Dakota before
climbing back in his cruiser. Just before he drove off, however, Clint hailed him. "Have you seen Homer around?
I've been trying to get in touch with him."

Rafe shook his head, looking up at them through his
open window. "It's been—oh, a couple of weeks, I guess.
Hell, you don't suppose he's been kidnapped again, do
you?"

Clint hesitated. "God, I hope not."

"Well, if I see him, I'll tell him you're looking for him.
If he doesn't show up soon, maybe we ought to go looking."

Back in their own vehicle, Dakota turned to Clint. "What
now?"

"I think it's time to pay Winona Cobbs a visit and see
if she's had any more spells lately."

Everybody in Blue Lake County knew Winona Cobbs
and her Stop 'N' Swap junkyard. Everybody also knew of
Winona's reputation as a psychic, and surprisingly few people pooh-poohed her skills. It was a testimony to the
woman's stature, personality and accuracy, Dakota supposed, that folks trusted her intuition to the degree that they
did. Still, whatever Winona's reputation, it made Dakota
uneasy to consult a psychic in relation to police business.

The sign that hung crookedly in front of the Stop 'N'

Swap was virtually illegible, not that it mattered. Nobody around here needed a sign to find Winona. The yard was cluttered with everything from rusting automobiles to chipped pink flamingo yard ornaments. Cats seemed to be everywhere, and a goat grazed lazily beside a 1953 Ford.

Behind the trailer where Winona lived was a ramshackle old barn that housed her more delicate treasures. Dakota had browsed there one day and had fallen in love with some old fern stands that now graced her own apartment. She also had her eye on a secretary that was in bad need of refinishing.

But as for Winona's psychic abilities…that made Dakota extremely uneasy.

Winona came out to meet them, her tanned face creased in a bright, welcoming smile. "I knew you'd show up sooner or later, Clint," she said. Then she turned to Dakota. "Good to see you again. I've been saving that secretary for you."

Dakota was astonished; she was sure she'd never let on how much she wanted the desk.

Winona's smile softened. "You touched it. When I touch it now I can feel how much you wanted it. Don't worry, honey. I'll keep it for you."

Winona could tell things like that from touching them! Amazed, Dakota stared at the other woman, uncertain how to reply. Winona didn't seem to expect an answer, though.

She invited them inside and offered them tea. Gathered around her dinette table, they chatted for a while of general things, of the off-again, on-again spring that didn't seem to quite want to turn into summer, of the upcoming rodeo and whether Winona was going to take a booth to sell her wild honey.

But finally Clint came to the point. "You had any more spells, Winona?"

"Related to little Jennifer's kidnapping?" Winona shook her head. "Lately I think my powers have hit a logjam somehow. No matter what I try to see, I get the same thing—a woman with two faces. Darned if I know what to make of it."

Dakota leaned forward, curious enough to forget her reservations. "What do you mean by a woman with two faces? Is it something you see, sort of like a Picasso painting?"

Winona shook her head. "It's hard to explain. What I see is…oh, it's not anyone I know. It's more like when you have a dream and you know what you're seeing is familiar even though your waking mind knows you've never seen it before."

Dakota nodded encouragingly.

"Well, what I see is a woman's face. Almost a mannequinlike face…and a hand keeps putting a translucent mask over it. Other times I just see…two faces overlaid, so that I can't make either one out clearly. I wish I could figure out what it means!"

"I'm sure you will," Clint said. "You usually do."

Winona favored him with a smile. "Usually. But then again, my talent may have just died. Never in all my days can I remember a time when I would have only one vision over and over again."

"It must be important somehow," Clint said.

"Maybe. Maybe not." She shrugged. "Was that what you wanted to know? It's scant help."

"Well, if all you can see is a woman with two faces, maybe we need to think about all the possible meanings that could have," Dakota suggested. "It could be metaphoric."

"That's what I'm thinking," Winona agreed. "Two faces could mean what—two-timing."

"Well, we'll work on it, too," Clint told her. "In the

meantime, I've been looking for Homer, but evidently nobody's seen him in a couple of weeks.''

"Homer? Heck, he's okay, Clint. He stopped by here just a couple of days ago to swap some agates for some of my sourdough starter.'' She chuckled. "He forgot to freshen his and it died on him. Silly old fool. Anyway, he asked me if I thought he could sell some geodes.''

"Geodes?'' Clint repeated.

"Hollow rocks with mineral formations inside,'' Dakota put in. "Some are quite beautiful. Did he show them to you, Winona?''

"Naw. Said they were big and bulky and he didn't want to be carrying them around unnecessarily. Some of them had amethyst in them, he said. Ought to fetch a few bucks from tourists.''

"I'm just glad the old cuss is okay,'' Clint said. "If you see him again, tell him I need to talk to him, will you?''

"I'll be glad to. I'll be surprised if he doesn't bring those geodes to me pretty soon. He seems to need a good sum of money for something or other.''

"What could Homer need a big sum of money for?'' Dakota asked Clint as they drove back to town.

"Maybe he thinks he's found a good place to mine. He'd probably need quite a bit of equipment to get any serious kind of operation going.''

Dakota leaned against the car window and watched the countryside speed by. The workday was over, but it was still bright. June evenings this far north were long and lingering. "Maybe he found some of those sapphires everyone keeps talking about.''

"The old mine?'' Clint shook his head doubtfully. "Well, he did find a small packet, but it was my understanding the stones weren't gem quality.''

"Would Homer know that?"

"That's what the assayer said. And Homer's eccentric, not stupid. The man knows which end of his pick is which, and I'd be damn surprised if he didn't know his minerals just as well."

"I wasn't trying to insult him, Clint. I just don't know him. Okay, so he's up on his minerals. We have to assume he wouldn't be misled by worthless sapphires. The point I'm trying to get at is that, if he found something of value, it would sure be an excuse for someone to want to kidnap him."

"To discover the location of whatever he might have found? Believe me, Winston, we considered that."

She could feel color bloom in her cheeks again, but ignored it. "There wasn't anything in the file about it."

"No?" He glanced sharply at her. "I'm sure he was questioned about that."

"Then something's missing from the file."

He swore, quietly but succinctly. "What the hell is going on around here?"

"Maybe it was misfiled. Maybe the report just slipped out of the folder somehow."

"Yeah. Sure."

She didn't believe it, either, but the alternative—that something had been deliberately removed from a police file—was more than she wanted to think could happen. "But someone *did* question him about any finds he had made, or whether his abductor questioned him about anything?"

"Of course he was asked. He was pretty incoherent at the time, and later couldn't remember a whole lot. Or claimed not to, at any rate. But that's why I want to talk with him again. I had a feeling at the time that he was too scared to tell everything he knew. Maybe some of that fear has worn off.''

Neither of them were willing to dismiss Homer's missing statement, so when they got back to the station, they went straight to Clint's desk to look through the file.

"You're right," Clint announced finally. "The statement's missing."

"Nobody could have walked in off the street and taken something from the file," Dakota said.

"Are you suggesting police involvement in Homer's kidnapping?"

She bit her lower lip. "I don't know."

"It wouldn't be the first time something's been removed from a file for a good reason, and the person who took it just never got around to putting it back. Or somebody could have shoved the statement back in without pulling the folder, and it might have gotten into another file."

Both possibilities were logical ones, but neither of them put her mind to rest. They didn't exactly seem to ease Clint's mind, either, because he helped her look through every folder in the drawer where the case file was supposed to be stored.

Just as they were about to give up, Dakota found the missing report. Somehow it had been shoved to the very back of the drawer and was crumpled behind the last file.

"Well, that's one less thing to worry about," Clint said. "I'm outta here."

But Dakota lingered, scanning the crumpled report before she tucked it back into Homer's file. He'd been incoherent, all right, talking about small, silver-suited aliens in broken phrases and making disjointed references to dark places where he'd supposedly been held prisoner. A cave, perhaps? Clearly the man had been terrified, but not even his terror could make Dakota believe that his abductor had been an alien. Oh, it was possible such things happened, and she was perfectly willing to admit that she didn't know everything there was to know about the subject. But from what she'd heard over the years, people who claimed to be abducted by aliens got returned pretty quickly...usually within hours of their abduction.

Except for that one case in Arizona where the guy had disappeared for five days... Naw. She shook her head and shut the drawer of the file cabinet. Something else had happened to Homer, and it probably had something to do with his prospecting.

"Dakota?"

Turning, Dakota smiled as she saw Tracy Hensley. "Where's the squirt?"

"I left her with Judd. He says you and Clint are looking into the Avery case again." Drawing close, she gazed anxiously at the younger woman. "Be careful, will you? Somebody is very serious about not wanting that case solved."

"Rafe found some footprints, didn't he?"

Tracy nodded. "Small moccasin prints. It was hard to judge the person's size because of all the regalia and the kachina mask he was wearing, but he couldn't have been all that big, according to Rafe."

"Ethan Walker's a big man."

Tracy nodded. "I never thought it was him—not the person who attacked me, anyway. I mean, at the time he *did* seem to be a likely suspect for the murder, but I was always sure he wasn't responsible for accosting me."

"You thought the regalia was all wrong?"

"It was a hodgepodge that no self-respecting Indian would have worn!" She smiled slightly and shook her head. "Honestly, Dakota, it looked like a costume thrown together from odds and ends. *I'm* convinced my attacker was some white person. Homer is convinced it was a spirit.''

''*Homer* saw him?''

Tracy nodded. ''He told Rafe he'd seen a restless spirit. From what Rafe could glean, it was the same character I saw. Unfortunately, it didn't help at all. We're pretty much guessing that whoever attacked me also attacked Judd…and that's why I had to come warn you to be careful. Somebody was scared by my poking around out there. Scared enough to try to kill two people.''

Seven

So Homer had glimpsed the figure that had attacked Tracy, Dakota thought later that evening. Stretched out on a chaise in the yard behind her apartment, she stared up at the brilliant stars. She wore a jacket and had wrapped a blanket around her legs to keep off the night chill.

Homer had seen a "spirit" that may have attacked Tracy and Judd. Much later, the old man had been abducted by aliens. On the face of it, with the two incidents occurring just over a year apart, Dakota wasn't inclined to think they were related…except that made one too many weird events involving one slightly weird prospector. And Clint kept arguing that while Homer was a little eccentric, he wasn't stupid.

Which, when she thought about it, was an interesting distinction.

Did Homer's eccentricities explain his report of the events? Not entirely, since he'd apparently seen the same thing Tracy had, but instead of identifying it as someone impersonating some ritualistic Indian figure, Homer had identified it as a "restless spirit." Which was a matter of interpretation that in no way devalued his report. If the same thing applied to his abduction by an alien or aliens…

Frowning thoughtfully, Dakota stared up into the night sky and wondered what Homer could have seen that he would have believed to be an alien. He hadn't been far off in his description of Tracy's assailant. Why should they assume he didn't know what he'd seen when he was abducted? The logical inference at this juncture was that Homer was inclined to give paranormal explanations to oddities. In short, his abductor could have dressed strangely and Homer would have easily leapt to the conclusion that he or she was an alien, just as he had leapt to the conclusion that Tracy's assailant was a spirit.

Therefore, Homer had been fooled, probably quite deliberately by someone who understood his inclination to misinterpret. Someone who had taken advantage of his eccentricities.

But why? It had been a year now since Homer's abduction. Logic suggested someone may have suspected that he had found a valuable mineral vein of some kind—gold, sapphires, whatever. Something valuable enough for someone to kidnap him to discover its whereabouts. But Homer hadn't found the real rich deposits so he couldn't have said where the sapphire mine was.

Still, maybe someone had thought he knew something anyway.... Damn, they needed to find Homer so they could question him. There were so many things he might have tucked in that crazy head of his that could be useful.

The soft swish of feet moving through the grass alerted Dakota, and she looked around to see a tall man approaching, his faced shadowed beneath the brim of a cowboy hat. Clint. It had to be Clint. Nobody else had quite that way of moving with the alert wariness of a wild animal. She sat up, swinging her cocooned legs over the side of the chaise.

"Don't get up on my account," he said.

"Did something happen?"

He dropped cross-legged on the grass beside her before he answered. "Not a damn thing. I ran into Tracy when I was leaving the station earlier. She said she was going to talk to you."

"She did."

"Did she manage to scare you off?"

"No."

He nodded slowly. "Somehow I didn't think she'd manage to. You got more hair than wit, Winston."

"Seems to go with the badge."

He startled her with a short bark of laughter. "Sometimes it sure does. Pretty out tonight."

"It sure is." Her heart leapt and began a slow, heavy beating as she suddenly remembered the way he had kissed her earlier. Was he remembering that, too? Was that why he had come by tonight?

But he didn't say anything to indicate that, and gradually she relaxed, settling back against her chair, swallowing a silly sense of disappointment. This man could have any woman he wanted for the asking, she was certain. There was no reason for him to come here tonight. That kiss earlier had been meant to intimidate her. Apparently Mr. Tough Guy Calloway couldn't stand a woman who talked back.

But he continued to sit beside her on the grass, and the evening was too beautiful to waste. Pushing away all thoughts of how he had treated her, she returned her gaze to the stars above. "I've been thinking about Homer."

"What about him?"

"It's just so odd that he saw the person who attacked Tracy, and then was abducted by aliens. Too coincidental, somehow. I keep trying to put my finger on why that bugs me, but I can't quite get at it."

"It bugs me, too. It's not the first time I've had the itchy feeling that a bunch of apparently unrelated things aren't unrelated at all. And the kidnapping. Jennifer McCallum's kidnapping..." He sighed heavily. "There's something about the way it happened that shows a lot of planning.

But who around here would want to kidnap that little girl? It's not as if somebody could keep her for their own. And if they wanted money, they'd sure have to hide it around here, because everybody would notice if somebody suddenly got rich.''

"But there's been no ransom demand," Dakota reminded him.

"I know. That bugs me as much as anything. When kids disappear like this—'' He broke off sharply.

Dakota was glad he didn't complete the thought. "Yeah," she said. "Yeah. Who around here would do something like that?''

"That's the sixty-four-thousand dollar question, Winston. Who around here could do something like that? Nothing like this has happened in the history of this county, as far as I can tell. Which is not to say it couldn't ever happen, but this just isn't the kind of place that seems to raise that type of sicko. So we have an apparently premeditated crime, no suspects, no evidence, no leads....'' He swore. "Hell, I don't think we've had this many murders around here since the range wars!''

"Spread out over all these years—''

"Patooey,'' he interrupted. "As a rule, people don't get too inclined to kill one another unless they're rubbing elbows all the time. Around here, most folks have enough space to avoid the urge. When I look back over the last twenty, thirty years, what I see are a couple of barroom brawls that resulted in a fatal injury and one guy who beat his wife to death. I don't think it's that we're any better than folks elsewhere as much as that most of us can avoid the people we want to.''

Dakota nodded, agreeing in principle. Crowding sure did increase the rate of violent crime.

"But all of a sudden we have a guy knifed at a wedding—a stranger, no less. Someone with no ties in the county, that we can figure. And then we have a thirty-year-old murder turn up that somebody wants to keep real quiet even now, and we have a major kidnapping, and…well, I'm not all that convinced that Dugin Kincaid's death was an accident, either.''

Dakota caught her breath sharply. An instant later, she sat up and threw the blanket back. ''If we're going to discuss this, I think we ought to go inside.'' There was no way of knowing how many open windows their voices could drift through on the still night air.

Clint rose to his feet in one easy motion and followed her into her apartment. When she stepped through the door with him on her heels, she experienced one of those discomfiting moments of seeing her apartment through a stranger's eyes. For the first time it struck her how little she had done to fix it up. Other than the fern stands she needed to refinish, it was basically just as it had been when she moved in. She hadn't hung anything on the walls or decorated in any of the smallest ways. The place looked bare, utilitarian.

Except for the small, stuffed pink elephant tucked in a corner of the couch. Dakota had bought it on impulse because it was irresistibly cute and squeezable. Now she wished she could hide it from Clint's sharp eyes. It exposed a part of her she didn't want any hard-bitten male to know about.

But he saw it. He saw it and then looked straight at her, his eyes full of knowledge. She shifted uneasily, sure that the elephant had somehow confirmed all his worst suspicions about her. But what could she do about it? It was there and he had seen it, and unless he wanted to say something about it, the best thing she could do was ignore it.

"Coffee?" she asked him, turning briskly to the counter. "Decaf or regular?"

"Regular, thanks."

"Now what's this about Dugin?" she demanded as she prepared the coffee. "I heard he died from injuries that happened in a fire."

"That's the story."

She glanced at him, watching the way he folded himself into one of the small chairs at the dinette table. Egad, his legs were long. It surprised her, even though her overall impression of him was one of massiveness. And that bulge at the juncture of his thighs... She dragged her eyes away quickly. "Then what's the problem? Kincaid was injured and died. Case closed."

"Yeah. Only he didn't die from burns. He theoretically died from the head injury that put him in intensive care."

"So?"

"Well, what bugs me, Winston, is that the man was recovering when he died."

"A final rally. It happens."

"The doctors were convinced he was pulling out of it and going to make it. Then boom! He stops breathing."

"The doctors could have been wrong."

He looked straight at her, his eyes a dark green. "The nurses don't think so."

Forgetting to be wary of him, she came to the table and sat across from him. "You talked to them?"

He nodded. "Yep. The attending physician left town rather suddenly, but the rest of the staff is troubled by it."

"Well, they hate to be patients."

"It's more than that. Dugin's nurse is convinced that something fishy went on. She said she's been wrong before and she'll be wrong again, but this one stinks to high heaven."

Dakota felt her pulse accelerate a little, the way it always did when she faced an interesting case. "Anything else?"

"The head injury. It was never really resolved how he got bashed at the very base of his skull. Everyone assumed that something fell on him, but to get hit there by something that fell, he'd have to already be facedown. How'd he get that way?"

"Smoke? Maybe the smoke knocked him out."

"Maybe. Except when they found him, there was nothing lying across him to indicate what had smashed his head. And a falling beam would have done a hell of lot more damage."

"You're saying someone knocked him out and then set the fire?"

Clint rubbed his chin a moment, almost as if he was reluctant to say what he was thinking. "It's a possibility, Winston. One nobody has really looked into."

It was remarkable, she found herself thinking, that he was telling her this, particularly after their explosion earlier over her suggestion that his motives might not be pure. Remarkable that it was she, his unwanted female partner, that he chose to confide in. Maybe he was beginning to appreciate her skills.

And maybe the moon was made out of green cheese, after all.

A couple of years as a cop had taught her not to trust too easily—not even her partner. People had private agendas all the time, and until you knew what they were, you could get into a peck of trouble. Maybe Clint was making these suggestions to send her off on a wild-goose chase that could make her the laughingstock of the department. Maybe this was his retaliation for what she had suggested earlier.

And maybe he was telling the truth. The only way to find out was to play along until she could be sure.

"What are you planning to do?" she asked finally.

His gray-green eyes became hooded. "I haven't decided that yet."

"You can't reopen the case on just a suspicion."

He made an impatient sound. "I know that."

The coffeemaker finished brewing, and she poured them each a cup. "Did Dugin Kincaid have a lot of enemies?"

"He wasn't real popular with most folks. He was pretty much a snotty, spoiled wimp. The guys at the Sundowner used to groan when they saw him coming, but I wouldn't have thought any of them hated him enough to want to kill him."

"So we don't even have a motive?"

"We? When did you get into this, Winston?"

"The minute you told me about it, Calloway. So why would anyone want to kill Dugin Kincaid?"

"He had a lot of money and a lot of land."

Dakota sat back in her chair and tried not to let Clint see what she was feeling at that moment. Essentially, he was implying that Dugin's wife had wanted him dead. While that wasn't out of the realm of possibility, the fact remained that the death had been ruled accidental. It was also true that Clint Calloway himself might have an interest in that same money, if Mary Jo Kincaid could be convicted of the murder of her husband.

Dakota didn't at all like the way her thoughts were running right now. It gave her the queasiest feeling to think that the man sitting across from her could be acting from such a base motive.

She admitted that she was seriously disappointed. For whatever reason, she had expected more from Clint Calloway. Maybe that was a foolish expectation from a man who had been raised as he had. More than one person had been eager to tell her that Clint had been raised by an alcoholic streetwalker. So far she had managed to avoid the assumption that he was no better than he should be, but perhaps...

"Anyway," he continued, "it's conceivable somebody has their eye on the land, maybe for ranching or even mining, and they couldn't get anywhere with Dugin. It wouldn't be the first time in history somebody's been murdered because someone else thought his widow would make an easier mark."

Astonished, Dakota tried to gather her scattered thoughts. Clint had come at this from an entirely unexpected angle, one that had never even occurred to her. She hoped she had been completely wrong in her suspicions. "Has anybody indicated serious interest in the Kincaid land?"

"That's what got me thinking about this. I was over at the Sundowner earlier, and Dick Harris mentioned that he'd had some queries from someone interested in purchasing twenty-five thousand acres of Kincaid land."

Dakota sat bolt upright. "Harris is a real-estate agent, isn't he? Does he have the land listed?"

"He says no, but he got the definite feeling that the person who called him had heard about it's being for sale from somewhere. He says he's going to go out and try to get Mary Jo to list it with him."

"Surely if she'd put up the land for sale the whole county would be buzzing about it!"

"You'd think so—unless she's doing it on the qt for some reason."

"I could understand her not wanting to keep the ranch. She's not a rancher, after all, and running the place must be one heck of a job. But I can't imagine why she would want to be secretive about selling it."

"Selling *part* of it," he corrected her. "Twenty-five

thousand acres isn't the whole place—which makes it even more interesting. Why would she want to sell just a parcel? Unless someone approached her with an offer for a specific part of the ranch, and that offer is what's getting around and causing other interested parties to try to find out about it.''

''Which would explain the calls Harris got, even if she hasn't listed the land.''

''Exactly.''

''But that still doesn't explain the secrecy.''

''That would probably be something the buyer wants,'' Clint said slowly. ''Maybe. If it's a foreign buyer, they'd definitely want it quiet until it was settled.'' There was more than a little resentment among Montanans when another piece of their state was sold to foreign interests. So far the sales had worked out well, but that didn't prevent initial opposition every time another one was in the works.

''That would explain it, all right.'' Dakota sipped her coffee and then pushed the mug aside. She didn't really want it, after all. She felt hyped-up enough as it was. ''What other reasons could there be for keeping it secret?''

''The Kincaids are wealthy, but most of that wealth is in land and cattle. I don't imagine they have all that much liquid capital beyond what they need at any given time for operating the ranch. If Mary Jo doesn't give a fig for ranching, she'd prefer to liquidate. She probably wouldn't want the whole county buzzing about how she's selling off her inheritance as soon as she got her delicate little claws on it.''

Dakota smiled wryly. ''You really don't like her, do you.''

A muscle in his jaw tensed. ''She's despicable.''

''How can you say that? Everyone else seems to think she's something wonderful.''

"Not everyone. Time is taking the shine from her image. But it doesn't matter what anyone else thinks. Look her straight in the eye sometime, Dakota. That woman is as hard as nails and as calculating as a computer. It wouldn't surprise me at all to learn she married Dugin for his money. Hell, what else could she have married him for?"

Dakota was amused by his gruff dismissal of Dugin's attractions. "I don't know," she said, deliberately baiting him. "From the pictures I've seen, he must have been a handsome man."

Clint snorted.

"What's the matter, Calloway? You don't think sex appeal matters as much to a woman as it does to a man?"

She knew instantly that she'd made a serious mistake of some kind. His face hardened to granite, and his eyes looked like twin chips of smoky glass. "Looks will never matter as much to a woman as the thickness of a man's wallet."

Dakota was stung. "Oh, come on, Clint! That's not true of *all* women, and you know it!"

"No, I *don't* know it," he said harshly. "I don't know it at all." Rising, he strode toward the door, pausing just long enough to say over his shoulder, "You're so damn naive, Winston. Coming from your background, you ought to know just how much money counts."

Dakota was still gasping in shock when the door slammed behind him.

She really didn't want to go to work in the morning. For the first time in her career, she dreaded getting up, getting dressed and going to the station. The rawness of what Clint had said last night left her feeling...vulnerable somehow. Which was utterly ridiculous, she assured herself as she smoothed her hair into a neat French braid. There was no reason on earth she should feel vulnerable because the man was a misogynist. That was *his* problem.

Something about what he had said last night led her to believe his problem with women didn't spring entirely from his mother. Had some woman scorned him in his youth because he didn't have enough money to suit her? The more she thought about that possibility, the more she felt it might be true. It would certainly explain some of the things he said.

But the fact that such things had hurt Clint so deeply told her more about him than any supposition could. He was a man who cared deeply. Too deeply. His scars were raw and painful, and he would not heal easily. Whatever had been done to him in the past, his pain was still with him, affecting his entire outlook. She wished there was some way to ease it, but she couldn't imagine what would help—except for him to meet a woman who disproved everything he had ever learned.

Not that he'd believe it. She found herself smiling sadly. No, he wouldn't believe it. He'd been hurt so badly he would probably never open himself up again, never trust any woman long enough to discover that she was a good person. Heck, he'd never let anyone get close enough to show him anything! He would probably continue to spew forth vitriolic statements as if they were gospel truth, and never once regret that they drove away one scheming woman after another.

Nor would he care who he might offend in the process. Not that Dakota was offended by what he had said. There was just no way she could take such a statement personally. The last thing she'd be looking for in any man was the size of his wallet. What she wanted—all she wanted—was a man who would love her with his whole heart. A man who would make her feel as if she brought joy to his days. A man who would try to bring joy to hers.

But although Clint's condemnation didn't apply to her, or to most of the women she knew, she was well aware that there were plenty of women out there who were exactly as Clint claimed they were. Her cousin Carlene was one prime example, the despair of the rest of the family.

Even if she asked, he wouldn't answer. Unconsciously she sighed, wishing he'd open up a little, tell her something about himself so she wouldn't have to keep wondering. Working with him would certainly be more comfortable if she felt she knew him. As it was, she still felt as if she were dealing with a total stranger.

Clint stared down at the piles of matchsticks on his desk. The morning light slanted across the street in front of him, but didn't enter the windows of his office. Without his desk lamp on, he sat in a kind of twilight, watching faint gray light slowly become golden and warm.

The matchsticks weren't answering any questions, or even providing any suggestions. Some nagging feeling kept telling him that a series of apparently unrelated occurrences were in fact related, but even he had to admit it sounded lunatic. How could the abduction of Jennifer McCallum, the abduction of Homer Gilmore, the murder of Floyd Oakley and the death so long ago of Charles Avery be linked? And why did he keep feeling that something wasn't right about the accidental deaths of Jeremiah and Dugin Kincaid? Accidents happened. Jeremiah was only one of many people who slipped and fell in a shower and died. Dugin had apparently gone into a burning barn to rescue horses. It was hardly surprising he'd been fatally injured.

But it nagged at Clint anyway, to the point that he was beginning to feel a little flaky. Dakota Winston probably thought he was losing his marbles after his suggestion that Dugin's death was suspicious.

But Dakota Winston was making him feel a little flaky, too. Damn the woman, why hadn't she just stayed home with Daddy and Mommy in Missoula—or at the very least stayed on the Miles City force instead of coming to Whitehorn? What the hell made a woman want to be a cop, anyway? Most especially, why would a rich young woman want to be? She had to have a loose nut or bolt somewhere!

He knew all about the Missoula Winstons. Years ago he'd worked his way through college at the university there, and like everyone in town, he'd come to know of their power and wealth. There had been one Winston female in particular who had crossed his path in an unsavory manner. One who had been a sugar-coated bitch to the core. He shook his head, denying the memory a foothold. He'd learned his lesson and he didn't need to rehash it.

Dakota would still have been running around in pigtails then, he figured. He wondered if the girl he'd had the run-in with was her older sister.

No, he decided. Dakota was too damn polite to have been raised in the same household with that woman.

Which brought him around to his own explosion last night. Dakota got under his skin in ways he didn't at all like, and consequently his temper had grown a little frayed. Damn it, she was a pain with her insistent questions. As his partner, she ought to be a lot more willing to heed his hunches without questioning them to death.

Last night he'd resented the hell out of the way she had questioned his dislike of Mary Jo Kincaid, implying he had some ulterior motive for distrusting her. He'd been a cop for the better part of twelve years, and his reputation for honesty was impeccable. How dare she imply he was acting out of personal interest?

But equally irritating were her wide blue eyes, so startling with her dark hair. They were innocent eyes, youthful eyes, and they didn't belong on a cop. Nor did her creamy skin, which must must be as smooth as satin. Nope, if a woman was going to insist on being a cop, then she ought to at least have the decency to be ugly.

But there wasn't an ugly thing about Dakota Winston, from her softly curling, dark brown hair to her narrow waist and small feet. She was the kind of woman who fueled a man's dreams. Not so much erotic dreams, though he thought she was sexy as hell, but dreams of softer things. Things he didn't dare let himself think about.

But she had him thinking about those things, so his temper was short, and he'd exploded at her. That line about women and money was suitable for barroom conversation, but not for the ears of a lady. Certainly not for the ears of a lady who was his partner.

Damn, she'd probably complain to Judd and accuse him of sexual harassment. That'd be just like a woman.

Frustrated with life in general, he pulled one of the case files off the stack and tried to concentrate on it. No luck. He needed a break—any kind of a break—on the kidnapping case. Please God, he found himself praying, just a small break to give us some idea where to look. Part of his problem with Dakota, he admitted, was the kidnapping case. He was pushing himself hard so he wouldn't have to think about what might be happening to the missing three-year-old girl, and so he was short-tempered from lack of sleep. To top it off, he felt Dakota wasn't experienced enough to be of any real assistance, and periodically he wondered if he would be getting somewhere faster if he had another partner.

But what other partner would he have? It wasn't as if he could think of anyone in the department he'd rather have

that he *could* have. Sterling McCallum certainly couldn't
work on his own daughter's kidnapping case. As the sheriff,
Judd didn't really have the time to devote to straight detective work. Basically, Clint was stuck with Dakota.

So naturally, he'd smoothed things out by making that
remark last night. That was really going to help matters.

But what was done was done, and she was just going to
have to swallow it, because he was damned if he was going
to apologize. She'd been pushing him and he'd reacted.
End of story.

He caught sight of her dark blue Chevy in the street
below as she zipped into the parking lot. That conservative,
moderately priced sedan of hers bugged him. A woman
with her money, a woman who wanted to be a cop, ought
to be driving a fire engine red sports car. Well, one of these
days she'd get tired of pretending to be ordinary.

The ringing of the phone was a welcome distraction from
his grumpy thoughts.

"Clint, it's Martha Preston." His elderly landlady's
voice sounded shaky. He was instantly concerned.

"Martha, what's wrong? Are you sick?"

"No! Oh, heavens no! Clint, those kids who tore up my
orchard? Well, I just saw one of them, I think. Hanging
around your cabin. And I don't like the way he was acting."

"I'm on my way. Just lock all your doors, Martha. And
stay away from the windows so he doesn't see you watching."

He grabbed his hat and headed out, catching Dakota
when she was halfway up the stairs. "My landlady called
to say there was a prowler at my place," he told her without
pausing. She turned immediately and followed him.

"We'll send a uniform," Judd said when he heard Clint
swiftly telling the dispatcher where they were going.

"No, *I* want to handle this. I'm going to get my hands on one of the little brats who tore up Martha's orchard and I'm going to make sure he learns his lesson."

Judd hesitated only a moment before nodding. "All right, you two. Just remember your backlog of work."

The ride out to Clint's place was short but seemed to take forever.

Dakota was mad at him all right, Clint decided. Hell, she wouldn't even glance his way. He damn well was *not* going to apologize to her, but he guessed he needed to know just how angry she was. Especially since they might be walking into a dangerous situation and he might have to rely on her to watch his back.

"You know a Carlene Winston?" he asked finally.

She didn't even turn her head to look at him. "Yes. She's my cousin."

"We were in college together, briefly."

"Well, that might explain your misogyny."

He almost laughed, but thought better of it. "You don't like her?"

"I can't exactly say that. I used to hate her. She was always completely selfish and self-centered...and nasty, too. I don't think she's improved much, but now I just feel sorry for her. She creates her own misery, you know?"

He glanced at her, feeling his perception of her alter markedly, but before he could explore exactly what had changed, they were pulling up to the Preston place. "Keep your eye out for anyone running away," he ordered as he wheeled into the driveway.

He stopped about twenty yards from the front of the bunkhouse, swearing when he saw that the door was ajar. Someone was inside. "The back door's there, to the right. You take that corner of the house so you can watch both entrances while I go inside."

"Got it."

He wondered if she did. He wondered if she would do as she was told this time, if she had learned anything from the night in the alley, or if she would be so angry at him over his comment last night that she would decide to try to show him up—and put them both in jeopardy.

He had to trust her, because there was no alternative, but it was harder to do this morning when he had been such a jerk last night. One of these days he was going to have to learn to keep his opinions to himself.

They climbed out of the truck and began to make their way quietly to the house. Both of them expected to find a juvenile who was looking for easy money. Although neither of them expected to encounter anything really threatening, it wouldn't pay to be lax. Even juveniles could be armed and dangerous.

Clint reached the front door and flattened himself against the wall beside it. Dakota took a moment longer to reach the corner, from which she could see both doors. The back door, she noted, was still closed tightly. Turning, she gave Clint a nod.

At once he swung around, kicked the door open with a bang and yelled, "Freeze!"

There was no sound at all within the bunkhouse. Dark inside because he had forgotten to open the curtains this morning, it seemed to harbor nothing but shadows. He stepped quickly to the side so he wouldn't be silhouetted in the open door and felt around for the light switch.

Light flooded the front room of the cabin, illuminating the kitchen, dining and living areas. Nothing stirred. Easing cautiously toward the bedroom, he avoided the planks that were apt to creak loudly. The bedroom door stood open.

Anyone in there knew he was coming, so this time he reached carefully around the doorframe for the light switch, keeping the wall between himself and the bedroom.

But the place was empty.

Eight

The very first thing Clint did was check up on Martha Preston. When he found his own place empty, his next concern was that the prowler might have disturbed her. She proved to be unharmed, albeit indignant.

"I don't know what the world is coming to," she said angrily when he told her someone had broken into the bunkhouse. "It seems every youth in the area is turning into a hoodlum! First my apples, and now your cabin!"

Dakota had checked around the outside of the old bunkhouse, looking for other signs of attempted entry but found nothing. It had been awhile since they'd had any significant rain, so there wasn't even a hope of finding footprints in the packed earth out front. In the tall grass behind, there was no sign that anyone had been around recently. She spread her hands and shook her head as she joined Clint and Martha Preston on the porch of Martha's house.

"Nothing else. We need to check inside to see if they disturbed anything."

"In a minute." Clint turned back to his landlady. "I need a description, Martha. The best you can give me."

"It won't be very good, I'm afraid. I have cataracts in both eyes. Oh, not bad enough to be operated on yet—leastways not to hear Dr. Finch tell it—but details escape me, Clint."

"Don't worry about it. Just tell me whatever you can."

"Well, he wasn't very big. I figured him to be about

twelve, maybe fourteen. Wearing jeans, I think, and a blue shirt.'' She frowned, straining to remember. ''Baseball cap, I think, but I couldn't see too clearly. I think it was a blue or black baseball cap. He was kind of creeping around the side of the bunkhouse, and I didn't like the way he was moving. That's when I called you, but by the time I came back to the window, he was gone.''

''Probably inside,'' Clint said. ''You're sure it was a boy?''

Martha looked surprised. ''Well…no. I just assumed…'' She shook her head. ''Didn't strike me as a girl, but it could have been, I guess.''

''Good enough.'' Clint touched her shoulder gently. ''You go on back inside and don't worry about it. It was probably just a kid looking for a few bucks of mad money.''

She nodded. ''Probably. I hope you catch him and tan his hide good.'' She looked at Dakota. ''That's the whole problem with the world today, you know. Nobody spanks children anymore.'' Muttering to herself, she turned and went back inside.

''What do you think, Winston?'' Clint asked as they walked back to his cabin. ''Did you ever get spanked?''

''Sometimes. Mostly when I was little.''

''I got beat up a lot.''

Dakota stopped dead in her tracks, but Clint just kept walking, as if he hadn't said anything remarkable at all. Her heart squeezed a little, aching for him. His childhood must have been hell.

At first glance, nothing in his cabin appeared to be out of place. They were both concerned that something of value had been stolen—the television, the stereo or other small appliances. Everything was in its proper place, though, and not even the change in a bowl on Clint's dresser appeared to have been disturbed.

"Something must have scared him off before he took anything," Dakota said.

"Maybe." Looking doubtful, Clint stood in his living room and turned slowly, checking everything one more time. Suddenly he froze. "The desk."

Dakota turned so she could look at it. "What about it?"

"Somebody was fooling with the desk."

She studied the apparently haphazard piles of matchsticks, books and manila folders. "How can you tell?"

"The matchsticks. They've been moved."

Dakota looked at the small mounds, unable to tell one from the other. "Are you sure?"

"They're not in the same order they were in last night. Yes, I'm sure. Somebody must have scattered them and then tried to put them back. Probably while they were looking for something on the desk."

Dakota looked doubtfully at the heaps of books and folders. "Will you be able to tell if anything's missing?"

"Of course." He was already going through the first stack item by item. "I know exactly what's here. I just can't imagine why anyone would want to go through it."

"Me, either, unless they're interested in one of your cases and think you might keep case notes at home."

He shook his head. "I'm not that stupid."

"Whoever it was wouldn't necessarily know that. If this is all that's disturbed, then that's the only conclusion I can reach. Opening the drawers wouldn't have messed up the matchsticks."

"Nope."

"What are those piles for, anyway?" She didn't expect an answer. He'd bluntly ignored her every other time she'd asked about them, and she didn't expect anything different now. But he astonished her.

"I color code them for people who are associated in any way with a crime. And then I put them in little stacks according to where they were at the time.... It's just an organization thing. No big deal."

She looked down at them again, thinking that it was a very clever idea. No one would ever guess what he was up to.

Just then a folder slipped from his hands and scattered the piles of matchsticks across the desk. "That's what happened," he exclaimed. "I'll just bet you that's what happened."

She looked straight at him. "Who would be that interested in our cases?"

"Maybe the same person who tried to keep Judd and Tracy Hensley from learning who killed Charles Avery."

"It doesn't add up," Dakota argued. They'd stopped for lunch at a burger joint just outside of town and were eating at a cement picnic bench away from prying ears. The sun was warm, the breeze light and dry. A perfect day. "Why would a kid be interested in your files?"

"A kid could have been paid to break in and look for something in particular. Or...the perp might just be small. Martha's eyes aren't all that great, Winston. You heard her. Cataracts."

"That's true." Martha Preston's eyes could be a lot worse than she was letting on. Whoever had broken in had tried to straighten up the piles of matchsticks, and that didn't sound like a kid, either. If something had been taken... But nothing had. Whoever had broken into Clint's home had had a purpose other than robbery, and had wanted to conceal it. That made Dakota far more uneasy than any robbery could have. "Nobody but Judd and Rafe know that we're looking into the Avery murder."

"Theoretically."

She put her hamburger down on the wrapper and looked at him. "Then maybe something else you've been looking into has attracted someone's attention."

"Could be."

She wanted to shake him. God, how she hated it when he turned taciturn this way. "It can't have anything to do with the kidnapping. Lord knows we haven't gotten anywhere with that. But we have been trying to get hold of Homer. Who would know that?"

"Rafe. And anybody who happens to keep an eye on Homer's place could have seen the notes I left."

"What I don't like is the feeling I'm getting that Homer's kidnapping may be associated in some way with the Avery murder."

"What makes you think that?"

It was a long stretch of the imagination, and Dakota shifted a little uncomfortably on her seat before she answered. "Well…someone tried to interfere with Tracy's investigation. Now maybe somebody wants to interfere with yours. It kind of seems unlikely that two different perps would attempt the same thing."

He smiled then, a real smile that reached his eyes. "Bingo. How about dinner tonight? I'm buying."

Much to Dakota's amazement, they didn't discuss business over dinner. By the time they got to dessert, she was utterly confused about why he had asked her out. She had honestly thought he wanted to discuss cases without interruption, but evidently not. Every time she edged the conversation toward their work, he steered her away. What he did want to hear about was her time on the force in Miles City.

"Sure I was harassed," she said in answer to his direct question. "Most women are when they step into positions that are traditionally male. It's probably not as bad now as it was twenty years ago, but there's still a lot of resentment. It wasn't as if I was the first or only woman on the force, but I think I had to prove more to everyone than I would have if I'd been a male rookie." She wondered if he could see the similarities to her position with him. Probably not. Advice columnists got wealthy because people couldn't see what was obvious to everyone else when it came to themselves.

"Did it wear off?"

"The harassment? Yeah, sure, from the people I worked with most frequently. I still got some, though."

"You could have reported it."

Suddenly she understood where this conversation was heading. "Yeah, I could have, but what would be the point? That's a two-edged sword, Clint. If I'd complained, it would have become impossible for me to work in that department, and I'm not at all sure I could ever have found a police job anywhere else. I decided I wanted to be a police officer far too much to just throw it away because I didn't like the way I was being treated."

He nodded in understanding, and for an instant she wondered if he were looking at her with greater respect, but she couldn't be certain. "Harassment is common enough, I guess," was all he said.

"I think most women face it sooner or later. It varies according to the type of job and the woman's position, but it happens. I've never talked to anyone who hasn't faced a little of it. But most of it isn't worth making a case out of."

"Some women ask for it."

She opened her mouth to tell him that line had been used as an excuse by men for everything from rape to murder, but she bit back the words. "Maybe so," she said, "but that doesn't mean the rest of us want to be treated that way. Or that we should be."

"It seems to me that some things are being called harassment that really aren't. Why should it be harassment when some cop isn't sure a female partner will be able to pull the trigger if it becomes necessary? Why should it be harassment that he isn't sure she's strong enough to back him up as competently as a male officer in a fight?"

"Why should he assume that she isn't just because she's a woman? She passed the physical requirements, didn't she? The same requirements he had to pass. Why not give her the same benefit of the doubt you'd give a male rookie?"

"It's different."

She just looked at him, realizing there was no way on earth she could change his mind, at least not through argument. He honestly believed that women weren't up to being cops. Period. Even though lately she'd been feeling that she was slowly gaining a measure of his respect, the bottom line was he was barely tolerating her.

So why the heck had he asked her out to dinner?

No longer thinking about work, she looked across the table and felt a sharp emotional rush. He wanted her sexually. That's why they were sitting in this restaurant talking about things that probably didn't interest him at all. Because this was a mating ritual, and he figured with her it might take dinner and candles to get her into bed.

She could have been insulted, but instead she was amused. He wasn't the first man who'd wanted her for no other reason. At least she didn't think Clint was capable of wanting her for any other reason. She might, in fugitive moments, think wistfully about him, but the bottom line was quite clear: this man was too emotionally scarred to ever really love a woman. And she was absolutely determined never to give herself to a man for any reason other than love.

Ignoring the pang beneath her breastbone, she gave him a sudden grin. "You wasted your money, Calloway. I'm not going to bed with you."

Something in his eyes lighted up. "I don't remember asking."

"Let's leave it that way, okay? I don't sleep around. Most especially, I don't sleep with my partner."

The light in his eyes grew brighter, hotter. "I sure never wanted to before."

The implication was unmistakable, and heat poured through her in a wild flush from the top of her head to the tips of her toes. He wanted her and he wasn't pussyfooting around about it. She should have been annoyed, and concerned about her job. Instead all she felt was a delightful thrill that plunged straight through her womb.

Madness, she thought. It was sheer madness to feel this way. The rush of attraction was both exhilarating and dangerous. It held the same fascination as driving a car at high speed on a winding road or skiing down the side of a mountain—both of which she loved to do.

Common sense dictated that she extricate herself right now, but a more adventurous part of her wanted to play out this hand, to see just how far this man would go. Some part of her wanted the exquisite rush that came from a dangerous game.

Common sense won. She gave him a smile that she hoped was wry, but suspected was disappointed. "My father always told me never to wager anything I wasn't fully prepared to lose. I'm not prepared to lose my job over you, Calloway.''

The gleam in his eyes never dimmed as he lifted one corner of his mouth in a half smile. ''Not much of a daredevil, are you?''

Amusement replaced the heady rush of attraction, and she laughed. ''Why don't you just double dare me?''

''Would it work?''

''I outgrew those games a long time ago.'' Reaching for her purse, she stood with a rustle of silk. Silk always made her feel so exquisitely sensual, even when cut as a simple black shirtwaist. Wearing silk with this man had been a mistake. ''I think I'd like to go home.''

''Sure.'' Pushing his dessert away, he tossed some folded bills on the table, then followed her out of the restaurant.

The evening was soft with the suggestion of coming rain. Clouds had filled the sky, bringing an early twilight.

Dakota felt confused, unsettled, wondering again what this dinner had been about. Clint was silent as he drove her home, offering no answers. It was too easy, she decided, to dismiss this as a poor attempt at a seduction. Clint must be as aware of the dangers of their involvement as she was. He could just as easily be dismissed as she could if she made a fuss about it. Perhaps more easily. He also had to be aware that it would only make it more difficult for them to work together, particularly if they had a brief affair and then called a halt.

All of which was borrowing trouble, she admitted. He hadn't made a pass at her—that one kiss he had given her must have been meaningless, a simple act of anger—and he wasn't likely to. She was probably reading too damn much into the whole thing. Maybe he had just wanted to buy dinner so they could get to know each other a little better.

Yeah. Right.

When they reached her house, he turned to look at her. "Invite me in for coffee."

"As long as coffee is all you expect."

He laughed then, a long, low sound that made something within her feel warm. "Coffee is all I want."

He followed her into the kitchen and leaned back against the counter as she prepared the coffeemaker. When she moved to step past him, though, he caught her almost gently by the arms and drew her into the V between his legs.

"Clint, no!"

"Dakota, yes," he said with a rough laugh. "Come on, admit you're wondering about it as much as I am."

"You don't even like me!"

"Who said you have to like someone to be attracted to them?"

Before she could object further, he pulled her snugly against him, catching the back of her head with one hand and pressing her hips to his with the other.

It was a consumingly sensual embrace, one that swamped her instantly in exquisite sensations: the slip of her silk dress against her skin, the feel of his large, warm hands on her hip and her head. The hard strength of his lean body pressed so intimately to hers.

Some things, she thought hazily, happened only once in a lifetime. This was a once-in-a-lifetime experience. No man had ever made her feel what this man was with so little effort.

A gasp caused her lips to part just as his mouth met hers, and he took it as an invitation. His tongue plunged unhesitatingly into its warmth, taking possession of her with unmistakable eroticism.

All that was wild and free in her rose to meet him with a joyous recognition. These were feelings she had only dreamed of, feelings so intense they overwhelmed mere fantasy.

She wanted him. She wanted to lean into him and give herself to him, to let him sweep her away on a journey to unknown lands of passion.

A long quiver ran through her as his hand slid from the back of her head to her hip. Demandingly he pulled her flush against his hips and urged her to rock against him.

Panic flared in her as she realized how close she was to capitulating. "No," she gasped, tearing her mouth from his. "No." Placing her hands on his forearms, she pushed away, and he let her go.

She turned her back to him, flustered and embarrassed and unwilling to look at him. "You said you didn't want anything but coffee."

"I lied."

She whirled, forgetting her embarrassment in sudden anger. "Do you lie very often?"

He was still lounging against the counter, looking as if nothing at all had happened. He was even smiling faintly. "I didn't think I was lying when I said it. I changed my mind."

"Maybe you'd better leave."

He shook his head slowly. "I want that coffee. You're as safe as you want to be with me, Winston. Just stop looking at me as if I'm candy and you're starving."

"I never—!"

"You did. You do. Whether you know it or not, you do. And you're a tempting woman."

It was, she thought glumly, the first real compliment he'd given her, and it managed somehow to sound like an insult. Grasping at her composure, she managed to speak firmly. "We have to work together. We'd better keep things strictly professional."

"Easy to say. This is another reason I don't think men and women can work together. It's easy to say we ought to keep things professional, but it's another to do it. Sex is a powerful drive." Even though he didn't move, he seemed somehow to come closer. He shook his head quickly, no longer amused by any of this. "I want you, Winston, but I hate wanting you. And I'd bet a hundred dollars you feel the same way."

Her cheeks burned. "*Mating* is a powerful drive, Calloway. That usually involves babies."

He shrugged one shoulder. "Sooner or later."

It astonished her somehow that he didn't blanch at the mention of babies, so she pushed it. "Babies mean commitment."

"Yep."

Speechless now, she simply stared at him. What the heck was he getting at here?

"You're right," he said, straightening and crossing to the coffeepot. "Commitment and mating are a little heavy to handle on the job. Let's just skip it, huh?"

Utterly confused, she could only accept the coffee he poured for her and plop into a chair at the table. He remained across the kitchen from her, returning to his post against the counter.

"So," he said after a moment, "you're beginning to come around to my conspiracy theory."

"Am I?" He'd made a swift change back to the subject he had avoided all evening. She probably would have been amused if she hadn't felt so knocked off-balance. "Maybe you'd better just tell me what your conspiracy theory is."

"I think I already did. That a series of apparently unrelated events are somehow related to the Kincaid ranch."

"But what could be the connection between someone stealing the evidence relating to the Charles Avery murder and someone kidnapping Homer Gilmore? That really bugs me. Did Avery and Homer have anything in common? Was Avery a prospector, too?"

"No. Although that would sure make a tidy link, wouldn't it?"

Dakota tilted her head, then shook it. "Not really. If Charles Avery found something of value, why would somebody murder him and then leave whatever it was undiscovered? No, if there's a link, it has to be something else. And I have to admit I can't escape the feeling there's a link between whoever stole the evidence and whoever kidnapped Homer. It's tenuous at best. Heck, it's not even tenuous. It's just an intuitive feeling."

"I suspect there's more than a tenuous link between a restless spirit and an alien abductor. Damn, I wish Homer would turn up. And tomorrow we're going out to the reservation with Rafe."

Dakota propped her chin in her hand and sighed. "I'd like to know who the woman with two faces is. Winona seems so convinced she's involved somehow."

"Anyone can have two faces. Half the world is two-faced."

"Don't you have a high opinion of humanity!"

"You wouldn't either, if you'd been where I've been."

"Where have you been?" She didn't look at him as she asked the question, and she expected a rebuff.

"You heard what I told that kid we found downtown. What more do you need to know?"

"Plenty. Didn't anybody at all try to get you a decent foster home?"

"What makes you think anybody gave a damn?"

Now she *did* look at him. "There are agencies—"

"*Agencies!*" He nearly spat the word. "They have to know you exist! And most of them don't care what's happening with a hooker who doesn't have a permanent address. If any of them ever wanted to find me, I never knew about it.''

''But the school—''

''Didn't see what it didn't want to. Times have changed, Winston. Thirty years ago, schools didn't particularly want to get involved. Nor did anyone else.''

It was true, she thought. Thirty years ago, public concern hadn't been as great, and neglected children were a dirty secret people didn't want to think about. The world had changed since then, but she could remember hearing her mother and father discuss how attitudes had changed on the subject, a discussion that had come about because her mother was volunteering for a citizens' group interested in child welfare. ''So nobody rescued you.''

''Nobody gave a damn.''

''Did she abuse you, as well as neglect you?'' He had said he'd been beaten up a lot, and she wondered if it had been his mother or someone else.

''It doesn't matter anymore, Winston.''

''Sure it does, Calloway. There has to be a reason why you have such a low opinion of women.''

''Experience is all the reason I need.''

''What experience? Just your mother? Maybe she was doing the only thing she knew how to do to keep food in her stomach and yours. Maybe she was trying the best she could.''

''Sure. That's why she drank like a fish. Turned tricks all night and drank herself into a stupor every morning. Never had enough money to rent a place to live. We moved from one of her 'boyfriends' to another all the time. I had to scrounge for what food I got. She couldn't even be bothered to toss me a piece of bread from time to time. I usually had enough clothes that fit me to get by in school, but I had to take care of them myself, wash them however I could. But I *did* go to school. Mainly because it got me away from her.''

Clint was angry with Dakota, angry at the way she had gotten him to admit all this. Angry at her for having spoken about babies and commitment. He wanted to tell himself that it was just a woman's trick to get a man to promise marriage, but he couldn't make himself believe it.

He had asked her out tonight, intending to prove once and for all that she was no different from any other woman, that in exchange for a little sweet talk and an expensive dinner she'd take him to bed. Instead she had refused to play the game, and no matter how hard he tried to tell himself she was just upping the ante, some part of him knew it wasn't true. Dakota Winston kept blowing apart all his preconceptions. Hell, she was even turning into a decent partner.

He pushed himself away from the counter. "Enough. I'll see you tomorrow, Winston. Bright and early. We're meeting Rafe at nine and I want to go over the files before we head out to the reservation."

"I'll be there."

How sad, she thought when he'd gone. How very, very sad. She guessed she could see why he would have a very poor image of women. It was equally sad that apparently nothing had happened in all his adult life to change his mind on the subject.

Rising, she carried her coffee mug to the sink and dumped out the contents. It was still early—only a little after ten—and the cloudy twilight had at last deepened to near dark. Evenings were long here in the summer, and with them came an urge to be active. Unfortunately, she didn't know precisely what to do. She was dressed up with absolutely no place to go.

Before she could decide whether to change into jeans and go out, there was a tentative knock at her front door. Clint? she wondered. She didn't know if she could handle any more of him tonight. He stretched her emotions in so many different directions that she wound up feeling exhausted.

But it wasn't Clint standing on her doorstep. Instead, Winona Cobbs stood there, smiling almost apologetically. "I hope you don't mind me dropping by. I was in town visiting friends when I had this feeling I just had to get over here. I'm not sure exactly why...." She trailed off.

"Why don't you come in?" Dakota suggested. "I just made coffee, and we can sit and chat awhile. I'd enjoy the company."

Winona's face relaxed and her smile became more natural. "That would be nice. It's time we got to know each other. If you're going to be staying here awhile, you might as well know all about my crazy abilities."

Dakota would have settled her in the living room, but Winona followed her into the kitchen, commenting that it was so much cozier to gather at a kitchen table. The woman's bright eyes followed every move Dakota made, but in a friendly way that didn't disturb her.

"I wanted more of a chance to talk with you when you came out to my place that day with Clint," she told Dakota, "but it wasn't the right time. He's a good man, for all he tries to make folks think otherwise, but he can have the most *damping* effect on a conversation when he wants."

Winona accepted with thanks the coffee Dakota poured for her and pulled a deck of cards from her voluminous purse. "Do you play pinochle?"

"Yes, as a matter of fact."

Winona's smile broadened. "Good. I love to play. Join me?" She began to shuffle the deck.

"Sure. Why did you have the feeling you needed to come over here tonight?"

"I really don't know." She shrugged a plump shoulder. "It'll come in it's own time, dear. I wish I could turn this talent on and off like a TV, and make it tell me whatever I want it to *when* I want it to, but it just doesn't seem to work that way. I'm hoping that something more will come to me while we sit here and chat. I can't escape the feeling that it's important."

"Have you gotten any more information about the woman with two faces?"

The older woman shook her head. "That's been plaguing me for a long time. At least a couple of years. Every so often I start getting visions about her, but so far nothing that's really of any use to anyone. It's a mystery I'd dearly love to see solved."

Dakota bid and Winona passed, so she laid out her meld and called hearts trump. "What else have you had visions about?"

"Just about anything and everything." Winona's eyes twinkled. "Even about tall, dark strangers and long journeys."

Dakota laughed and gave her attention to the game. They played companionably for a couple of hours, talking casually about recent events in and around Whitehorn. Along about midnight, Winona started gathering up the cards, apologizing for keeping her up so late.

Dakota waved the apology aside. "It's been fun, Winona. Exactly what I needed tonight."

Just as she was about to rise from the table, however, Winona froze and her eyes grew glazed. "I'm seeing something...."

The skin on the back of Dakota's neck prickled as she realized that Winona was having a vision. The older woman swayed slightly in her seat, and her face grew unnaturally slack. Her eyes appeared to be fixed on something far beyond the room. After a minute or so, life seemed to return to her, reanimating her face, relaxing her posture. Little by little she came back to the present.

"Oh, no," she said. "Oh, no!"

"Winona?" Dakota leaned toward her. "Winona, what is it?"

"Clint. Someone is…" She trailed off, shook her head and suddenly looked straight at Dakota. "Get out to Clint's place," she said urgently. "Now! Someone is trying to kill him!"

Nine

Winona wanted to come along, but Dakota refused. No way was she going to drag a civilian into the middle of a potentially dangerous situation. If there was a situation. What she believed or didn't believe about Winona's psychic talents didn't matter at the moment. What mattered was that with a life in the balance, she couldn't afford to take the chance that Winona was wrong.

Clint seemed to believe in the woman's psychic ability, though. He hadn't brushed it aside the way Dakota had half expected him to, she thought as she drove as rapidly as she could toward his place. But then, even in her short time in Whitehorn, she'd discovered that very few people ever dismissed Winona Cobbs's talent.

If only Winona had had some idea of what the threat was! It would have been very useful. Instead Dakota was driving into the dark with absolutely no idea what she might be facing. There were any number of ways someone could menace Clint, some of which might be difficult to detect.

She hated not being able to call for backup, but what could she say? That Winona thought someone might be trying to hurt Clint? If she asked a unit to go out there on a call like that, she might very well wind up being the laughingstock of the sheriff's department. Worse, the next time she wanted backup, she might not get it.

So she had to go in alone, and she didn't like that at all.

When she turned onto the road that ran in front of the Preston place, she slowed down and began a cautious approach. Switching off her headlights, she drove slowly, wishing the clouds would blow away. The moon, full tonight, would have been almost as good as daylight. The little bit of light that penetrated the clouds was barely enough to see by.

She parked at the end of the driveway and went the rest of the way on foot through the grass, with her radio clipped to her belt and her shotgun at ready. The gravel on Martha Preston's driveway would have made too much noise, warning of her approach. If someone were indeed trying to hurt Clint, Dakota wanted to catch him red-handed.

She paused, sniffing the air, wondering if she smelled cigarette smoke. No. Wood smoke. It was a common aroma at night, even this late in the spring, as a great many folks relied on wood stoves for warmth. Nothing else disturbed the night.

Keeping to the side of the driveway, off the gravel, she hurried up toward the house and the cabin. She found herself hoping with every fiber of her being that Winona had been wrong. Irritated as she was with Clint for the way he had treated her this evening, she didn't want any harm to befall him. All she wanted, in fact, was for him to wake up and start treating her like a human being instead of an object.

A *sex* object. That's how he saw her. She should have found that pathetic. Or amusing. Or even infuriating. But not disappointing. And disappointment was exactly what she felt. She wanted more from Clint than mere physical passion. Much more. Like maybe a little bit of respect?

Smiling sourly to herself, she focused on the cabin ahead, trying to see if anyone was around. The shadows were deep, dark, impenetrable. The smell of wood smoke was stronger. Maybe Clint had built a fire this evening. He did have a wood stove, after all.

As she drew closer, she could see the smoke hanging low, like a wreath around the bunkhouse. On the still air, that wasn't surprising.

But there was far too much of it, surrounding the building like an evil fog.

A tiny glimmer of orange leapt out at her, brilliant against the colorless backdrop of the night. Dakota froze, uncertain what she had seen. Was someone creeping along the front of the bunkhouse with a lit cigarette? She saw it again, and an instant later understood exactly what it was.

There was a fire inside the cabin!

Every other thought fled except that she had to get Clint out of there. She paused just long enough to radio the department, explain what she had found and request a fire truck, ambulance and backup. Then she took off at a run for the cabin.

As she approached the front porch, she could see the fire more clearly. The curtains were drawn, and glimmers of orange seeped around the edges. It wasn't too bad yet, she thought. If it was, she'd be able to see the glow from all the windows.

The door was locked. Of course. Having found evidence of a trespasser earlier, Clint was hardly likely to sleep tonight with his doors unlocked.

"Clint, wake up!" She shouted again and again as she threw herself against the door, trying to open it. After three or four tries, she gave up. She had to break the window.

Using the butt of the gun, she smashed out the front windowpane and then jumped swiftly back, expecting the sudden influx of oxygen to cause the fire to nearly explode into roaring fury. When nothing happened, she reached in and pulled the curtains down.

And gasped as she saw straight through into Clint's bedroom. By the hellish glow that came from the burning wall at one side, she could see him sprawled facedown across his bed. The fire hadn't yet spread out of the bedroom, but a pall of smoke hanging low in the interior warned that it might not be long until flashover, the point at which all the smoke ignited with explosive fury and spread the fire everywhere.

She had to hurry. Swinging the butt of her shotgun, she broke out the jagged pieces of glass from the window frame and crawled through. Inside, the dense smoke was suffocating. Dakota dropped to her knees and unlocked the front door, opening it wide in the hopes that some of the smoke would escape. Then, crawling, she made her way to the bedroom.

It was hot in there. Hot enough that surely Clint should have awakened. Maybe the smoke had rendered him unconscious. He certainly didn't respond when she at last reached the side of the bed and tugged on his hand.

Having no other choice, she grabbed his ankles and tried to find enough leverage to pull him off the bed. He was dead weight and didn't budge. God, how could she get him out of here without standing up and running the risk of knocking herself out with smoke inhalation?

The smoke was growing thicker, the fire hotter. Flashover was becoming more and more of a risk. If she didn't hurry, they might both be dead. Taking the awful chance, she drew a deep breath of the cooler, clearer air at floor level, rose up and grabbed Clint by his belt. With one mighty heave, she dragged him off the bed and down onto her.

Not even then did he stir. That terrified her as much as the fire did. God, let him be all right!

Twisting, she managed to turn facedown beneath him.

Then, reaching behind her with one hand to cling to his belt, she began to crawl on her belly back to the living room and the front door.

Her own mind began to grow as hazy as the air. Her lungs burned, and sweat ran in rivers down her forehead and cheeks. Her eyes felt like hot coals in her head, and only one thought remained clear: get outside. *Get outside.*

The smoke was much denser now, and even down at floor level it was hard to see. She began coughing—deep, hoarse, racking coughs as she tried to expel smoke. Damn, she couldn't even be sure now that she was still heading toward the door.

"Help!" She choked on the word, coughing violently. "Help! Somebody…"

"Oh, my Lord!" Martha Preston's voice came out of the haze. "Oh, my Lord…Clint? Clint, are you in there?"

Dakota began to crawl toward Martha's voice, assuming the woman to be outside, beyond the open door. "Please," she called, and coughed again. "Please, keep… t-talking.…"

"Is that you, Dakota?" The woman understood and kept up inane chatter, her voice growing more and more strained as her fear mounted. "I hope you have that Clint Calloway with you. I have a few words for that young man, setting my bunkhouse on fire.…"

Dakota knew when she was on the porch by the way the air suddenly seemed cooler, by the way it filled her lungs almost icily. Now all she needed to do was stop coughing long enough to breathe.…

The world seemed to spin darkly. She felt herself tumble off the edge of the porch, heard herself grunt as Clint's heavy weight fell across her, and then she spun away into a deep, velvet night.

* * *

When she came to, she was lying on a stretcher with an oxygen mask over her mouth and nose. Every breath seemed to hurt. Someone bent over her, his head silhouetted against the orange glow of fire.

"Welcome back, Winston," said Sheriff Judd Hensley. A concerned smile creased his face. "Guess you get to be hero for a day."

"Clint?"

"On his way to the hospital. Thanks to you he doesn't seem to be burned, but they can't rouse him. Too much smoke, I guess."

"Arson." Her throat was raw. "Look for...arson."

"Believe me, that's exactly what we're going to do. Just you relax, Dakota. I'll want to question you later, but for now you just take an easy ride to the hospital so a doctor can check you out. I'll follow along later and look in on you."

She wasn't given an opportunity to say anything else. The paramedics scooped her up and slid her expertly into the ambulance. Moments later they were rolling down the road away from the scene of the fire.

By the time they reached the hospital, the oxygen had cleared Dakota's head, and her lungs were starting to feel a lot less raw. A half hour later, a doctor declared her fit and released her. Her immediate concern was for Clint, but no one could tell her anything except that he was still unconscious. She wound up sitting on a hard plastic chair in the waiting room, impatient for some kind of news.

Judd showed up an hour later, looking tired. "The fire's out, but I'm afraid they weren't able to save much. That's going to be hard on Clint."

Dakota nodded, finding it not at all difficult to imagine how she would feel if everything she had in the world were destroyed in a fire. And for Clint, it had to be worse. That had been his home for a quite a few years, and he had nothing outside it except his job and a few friends. Whereas she would have turned to her family for support, Clint had no one.

"No word yet?" Judd asked.

Dakota shook her head. "I'm really worried about him, Judd."

"So am I. He must have been asleep when the fire started and just breathed in too much smoke. But he was still breathing when you found him, wasn't he?"

"Well, he groaned when we fell down the front steps."

A faint smile creased the corners of Judd's eyes, then faded. "But he didn't wake up."

"No." And now that she was thinking back over events, something else began to bother her. "It was funny, Judd. When I got there, he was sprawled fully clothed across his bed. That seems like a funny way to fall asleep, but if he wasn't asleep before the fire started, why didn't he get out?"

"Smoke inhalation."

Judd apparently wasn't going to entertain any other possibility, and Dakota wished she shared his optimism. Right now the specter of Clint's death wouldn't leave her alone. Irritated as she was with him, the thought of losing him made her ache.

Judd spoke. "Why do you think the fire was arson?"

How Dakota would have loved to have some piece of hard evidence to offer him! Instead, all she had was the truth, and it sounded lame. "I went out there because Winona Cobbs told me to. She said someone was trying to kill Clint."

She expected Judd to grimace or chuckle or otherwise

make her feel like a fool, but he didn't. "Winona's usually right. Damn, what now?"

It was a question with no answer. There were probably a hundred reasons someone would want to kill a police detective, but it was going to take more than a mere reason to point a finger of blame at someone. More than a feasible motivation to be able to determine who might have started the fire. *If* someone had done so. Dakota was reluctant to close out the possibility of it being an accident, despite the accuracy of what Winona had said. After all, Winona might have been right about the danger, but wrong about the cause. Only the arson investigators could tell for sure.

Judd restlessly paced the length of the room, stepping carefully around a woman whose hand was wrapped in a towel and a man who had been hit in the eye by a baseball earlier that evening. "Didn't worry me at first," the man told Dakota, "but it keeps swelling more and hurting more."

She nodded sympathetically, but hardly heard him. Clint filled her thoughts.

At long last, just as dawn was nearing, a doctor came to the doorway and motioned for Judd and Dakota to follow him. He took them down the hall to an empty cubicle and faced them.

"This whole situation stinks to high heaven, Judd. Detective Calloway wasn't unconscious because of smoke inhalation. We found both alcohol and barbiturates in his blood, a hell of a dangerous combination. He might have died regardless of the fire. Anyway, he swears he doesn't have any barbiturates, or any kind of tranquilizers or sleeping medications, and that even if he had them, he wouldn't be stupid enough to take them on top of a whiskey double."

Dakota and the sheriff exchanged looks. Judd spoke to

the doctor. "Are you saying somebody slipped him a Mickey Finn?"

"I'm not saying anything one way or another. I'm just telling you the way it is. If Detective Winston hadn't come along when she did, Calloway would be dead. There's not a chance he'd have regained consciousness before the fire killed him."

Dakota stationed herself in Clint's room, sitting in the corner on a chair that was surprisingly comfortable. If Clint had said he hadn't taken any barbiturates, she believed him. And that meant somebody had tried to kill him, just as Winona had said.

That made her uneasy, too—Winona's ability to know such things by means of a sixth sense. It must be terrible to have "spells" like that and know things she shouldn't be able to know. Dakota couldn't imagine anything worse than sensing that something terrible was about to happen to someone and being unable to prevent it. Or to have bits and pieces of information, as Winona seemed to have about the Jennifer McCallum kidnapping, yet not enough to find the child.

But she was thinking about Winona's talents simply because she didn't want to think about what had almost happened to Clint. About the fact that someone had tried to murder him. About how he might not even be safe here in the hospital, which was why she was going to sit right here all night. The doctor had said Clint was going to be all right. But a doctor had said that Dugin Kincaid would be all right, too, yet he had died in this very hospital.

Clint had thought that was suspicious, and now he was lying in a hospital, nearly killed by a fire, saved only by...

Dakota's thoughts sputtered to a halt and her stomach knotted with apprehension. The similarities between what had happened to Dugin and what had nearly happened to Clint were enough to make her hair stand on end. Had someone twice attempted murder, hoping to cover up the evidence by burning it? Maybe switching to a barbiturate this time, because last time the blow to the head had been insufficient? Hoping that this time the drug would kill if the fire failed to?

No, it was too wild. Too, too wild. It had to be just a coincidence.

But even as Dakota's mind argued against leaping to such crazy conclusions, there was a knot in the pit of her stomach that told her Dugin Kincaid's death had been no accident, that Clint was right about it being too damn suspicious. She wouldn't have believed it before, but now, with Clint lying in a hospital bed after a distressingly similar occurrence, she couldn't believe the two events weren't linked.

If someone had tried to kill Clint, then it was dollars to doughnuts they'd also tried to kill Dugin. And perhaps had succeeded.

"'Morning… ''

The sleepy drawl drew Dakota out of the doze into which she'd fallen. Blinking fully awake, she found herself looking straight into the stubbly face of a groggy Clint Calloway.

"What're you doing there?" he asked.

"Making sure nobody slips you another Mickey Finn."

His gray-green eyes cleared a little. "I thought it was a freight train."

"Do you remember anything about last night after you got home?"

"Yeah. I poured myself a double whiskey like I always do. Must've downed it too fast. Hit me like a ton of…''

Recognition dawned in his eyes. "That's why that doctor was asking me about sleeping pills."

"Bingo. It seems somebody slipped you something, probably in the whiskey. You didn't even wake up for the fire."

"Fire? My place?" He pushed himself up on his elbows. "Damn it, Winston, fill me in!"

"I don't know a whole hell of a lot more, Calloway!" She scowled and wiggled her shoulders, trying to ease some of the stiffness that came from dozing in a chair. "Winona stopped by last night and told me to get out to your place, that somebody was trying to kill you. I raced out and got there just in time to drag you out of your burning cabin. At this point I don't know if any of it is still standing. Anyway, the doctor said you had barbiturates in your blood, along with alcohol. Since you told him you hadn't taken anything except whiskey, it seems obvious that somebody slipped you a Mickey Finn."

He swore.

"I kind of figured you'd feel that way," she said dryly. She didn't mention her suspicions about the similarities with what had happened to Dugin Kincaid. In the bright light of morning, it seemed like a long stretch. Dugin and Clint had nothing in common that would make anyone want to kill them. Nothing at all.

"I'm getting out of here now." He threw back the sheet and sat up, swinging long, hairy legs over the side of the bed. Almost immediately he grabbed the edge of the mattress to steady himself and squeezed his eyes shut. "Damn, what a headache."

Dakota tried to tear her gaze away from him, but found it impossible. He was a powerful, attractive man, and right now, clad in nothing but a hospital gown, he was even more powerful and attractive looking. Nothing could diminish him, she realized. Nothing would ever make this man appear weak, foolish or helpless.

She had to fight a terrible urge to reach out to him. Some part of her felt the most ridiculous need to tell him he didn't always have to be strong, that he could stay in that bed awhile longer, until his body recovered, and no one would think the worse of him.

But he probably wouldn't believe that. Given his origins, he'd probably spent his entire life trying to prove that he was as good as everyone else. And he was probably his own worst critic.

Still, she had to try. "I don't think you ought to get up until the doctor says you can, Clint. Someone tried to poison you last night."

His eyes snapped open. "I'm all right. I just sat up too fast."

"I know you're all right. It just may be too soon to get up." Why was she even bothering? she wondered. This man probably hadn't listened to anyone in his entire life. Certainly not to a woman.

"The best thing to do for a little light-headedness is to get up and get moving. Now get out of here so I can dress."

"I'm not sure you have anything to get dressed in."

"Oh for Pete's sake..." Scowling, he slipped off the bed and headed for the small closet, giving her a rather breathtaking glimpse of his backside. This time she managed to look swiftly away.

He swore once, succinctly, and then she heard the bathroom door close behind him. She seized the opportunity to go hunt up a nurse.

"Oh, it's all right, Ms. Winston," the charge nurse told her when she expressed her concern. "Doctor said if Detective Calloway felt well enough this morning, he was free to leave."

Her concern relieved, Dakota returned to Clint's room in time to find him pulling on his boots. "You need to stop by Admissions to take care of your insurance information before you leave," she announced. "Other than that, I guess you're free as a bird."

He turned to her abruptly as a thought struck him. "I don't have a car here."

She couldn't prevent it; a wicked grin turned the corners of her mouth upward. "I guess not."

He tilted his head a little as he looked down at her thoughtfully. "You could offer."

"I suppose, but it's not half so nice as being asked. Politely." It was all she could do not to laugh.

"We're partners, Winston."

"Ah! Finally he admits it!"

He scowled. "Cut it out. I need a ride to my place."

"That's what I hear."

"Damn it, Winston, will you give me a ride or won't you?"

"I don't hear the magic word." For an instant as he loomed over her, his eyes darkening with annoyance, she thought she might have gone too far. Learning to shut her mouth, she thought uneasily, was a skill she needed to work on. But then Clint seemed to relax in some indefinable way.

"I never learned magic words," he said almost gruffly. "So you'll have to settle for persuasion."

Before she knew what he intended, he had caught her up in his arms and she was pressed full-length against him in a snug embrace. An instant later, his hot mouth claimed hers.

Some part of her wanted to resist, wanted to show him she was in command of herself and that he couldn't just grab her and turn her into a limp noodle anytime he chose. But some other part of her softened, sinking into the embrace with an eagerness that should have warned her she was in serious trouble. She responded to Clint Calloway with more than she had ever responded to a man with. She responded with more than passion—she responded with her feelings. Some deeply rooted part of her wanted him in ways more essential than mere desire.

She was softening, opening, yearning to receive him in the most private and tender portions of her being. She wanted Clint...only Clint....

Fear slashed through her, dousing her warm, surrendering state with shocking, icy clarity. What was she doing? This man hated women. He wasn't offering her anything except an illusion of warmth and love, and she didn't want an illusion. She certainly didn't want the pain that would come from being *dis*illusioned.

With a twist, she broke free and backed away three steps. "Paws off, Calloway," she said, trying to sound gruff but managing only to sound uncertain. "There's no room for that kind of stuff between partners."

It seemed to her there was an odd glimmer in the depths of his gray-green eyes, but it vanished before she could interpret it.

"What about that ride?" was all he said. She was content to let it go.

The morning was almost unbearably beautiful, with the air dry and so clear the mountains looked close enough to touch. The blue of the sky was brilliant, undimmed by even a hint of dust.

Beneath it, the charred wreckage of Clint's home seemed obscene. There appeared to be nothing at all of value left.

Clint stood there with his hands on his hips and just looked around, as if he couldn't quite believe it. Martha

Preston came out of her house and stood beside him, sharing the moment in silence. It was Clint who finally spoke.

"First the orchard, now this. You're taking a beating, Martha."

"What happened to the orchard?" Dakota asked.

"Somebody pulled all the apples off the trees," Martha answered. "Kids, probably. Don't worry about me, Clint. The apples will grow back next spring, and the bunkhouse wasn't really mine. It was yours. You fixed it all up. I'm so sorry...." Her voice trailed away, as if she couldn't bear to continue.

"It's okay," he said gruffly. "It's okay. There wasn't anything in there that can't be replaced. Not a damn thing."

"It was your home. That hurts."

He didn't reply. Maybe there just wasn't anything that could be said to something like that. It had been his home. His first *real* home. The only one he'd ever truly had. Now this. He felt like strangling somebody, but he hadn't any idea who had done this.

Nor was there any reason to believe it had been accidental. Not coupled with the barbiturate cocktail he must have swallowed. Someone had meant for his charred bones to be found among the blackened beams that were all that remained of the cabin.

"You move in with me," Martha offered. "I've got plenty of room, Clint, and you can stay with me until we get the cabin rebuilt."

But he shook his head. "No, I don't think that would be wise. Trust me, Martha. It's best if I don't stay with you." He glanced at Dakota over the top of Martha's head and saw understanding dawn on her face. If someone was trying to kill him, he didn't want to risk Martha Preston getting in the way and possibly being hurt.

The bunkhouse ruins were still smoldering a little, but

he walked into them anyway, kicking cautiously at blackened mounds, needing somehow to assure himself that everything really was gone. That there wasn't some overlooked item he could take with him.

But what would he want, anyway? What had there been among his possessions that was irreplaceable, except possibly a few out-of-print books? It didn't seem right, somehow, that his home could be reduced to a pile of soggy ashes and that there wasn't one thing he'd lost that he'd truly miss.

Other people had photographs, mementos of some kind that they would forever regret losing. Not him. He didn't even have a photo of his mother—as if he had ever wanted one. The old bitch was probably still soaking up the booze and sleeping it off in the gutter over in Billings or Butte or wherever she had gone to with that last down-at-the-heels drifter.

Nope, not a single family picture. No trophies, no stuffed fish or elk antlers or anything else. Damn, that probably said something about him, and he didn't think he liked what it did say. An unwillingness to form attachments, probably. Only there was most likely some fancy psychological name for it, not that he cared.

Glancing up, he saw Dakota watching him, those big blue eyes of hers almost exactly the color of the sky overhead. She looked so sad, as if the loss of his home hurt her somehow. Ridiculous. This place couldn't mean a damn thing to her.

He kicked at another clump of ash and saw the melted edge of his clock radio emerge. Nothing he wanted.

Dakota was still watching him, and he turned his back on her, not wanting her to see his face. Sometimes he had the feeling she could look past his eyes to his brain and read the thoughts there. Stupid. Obviously she couldn't do that, or she'd be running from him as if all the hounds of hell were on her heels. What he wanted was to bury himself in that lush body of hers so hard and so deep he'd feel as if they were fused together. What he wanted was to feel her damp velvet depths close around him and draw him into oblivion. What he wanted was to ease the endless aching of his body in the release that hers would grant.

What he wanted was Dakota Winston beneath him, as wild for him as he was for her. He wondered if she even guessed how much he wanted her. He wondered if she was even capable of wanting him as much.

Naw. Not a spoiled little debutante who'd probably never sullied her mind with a lascivious thought in her entire, sheltered life.

But even as he had the notion, he caught himself up sharply. She may have been spoiled once, but she didn't seem too terribly spoiled now. And fancy her telling him to keep his paws to himself. He'd liked the way she'd melted into him at the hospital, but he'd also liked the way she'd stood up to him. You couldn't respect anyone, man or woman, who didn't possess self-respect.

He looked down at his feet and felt a sudden, painful wrench in his gut as he recognized a piece of porcelain that poked up out of the ash. Squatting, he used his forefinger to brush it clean. Lying there undamaged was the top of a heart-shaped whatnot container that he had purchased long ago for a woman who had taught him that fairy tales did not come true. White porcelain with little pink rosebuds. She had once used it to store her rings in. Then, when he had caught her being unfaithful, she had hurled it at him. The top was all that was left, and he had kept it as a reminder.

He reached for it, reluctant to part with the tangible evidence of betrayal, a reminder that had kept him strong for a long, long time.

"Clint? Are you okay?"

Dakota's light voice drifted to him, carried on a breeze as gentle as a loving caress. He straightened, leaving the porcelain in the ashes.

"I'm fine," he answered. "Fine." He glanced down one more time, then strode among the smoldering ruins toward Dakota, feeling as if the fire had burned away something inside him, too, leaving him feeling freer. The sensation made him uneasy, and in a moment of revelation he was stunned to realize that he had clung to the painful bonds of his past as if they were a security blanket.

He stopped dead in his tracks, staring blindly toward the mountains as he realized that he had placed his bitter memories between himself and life. Had used them as a shield to protect himself from involvement.

But the protection hadn't been absolute, he thought, letting his eyes stray to the young woman who waited so patiently for him to deal with his demons. The most unnerving realization of all was that he wanted more from Dakota Winston than her body, and that he'd never be happy with less.

He could drive her away; of that he had no doubt. Oh, she'd withstood more of his misogyny than any other woman who'd ever passed through his life, but if he poured it on full strength, she'd flee eventually. But he didn't want to drive her away. He was actually getting to like having her for a partner, much as he hated to admit it. Just as a partner, though. Anything else would be too messy, so he had to keep his hands to himself...and that was growing increasingly difficult.

"Clint? Are you okay?"

With a start, he realized he'd been standing among the

ashes like a statue long enough to grow weeds. "We need to get back to town and meet Rafe," he said gruffly, masking the internal earthquake that was shaking him to his very core.

"I called him first thing this morning. I didn't know then if you'd be up to going out to the reservation. He suggested we get together tomorrow morning."

He wanted to resent her unilateral action, to tell her that he was the senior partner and she shouldn't be making arrangements without asking him, but somehow he couldn't stir up even mild annoyance. Somehow, he was just glad he didn't have to deal with that stuff today.

"Okay. Tomorrow's great. I need to get back to town and find a place to move into, anyway. Pick up a few things, like a toothbrush." His mouth felt as if it were growing moss.

"You can stay at my place," she blurted.

Startled, he looked down at her and saw that she was as surprised as he was. He ought to politely decline, but some devil drove him to smile and say, "Thanks. That'd be great."

He liked the way her lips parted and her eyes darkened. She might tell him to keep his paws off, but that wasn't what she wanted at all. An alarm bell sounded at the back of his brain, but for once in his life, he completely ignored it.

"Just temporarily," she hastened to add. "Just until you can find some place you really like. So you don't have to take the first thing you come across."

"Sure," he agreed. "Just temporarily." Temporarily was all he wanted anyway. Wasn't it?

Ten

Somebody ought to commit her.

As Dakota led Clint toward her apartment in order to let him in and give him a key, the conclusion she came to was inescapable. Yes, she definitely needed to be committed. She was obviously a danger to herself. Obviously incapable of looking after her own best interests. Asking this hypersexual, overly attractive man to share her apartment after he'd made no bones about wanting to sleep with her surely indicated that she had lost her mind.

Temporarily. Somehow she hadn't at all liked the way that word had sounded coming from his lips. From her own it had merely sounded weak. From his it had sounded like a threat—the kind of threat that is offered with a satisfied smile.

She had played right into his hands. Damn it.

At least for the moment he didn't appear to be gloating, not even when she assigned him the sofa bed in the living room. The coat closet by the front door didn't have anything in it, so she gave it to him to use—not that he had anything to put in it yet. All he owned in the world right now was his car and the clothes on his back.

While Clint took the rest of the day to buy some clothes and talk to his insurance agent, Dakota went back to work. There wasn't a whole lot to do except ponder all the unsolved cases on her desk, cases that spanned more than twenty years. As a detective in Blue Lake County, she'd expected to spend most of her efforts on burglaries and other similar crimes, but lately there weren't even many of those.

Instead there was the unsolved kidnapping of Jennifer McCallum, and the ever-more-drawn face of Sterling McCallum, who by now certainly must believe his daughter was dead. She ached for him and his wife, and for the little girl who must be terrified out of her wits—if she wasn't already dead.

What Dakota wanted was a clue. Any clue that would lead her to the child. The most frustrating part of this case was the utter absence of anything useful in the way of clues. Yes, whoever had taken the child was familiar with the library, but that could be anyone in the county, and probably plenty of people from elsewhere. After all, how long did it take to become familiar with a single building? A kidnapper from as far away as New York could have targeted the child, watched for a few weeks to determine her routine and then cased the library to make his plans. No, that was hardly useful information.

But they didn't have one other damn thing. It was almost possible to believe that aliens had spirited the child away. Other than Winona's assertion that Jennifer was alive and living with a couple somewhere, they had nothing to go on.

At five o'clock, she started to leave, then hesitated. Clint would probably be at her apartment. What had once been her sanctuary suddenly seemed to resemble an alligator den. She wasn't sure she wanted to stick her toe in those waters. Good grief, there were a million things they hadn't even settled about being roommates, not the least of them what they were going to do about dinner. She was damned if she was going to do all his cooking. And what about cleaning?

And what about that look on his face when he had been

walking through the ashes of his home earlier? Something had shaken him seriously, something more than sorrow and anger over his losses. When he had finished scouring the ruins and had come walking toward her empty-handed, there had been something in his eyes that had scared her more than all his hostility. It had been a lost, hungry look. A look that made her want to wrap him in her arms and promise him that everything would be okay. A look that seemed to be an appeal for...for what? Love? Understanding?

The expression that had been on his face was engraved on her mind, a mystery that seemed to reach out to her. She couldn't escape the feeling that something other than the fire had shaken him to his very core.

But none of this was solving the practical difficulties of the two of them living together. She was just grabbing at excuses in order to avoid going home and dealing with the situation.

She was just pulling her purse from the bottom drawer when Mary Jo Kincaid arrived. "Hi, Dakota. Is Clint around? I heard about the terrible fire last night and I just wanted to see if there was anything I could do to help him out."

Dakota's teeth were instantly on edge. "He's not here. He had business to take care of."

"Well, do you know where he's staying?" Mary Jo smiled prettily. "I'd really like to see if there's anything I can do."

Dakota hesitated. She had the worst urge to lie, for reasons she couldn't explain. She was also reluctant to state the truth, because she knew what Mary Jo was going to assume. And yet some wicked imp inside her was delighted to be able to say, "He's staying with me."

Mary Jo's saccharine smile never slipped. "How sweet

of you! But that's what partners do for each other, isn't it?''

The memory of Clint's less-than-kind comments about this woman helped Dakota keep her smile in place, too. ''That's what they say. Listen, I'm heading that way right now. Would you like me to pass a message to him?''

Something hard seemed to glitter in Mary Jo's eyes, then vanish. ''No, but thanks anyway. I'll just get in touch with him later. Is there anything I can do to help *you* out? It must be difficult having someone move in with you this way.''

''It's not difficult at all,'' Dakota lied, mentally crossing her fingers. ''Clint's a wonderful...companion.''

The hesitation didn't go unremarked by Mary Jo. Her eyes darkened. ''Well, I guess I'll just ask *him* then. Good night.''

Dakota watched Mary Jo flounce away and wondered what it was about the woman that had set her teeth on edge so quickly. Her sudden interest in Clint, perhaps?

She hated to think she might be that catty and jealous. In her entire life she had never permitted herself to be either one. Now here she was, feeling both, and over a man she cordially disliked. Or wanted to believe that she disliked.

Okay, she was confused. She could admit that much. She didn't want to like the man, but found herself liking him anyway, even when he was being thoroughly obnoxious. That was surely proof that she needed to have her head examined.

Slipping her purse strap over her shoulder, she double-checked to make sure her desk was locked, then headed for home. It was surprising to discover that she actually wanted to hear what Clint would say when she told him Mary Jo had been looking for him. He didn't seem to like the woman very much.

On the other hand, men were sometimes ruled by their hormones rather than their heads, and Mary Jo Kincaid was both beautiful and available. Clint might well be able to forget his dislike of her if she paraded her charms obviously enough. And her interest would flatter him. Most men were suckers for that. She wondered if Clint were one of them and sincerely hoped he was not.

It therefore dismayed her when she saw him standing in front of the apartment house talking to Mary Jo.

Worse, this was something she hadn't considered when she'd invited Clint to stay with her. He would certainly have friends he would want to see, or even invite over, and she might not like them very much, the same way she didn't much care for Mary Jo. The realization soured her mood even more.

"Hi," Clint said pleasantly when Dakota climbed out of her car. "Mary Jo stopped by to see how I was making out."

"How sweet."

"I thought so." He smiled at Mary Jo.

Dakota felt stunned. Was this the same man who only a couple of weeks ago had been telling her that Mary Jo Kincaid was some kind of ice queen? Was this the man whose dislike of the woman hadn't been exactly subtle?

"We're going out to get some dinner," Clint told Dakota. "See you later."

Her jaw nearly hanging, Dakota watched Clint and Mary Jo climb into Mary Jo's car and drive off.

"Well, if that isn't just like a man!" said a disgusted voice from above.

Dakota looked up to see her upstairs neighbor leaning over the porch railing. She liked Nita Wilkins, a woman of about forty-five who was comfortable with herself, her marriage and her status as an expectant grandmother. "Hi, Nita."

"Hi. Didn't that hunk just move into your apartment? You ought to shoot him!"

Dakota shook her head. "I'm only letting him stay for a couple of days because his place burned down. We just work together." Which was the absolute truth. So why didn't she feel as if that was all there was to it?

"He's still a brass-plated bum. You're rescuing him. The least he could do is take *you* to dinner."

That's what Dakota thought, too, but she didn't say so. What was the point, after all? Clint was Clint and always would be. And she was better off not getting involved with him.

The evening dragged. She told herself he probably wouldn't come back that night. She seriously doubted that Mary Jo had gone this far out of her way just to offer her assistance to a fire victim. No, the widow wanted Clint Calloway, and before two hours had passed, Dakota was telling herself that she was welcome to him.

That didn't prevent her heart from leaping when Clint suddenly walked through the front door. Alone.

"Where's Mary Jo?" As soon as she asked, she wanted to snatch back the words. She didn't want to know, and she didn't want Clint to think she cared.

"Going home, I guess."

"I'm surprised you didn't go with her."

Clint snorted. "With *that* woman? I'd as soon spend the night in a den full of rattlers."

Unreasonably cheered and relieved, Dakota couldn't resist giving him a hard time. "Come on. She couldn't be that bad."

"Oh, no? Trust me. She's a black widow."

Part of her was thrilled that he didn't like Mary Jo, part

of her was disgusted with herself for being thrilled about that and part of her was suddenly a cop on duty. "Are you saying she killed Dugin?"

"I don't recall saying anything of the sort." He sat on the couch facing her, and she forced herself to continue to rock placidly, as if the room wasn't suddenly awash with the tension of unspoken accusations.

"That's what people usually mean when they call someone a black widow."

"Maybe." He let his head fall back against the couch and closed his eyes. "Let it go, Dakota."

He couldn't have said much that would have made her less likely to comply. "Why should I? Damn it, Clint, we're partners, and it's high time you started treating me like one! You meant something by that remark and I want to know what it is!"

"You sure can be a pain in the butt, Winston."

"So can you. Why did you call her a black widow?"

He opened one green eye. "What difference does it make? You think I've got a personal ax to grind when it comes to the Kincaids."

"Don't you? I'd be real surprised if you don't. After all, Jeremiah Kincaid was your father, but he never did a damn thing for you. He didn't even acknowledge your existence. You'd be *weird* if you didn't have a problem with the Kincaids."

"Mary Jo isn't a Kincaid," he reminded her.

"No, but she inherited the money that should have been yours."

He sat up abruptly and slapped his palm on the sofa cushion beside him. "I don't want any of the stinking Kincaid money! I guess you just can't conceive of somebody who'd rather work for his money than have it handed to him the way yours was handed to you."

Her head jerked back as if she had been struck, the viciousness of his attack leaving her stunned.

He rose to his feet and towered over her, his eyes as hard as chips of agate. "Let me tell you, Little Miss Rich Girl, that even if I had inherited the Kincaid money, I wouldn't soil my hands with it. I wouldn't soil my hands with *anything* a Kincaid had touched!"

He snatched his hat off the table, then stomped out the door, slamming it behind him.

Dakota stared at the closed door, feeling as if her knees had turned to water. Something about Clint's anger with her had left her feeling more drained and upset than an encounter with an armed assailant. Her immediate impulse was to go running after him and apologize, but she stopped herself.

He'd had no call to attack her the way he had. She had only been insisting that he treat her like the partner she was, instead of like unwanted baggage. Was that too much to ask?

No, damn it, it wasn't! If they were going to work together, he had to stop keeping her in the dark. And from what she'd seen of Clint Calloway, he didn't make offhand remarks that had no basis in reality. If he had called Mary Jo Kincaid a black widow, he had done so for a reason.

And there was only one reason to call a woman that.

Could Mary Jo really have murdered Dugin? Dakota felt frustrated that she hadn't been here in Whitehorn at the time of his death and so knew very little about the circumstances surrounding it. Since it had been determined to be an accident, there probably wasn't any really useful information in the police files, either.

If only Clint would talk to her about it! How could she possibly help if she didn't know what ideas he was pursuing? And it would also be nice if he'd quit trying to use her family's wealth to tar her with. She was perfectly willing to concede that the harshness of his childhood had taught him things she would never learn. But the relative ease of her own did *not* mean she was a soulless, brainless, heartless, incompetent bimbo. Why was he so determined to dislike her?

Because he hadn't wanted a female partner. Because he didn't believe women should be cops. Because he had wanted to sleep with her and she'd refused. What other reasons could anyone need?

She had been trying so hard, and she had actually begun to believe that he might like her, just a little bit. That he had begun to respect her work. Over the last few days she had actually begun to feel as if they were becoming comfortable as partners. Now this.

Disappointment rested heavily on her, a weight she would never be able to shake loose. Maybe she should give up and ask Judd to assign her to Sterling as a partner. Sterling didn't seem to have a problem with women cops. Of course, he might seem comfortable with the idea only because he didn't have to work with her. Maybe he'd be every bit as frosty as Clint if she were assigned to him.

Maybe she ought to try another law-enforcement agency, somewhere far from here. Maybe she ought to look into a position in Wyoming, or Colorado.

All of a sudden she caught herself sharply. This was nothing but a personal pity party, and she wasn't going to give in to it. She'd been working with Clint for only a few weeks. She owed it to herself to stick it out longer. In a month, or two months, she might even be able to convince him that she was a pretty damn good detective. She certainly wouldn't be able to do that if she backed out now.

Besides, wherever she went, she would meet the Clint

Calloway types who didn't want to work with women. She might as well get used to it right here.

It was just a shame that he was such an impossible man, because he was sure the sexiest one she'd ever met. The thought lifted her spirits just a little and made her giggle to herself. What in the world would Clint Calloway think if he knew he was a sex object?

What a hoot!

How in the *hell* could that woman claim the right to be his partner when she suspected him of acting out of a desire for the Kincaid money?

And why the hell did he even care what she thought?

The questions followed Clint as he stalked angrily through the night. Damn, she was a maddening woman. She could blow his fuse faster than anyone he'd ever known. When he was angry, he didn't rant and shout, but instead grew bitterly sarcastic. He wondered if she even realized that she was provoking his nastier remarks by irritating him half to death with her Pollyanna optimism and her Goody Two Shoes manner. With her unceasing determination to be *perfect*.

God, it was painful sometimes to watch her hold herself in, swallow her own anger. He wished she'd just explode and tell him what she really thought of him. Or at least tell him where to stuff it. Instead she fought to remain calm and wound up making him feel as if he'd just kicked some poor little puppy—which only made him angrier.

She kept demanding to be treated like his partner, when she refused to *be* his partner. A partner wouldn't suspect him of trying to find a way to wangle a piece of the Kincaid fortune. Nope. A partner would trust his word that he didn't want the damn money.

Instead she looked at him with a question at the back of

those big blue eyes, a question that said she wasn't sure his motives were pure. That look was turning him into a mad dog. Twelve years on the force evidently wasn't enough to establish his reputation with Dakota Winston.

But of course not. She came from wealth and privilege and had probably been taught from the cradle that the poor, unwashed masses would rob you blind if you looked away for an instant. She probably couldn't imagine that someone from his background actually had scruples, morals and standards.

Nope. She probably thought morals and standards were luxuries that didn't belong to the homeless and unfed. Anybody who came from the kind of background Clint Calloway had couldn't be trusted farther than you could throw him.

But maybe he was being unfair to her. He paused near the park, looking across the grass toward the library. The place was dark and the big windows stared blankly back at him. Maybe Dakota Winston wasn't a snob. She hadn't acted snobby, not even once. In fact, if he were to be fair about it, she hadn't once acted anything like her cousin, and he should stop assuming they were peas in a pod.

But even if he put aside that presumption, all the other problems remained. She'd still look at him with doubt in those brilliant blue eyes of hers. And every time he looked at her he'd still feel a rising surge of desire that could almost drive him insane.

That was why men and women shouldn't work together; it was as simple as that. How could a man keep his mind on work if he was forced to associate with someone who made his thoughts turn to the bedroom all the time? Fifteen years ago, if he'd been forced to work with someone like Dakota, Clint would probably have blown a gasket. As it was, maturity was scant help.

He wanted that woman like hell on fire, yet she looked at him with cool blue eyes as tranquil as a glacial lake. If she felt the attraction sizzling between them, then she was a far better actor than he.

Of course, they were both trying to behave professionally. He'd kind of blown it last night by taking her out to dinner and then making that stupid pass, but she hadn't let it affect anything today, at least not as far as he could tell. He had to give her credit for that.

Now if only she would trust his integrity…

A quiet voice at the back of his mind reminded him that he hadn't actually done anything to encourage her trust. In fact, he'd done a number of things to *dis*courage it. Like a fool, he wanted her to trust him for no reason other than that he was Clint Calloway. It was unreasonable and he knew it, but he couldn't keep himself from feeling betrayed when she didn't.

Whoa, he told himself. This is getting a little heavy here. It had been a long time since he'd given a damn whether a woman trusted him or not.

But Dakota was different. That fact stared him starkly in the face. She was different. He cared what she thought, and no amount of telling himself that he didn't was going to change that. He cared. He was beginning to like her as a partner and as a person. His feelings for her were running a whole lot deeper than simple lust. The woman was getting under his skin in a big way. All he could do was keep trying to shove her away, before she took up permanent root in his heart.

Swearing quietly, he turned and headed back to her apartment. They were stuck together as partners, and she'd been decent enough to offer him the run of her place until he could figure out what he was going to do. The least he

could do was try to behave like a civilized human being.
At least try to make it a little easier on her.

And hell, if he were honest about it, she wasn't half bad
as a partner. Not the best he'd ever had, certainly, but not
half bad, and getting better all the time. She'd been pretty
observant and clever at the library when she was checking
out the information on the kidnapping....

Thinking about that, he halted and looked back at the
darkened library. There were too many coincidences, if you
looked at all the unsolved cases around here. Too many.
Maybe he was just being paranoid, but he didn't think so.
Each and every event had some similarity to another inci-
dent, and if you followed that chain of similarities, you
wound up thinking there were just too damn many coincidences.

The problem was he needed something besides a bunch
of interesting coincidences before he could do anything. If
he put his suspicions in front of Judd Hensley right now,
the sheriff would be justified in telling him he was really
stretching it. And he was. But time had also taught Clint
to trust his intuition, and intuition was telling him the coincidences he perceived were more than accidental.

Sometimes he thought Dakota was on the edge of rec-
ognizing them, too, but then something in her would pull
back and let go of the suspicion. She didn't yet trust her
intuition the way he trusted his, but she would in time…if
she stayed in this business long enough. In the meantime…

In the meantime they had a missing child to find, and
Clint was likely to start chewing holes in steel if they didn't
get a lead soon. Damn! Poor Sterling and Jessica. Somehow
he had to find a way to trick the perp into revealing the
kid's whereabouts. Somehow.

Dakota had her nose buried in a book when Clint returned. She hadn't read a single word, but had instead

stared blankly at the same page for the last hour as she wondered if he would come back, and if he did come back, how he would act. She had wanted to go to bed and pretend she didn't care at all, but when faced with the prospect of waiting until morning to talk to him, she found herself incapable. She had to know tonight.

He closed the door behind him and then stood there until at last she looked up at him. She forced a casual smile to her lips. "Have a nice walk?"

Catching her completely by surprise, he laughed. "What, no nasty comment?"

"As a rule I try to avoid being nasty."

"You have a right to take a potshot or two. I said some pretty nasty stuff to *you*."

She closed her book and tilted her head a little as she continued to look up at him. "Why do you keep picking on my background? You of all people ought to know that each of us is entitled to be measured by his own actions, not by the circumstances of his or her childhood."

He looked a little startled, as if he hadn't thought of it that way before. "You're right," he agreed after a moment. "You're absolutely right. So if you'll stop judging me by mine—"

"I'm *not* judging you by your childhood!" Incensed yet again, she leapt to her feet. "How can you even think such a thing?"

"By the way you keep presuming that I'll do anything for money. By the way you seem to think scruples are above me."

"Good grief! Clint…" Completely floored by his supposition, she could hardly marshal her words. "That has nothing to do with your background. Nothing at all! Actually…actually, it probably has more to do with mine. I've known so many people who were interested in me only because of my money, and I've got some cousins who—'' She broke off and shrugged. "Let's just say I wouldn't exactly be surprised if they stooped to anything short of murder. I guess that when I hear about large sums of money, I get cynical. You're right. That isn't fair to you.''

"I *do* have scruples, you know. Plenty of 'em.''

She nodded; she quite honestly believed he did.

"And that's the only reason you're going to sleep unmolested in your chaste little bed tonight.''

It was as if some giant vacuum sucked all the air from the room. She couldn't breathe, and a hot flush poured through her, making her skin tingle. In an instant she became acutely aware of the thudding of her heart in her chest, of the rise and fall of her breasts as she struggled vainly for air. Each and every nerve ending in her body awakened to exquisite life, so that the merest brush of her clothing against her skin became intensely sensual. And down below, in the very center of her womanhood, a slow, deep pulsing began.

There had been times before in her life when she had felt aroused, times when she had yearned to cast off her virginity and discover the mysteries of womanhood. Something had always stopped her, prevented her from giving the most intimate part of herself in the most intimate way imaginable. Always, some doubt had reared its head and cooled the fires.

But not this time. Never before had she felt such an intense yearning. Perhaps, she thought hazily as the pulsing in her womb gradually seemed to spread to her entire body, perhaps she had never truly been ready before. Perhaps the time had never been right.

Warm molasses seemed to fill her veins, making her body feel heavy. Oh, heavens, she wanted him, and he hadn't even touched her yet. He just stood there and looked at her, and she couldn't tell if he was feeling any of what she was feeling. Couldn't tell if he still wanted her, or if he had just said that to annoy her.

His eyes dropped from her face to her breasts. Almost automatically she looked down at herself and saw that her nipples were plainly erect, that the layers of T-shirt and sports bra did nothing to hide her arousal.

A hot flush stained her cheeks. Part of her wanted to turn away, to act as if nothing out of the ordinary were happening. To laugh the moment off with sophisticated disdain. The problem was, she couldn't have moved to save her life. Her feet seemed to be rooted to the floor. Her arms were too heavy to lift, so that even an impulse to fold them protectively over her breasts died stillborn.

Slowly, slowly, she lifted her head and looked into a pair of gray-green eyes that were dark with knowledge. He knew she wanted him. He understood the paralysis that held her where she was.

He wanted to take advantage of her wanting.

He took a single, heavy step toward her. It seemed loud in the hush that had fallen over the room. Another step brought him closer, and now she could almost reach out and touch him, if she stretched her arm far enough. She didn't move. Instead she licked her lips nervously and searched his face, suddenly as afraid as she was eager.

He seemed to catch a glimpse of the fear on her face. "Dakota?"

Oh, Lord, she thought, feeling suddenly wild and terrified. She didn't know if she could do this. As much as she wanted this man, she didn't know if she could bring herself to do this. She didn't even know how! What if she made a fool of herself?

"Dakota?"

She loved the way her name sounded when he said it. Something about the way he pronounced the consonants softened them just a shade, made the name into a caress. So different from when he called her by her last name.

"Dakota? Are you all right?"

She licked her lips again and forced herself to speak. Perhaps if he understood, he would help her and keep her from making a fool of herself. "I—I...n-never..."

Understanding dawned on his face. He froze where he was, looking first stunned, then disbelieving. "Oh, come on. You're twenty-four. You can't expect me to believe you've never..." He trailed off when she shook her head. "Never?"

"Never." She was shivering now, cold to the bone, as if a chilly wind had blown into the room. She felt exposed, emotionally naked, and found the strength to wrap her arms tightly around herself. Now she wished she had taken just one of those earlier opportunities, because she suspected Clint Calloway wouldn't consider her virginity to be an asset.

He swore. The sound was harsh, and it struck her like a blow. He found her wanting. She was a disappointment. Why that hurt so much she couldn't say; it just did. The room seemed to tip slightly as all the blood drained from her head.

He swore again. "I'm going out," he said almost savagely. "I don't know when I'll be back."

He brushed past her, and a second later she heard the door slam once again.

Alone, cold and shivering, she could only stand there and wonder why everything she did with Clint Calloway was wrong.

Eleven

The silence in her cubicle was stifling. Clint wouldn't look at her, and Dakota didn't want to look at him—except she seemed unable to do anything else. She didn't want much, just a glance that said he didn't hate her—even though he had no right to hate her. None at all. But this morning her backbone felt like a wrung-out rag, and all she wanted in the world was for things to be right between her and Clint Calloway.

Stupid, she told herself over and over. Stupid. Things had never been right between them. Somehow it seemed apropos that he should first dislike her for being a woman, and now should dislike her because she wasn't experienced.

What's the matter, Clint, she wanted to say, *don't I live down to your expectations of women?*

But she kept her mouth shut because nothing she could say would change what lay between them now. She had offered herself to a man for the very first time in her life, and he had found her wanting. She didn't think even a smile from him, a signal that he was no longer angry, would ever take the sting out of that. Maybe she should be the one furious at him.

But she didn't want to be mad at him or at anyone. All she wanted was for everything to be all right, and that wasn't going to happen. Stiff-upper-lip time, she told herself. Chin up and carry on. What else could she do?

The intercom buzzed and Clint answered it. "Homer Gilmore is here to see you," the tinny voice said.

"Send him on up." Clint turned to Dakota for the first time that morning, and it was as if last night had never happened. "It's about damn time," he said, looking satisfied. "I was beginning to wonder if he'd stepped off a cliff out there."

Homer was a funny-looking little man with long, grizzled hair and blue eyes nearly as bright and brilliant as Dakota's. The cowboy hat he wore was stained with many years of sweat and dirt, and the bandanna around his neck was frayed. "How you doin', boy?" was the first thing he said.

Clint smiled and shrugged. "Same old, same old, Gramps."

"You sure got a fire lit under you about talking to me," Homer remarked as he straddled a metal chair. "Who's the gal?"

"My partner, Dakota Winston. Yeah, I need to talk to you about that alien who kidnapped you last year."

Homer's bright eyes darted from one to the other. "I don't like to talk about that. They might hear me."

"The aliens?"

"Somebody. There're spirits all over them hills. Sacred ground, y'know."

"I know, but aliens aren't spirits, Homer."

"Mebbe. Mebbe not." Homer tapped the toe of one worn, filthy boot. "They're small like." He pointed to his chin. "Mebbe that tall. Mebbe a little more. Seen spirits that size."

"I've heard about the aliens, Mr. Gilmore," Dakota said. "Lots of people have seen them." She almost wished she'd remained silent when his blue eyes fixed sharply on her. They were clear—too clear. And they had a wild glint that was just a little scary.

"You ain't heard right," he said shortly. "I know they talk about them bug eyes and things, but this alien didn't have no big eyes."

"Did he have eyes at all?"

Homer closed his own eyes, squeezing them tight as he strained to remember. "Couldn't see none. Looked to me like it had a coal bucket on its head."

"A coal bucket?" Clint took a legal pad from his desk and passed it to Homer, along with a pencil. "Can you sketch it for me?"

Homer nodded and with an unsteady hand drew what looked vaguely like an upended coal scuttle. Dakota stared at it a moment before looking up at Clint. "Helmet?"

Clint nodded, then turned again to Homer. "Could you see anything at all?"

Homer shook his head. "Didn't really want to. Might be something ugly. Maybe it was a helmet, maybe it wasn't. Didn't see any breathing gear, nothing like that."

"How many of these aliens did you see?"

Homer sighed. "I done told you all this before! There was only the one."

"And it had a weapon?"

"Sure looked like a gun to me. I wasn't going to argue about it."

"What did it want?"

"To know where the sapphires was." All of a sudden, Homer cackled. "Never did tell her."

"Her?" Clint was suddenly tense, leaning toward him. "Why do you say *her?*"

Homer looked suddenly befuddled, as if his choice of pronoun confused him. "I don't…hell, I don't know! I just thought it was a woman!"

Clint didn't reply immediately, but let the silence drag out. Dakota had already realized that Homer was not nearly as willing to speak to her as he was to Clint, so she kept silent, too.

After a while some of the tension seemed to seep out of the old man, leaving him more relaxed. "My brain works funny," he told Clint. "Sometimes everything jumbles up."

"It's okay, Homer. You take your time. I'd just like to know why you think the alien was a woman. Something must have given you that impression."

Homer nodded and closed his eyes, apparently letting his jumbled brain do what it could. It must be terrible, Dakota thought, to know that you got mixed up, but to be unable to do anything about it.

After a few minutes, he opened his eyes. "I need to think about it some more. She wanted to know about my sapphires, but I didn't tell her. That's why she wouldn't let me go. I didn't tell her." He smiled. "They're mine, you know. I found them."

"You found sapphires?" Clint asked.

Homer's expression became crafty and evasive. "Coulda been. Could be. Time will tell."

And that, thought Dakota, was the last useful thing he was going to tell them this morning.

"You let me know if you remember any more," Clint said to Homer. "I really need to know."

Homer nodded and rose, turning toward the stairway. He paused briefly to look back. "You were a good boy, Clint Calloway. Woulda liked it if'n you'd been mine."

"I'd have liked that, too, Homer. I really would."

Homer smiled, then departed.

"He knows something," Clint said. "Damn it, Winston, he knows something. I wish there was some way to get at it, but my experience with Homer is that we're going to have to wait until it bubbles up to the surface. I just hope he remembers it long enough to tell us.''

Us. The word seemed to slip through her, easing the tension left from last night. Us. They were a team. Clint had just said so.

Twenty minutes later Rafe arrived to take them out to the reservation. Along the way he spoke of the times he'd come out here with Tracy Roper Hensley, Judd's wife, while they'd worked on retrieving the remains of Charles Avery and any evidence that might have been left.

"It's as plain as day to me," Rafe said, "that whoever went out there and pretended to be some Indian spirit had to be involved in the murder. Who else would have any reason to steal the evidence bags?"

"That's what I'm counting on," Clint said. "Just keep it to yourself, okay?"

"I kind of thought that's what you were up to." Rafe flashed an attractive grin.

"Mainly I'd like it to get around that I think I've found some new information and am reexamining the case."

"How soon do you want me to start talking?" Rafe shook his head. "It's easy enough to get gossip started around here."

Rafe had an excellent memory. He didn't hesitate once as he led them through the woods to the overhang where Charles Avery's remains had been found. The wind whispered in the treetops and running water gurgled nearby, making Dakota feel as if the woods were alive.

"They tell me I was found not too far from here," Rafe commented. "When I was just a little tyke. I have to admit, though, I wonder what kind of bitch abandons a little kid in the woods."

"It's a miracle you were found," Dakota said.

He smiled at her. "Lately it's a miracle I'm grateful for."

"Do you ever wonder what became of your mother?"

"When I was a kid I used to wonder a lot, but not anymore. To my way of thinking, she must have been subhuman."

That afternoon, Dakota and Clint went over the Jennifer McCallum kidnapping case one more time. There wasn't anything new to consider, but neither of them was prepared to give up. Each time they reopened the folder and reconsidered what they knew, they hoped that something would suddenly leap out at them and shed light on the situation. Unfortunately, nothing so far had, and this afternoon was no different. Dakota rubbed her forehead with her fingertips, attempting to ease the tension there, and tried not to think about Sterling McCallum. About how he had to be hurting.

"The library, the library, the library," muttered Clint. "It has to do with the library. Damn it, Winston, if I were going to kidnap a kid, I don't think I'd steal her from the public library in broad daylight."

"Actually, it was probably the easiest place to stage a snatch, short of a crowded mall. Think about it, Clint. Where else was the kid as likely to be separated from her mother—who is probably the only person who would notice *immediately* if Jennifer disappeared?"

"Good point."

"Snatching her out of her bed at night would be too risky. Somebody might see, the family might wake up, especially if the kid cried—"

Clint sat bolt upright. "That's it!"

"What is?"

He turned to her, his gaze sharp. "Damn it, Winston, why didn't the kid cry?"

"Who says she didn't?"

"Someone would have noticed if she had. These are pre-schoolers, all of them around four years old, who come to the library every week for story hour. It wasn't as if a whole bunch of kids had just been dropped into a strange situation and were scared and crying. Nope, if any one of those kids had cried, someone would have noticed. They'd have wanted to know what was wrong—had she hurt herself or anything. No one noticed a thing. Ergo, the kid didn't cry."

"Which means?"

"Either the kid knew the person she went away with, or she went of her own free will—which with a kid that age probably amounts to the same thing. Sterling and Jessica had already given the standard 'don't talk to strangers' lectures."

"But a child that age…Clint, it would be so easy to lure a little girl like Jennifer, especially if she was in what she believed to be safe surroundings."

"To a point. But what happens when she's lured up the stairs away from everyone?" He shook his head. "It's very unlikely that she would have gone willingly up those stairs with a stranger, especially since she had been repeatedly warned not to."

"You're saying she knew her abductor."

"Precisely!"

"Then whoever took her was someone Jennifer had been given permission to trust?"

"Directly or indirectly. I'm sure there are a number of people a child would learn were okay. Neighbors, parents of friends, teachers at Sunday school—bunches of folks. The question is who was at the library that day that Jennifer would have thought it was okay to go away with."

"The best place to learn that would be from her parents."

Clint nodded. "Let's do it."

Jessica McCallum was a lovely woman who managed to control her grief and worry well. It was plain to Dakota that she was teetering on the brink of exhaustion and that she wasn't able to think about anything but her missing daughter. Jessica could have been excused for almost any behavior under those circumstances, but she remained gracious and self-contained.

"Jenny had been going to the story hour for the last three months," she told them. "I imagine she felt familiar with all the library employees and volunteers who were present at those times. She's a very outgoing child." Her voice broke almost imperceptibly, then steadied.

"You stayed at the library during the story hour, didn't you?" Clint asked.

Jessica nodded. "I was tutoring in the literacy program at the same time."

"Were there other people at the library that day that Jennifer might have felt friendly with, besides the usual library crew?"

She hesitated, then shook her head. "No, I don't think so. It's conceivable she felt friendly with some of the other children's parents, but most of them go do something else until the story hour is over."

"Would Jennifer have cried if a stranger had tried to take her from the library?"

Jessica's lips quivered and she blinked rapidly. "Yes. Yes, she would have. It's terrible, but even at her age children have to be warned about strangers, and we warned her repeatedly. She's such a good child. She's been taught to cry and scream if a stranger wanted her to go anywhere with him, and I believe she would have done exactly that.''

"Bingo,'' Clint said as he and Dakota climbed into their cruiser out front. "Slam dunk. Touchdown.''

"There were a lot of people in the library that day,'' Dakota reminded him.

"But a limited number of them would qualify as friends. People that she would have felt safe with.''

Dakota nodded slowly. "We're really snatching at straws here, you know.''

"Give me something better and I'll snatch at *it*. Let's get back to the office. I want to think about this a bit before I go charging ahead.''

When they arrived, they talked with Sterling McCallum for a few minutes. He was emphatic in agreeing with his wife that Jennifer would have cried out if a stranger had tried to take her away. "Just think about that,'' he told them. "Someone she *knows* must have done this. Someone she *trusts*.''

Back in their own cubicle, with Sterling's footsteps fading down the stairs, they looked at one another.

"Hell,'' said Clint succinctly.

"I don't know how he keeps from wringing the necks of everyone at the library,'' Dakota said presently. "I'd sure be tempted if she were my kid.''

"Me, too.'' He shook his head. "Okay. Tomorrow we'll go around and question folks again about whether anyone noticed anything unusual, whether anyone heard Jennifer cry or call out. And while we're at it, we'll double-check on who was at the library when she disappeared. Could be something got overlooked. If not, we'll at least have a solid list of suspects.''

Dakota nodded her agreement. "I've been thinking about our talk with Homer this morning, too."

He leaned back in his chair and propped his hands together, making a steeple with his fingers. "What about it?"

"Just that it was kind of odd the way Homer lumped his alien and the spirit he'd seen near the Avery remains into the same category."

"Homer's mind works in funny ways."

"I've noticed. But I also think that however odd his way of thinking, he has reasons for what he thinks. They could be worth looking into."

He nodded, his gaze sharp. "Anything else?"

"Most particularly, I'd like to know why he's saying that alien was a woman."

Clint swiveled his chair so that he faced his desk. While Dakota watched, he moved some of his matchsticks from one pile to another.

"What *are* you doing?" she demanded, forgetting caution in her irritation.

"Keeping track of persons, places and things," he answered. "Come on, let's get out of here and have some dinner."

Dakota was surprised to realize it was already past six, and well past quitting time. As she grabbed her purse and slipped it over her shoulder, she paused to look down at the piles of matchsticks. *People, places and things?* No way. There were too many colors for that.

Leaving the mystery behind, she followed Clint from the building.

After dinner they decided to play a couple of games of miniature golf. Unspoken between them was a reluctance to go back to her place together, after last night. As dusk descended, tension rose, until they were saying almost nothing to one another.

It was so ridiculous, Dakota told herself. Clint could have moved into a motel if he was uncomfortable about what had happened. Apparently he wasn't. She was simply imagining his tension, a reflection of her own. And if she couldn't handle it, all she had to do was ask him to leave.

Somehow she couldn't bring herself to say the words.

By the time they pulled into the parking space in front of her apartment, night had fallen. Dakota was grateful for the lack of light because it prevented Clint from reading the nervousness in her face—and because it prevented her from seeing his own expression. Now if she could just slip into the house and get to her bedroom without looking at him…

That was exactly what happened. He entered behind her and said only a perfunctory good-night as she hurried down the hallway to her bedroom. A few minutes later she heard the front door close behind him and his car start up.

He was going out again, leaving her alone with the darkness and the silence—and the loneliness. Oh, how she wanted to cry.

She couldn't sleep. Alone in the dark, she lay awake and stared at the patterns cast on her wall by the moonlight that was creeping past her curtains. She wanted to sleep. She wanted to forget about Clint, to close her eyes and dream of girlish things. She wanted to believe that her hunger for him was merely a crush, a passing phase that would soon vanish.

Instead she lay there with sinuous, steamy images of passion storming her brain, while her body ached for answers and her heart called out for love.

She had it bad. As desperately as she wanted to believe

this was all some desire-induced case of temporary insanity, she was terrifyingly certain that it was more.

Was it possible to fall in love so quickly, with someone who was often scarcely civil to her? Could such a love last? Insanity was the only name for what she was feeling. That or lust.

Lust. Even that word didn't shake her into cold clarity. If this was lust, then it was not the ugly thing she had always believed it to be. Instead it was haunting, compelling and strangely beautiful. It was as if her body were awakening from a long sleep and stretching luxuriantly as life returned.

But these feelings could do her no good. Clint didn't want her—he'd made that painfully obvious—and she didn't want anyone else. Besides, did she really want to give herself to a man whose only interest in her was a brief fling? She wasn't crazy enough to believe Clint cared for her, when he could hardly tolerate working with her.

So it was best for both of them that he had walked out last night when she had been so vulnerable. Lord! Just think if she had given herself to him. She'd probably be feeling even worse tonight, feeling cheap and used and wounded.

Instead, she was lying here feeling…deprived. But she could live with that a lot easier than with feeling she had been used. Of that there was no doubt.

Outside, she heard a car door slam. The breeze stirred the curtains at her window and slipped like a gentle hand across her naked body. It wasn't that warm tonight, but somehow she couldn't bear to put on a nightgown. The brush of it against her skin had been sensual torture.

Another car door slammed. Neighbors coming home from the bar, she thought. She heard a woman's laughter, husky and intimate. The sound made her throat tighten for some absurd reason. Maybe because it was the sound of a happiness that was denied to her.

The breeze stirred again, stronger this time, and with cool fingers tickled along the length of her body. It was so nice to sleep with windows open and the curtains stirring in the air. The nights were rarely sultry here, but she found herself wishing tonight were, just so she could blame something else for the heat that prickled along her skin.

"Dakota?" She heard a husky whisper in the darkness.

Oh, God, surely she must be dreaming. That couldn't be Clint standing beside her bed in the dark, looking down at her moonlight-touched nakedness. This had to be a dream, even though her heart leapt and then hammered wildly with a mixture of fear and yearning. This couldn't possibly be real.

Moonlight caught him from the side and bathed him in silver. He wore nothing but a pair of unbuttoned jeans, and he was magnificent, an awe-inspiring creation of muscle, bone and skin. If she had been able to move, she would have reached out with both hands to touch him, to assure herself that he was real, not some mythic hero dredged up from her deepest fantasies.

"Dakota, I'm sorry I walked out of here last night. I didn't mean to hurt you."

Now she was *sure* she was dreaming. The Clint Calloway she knew couldn't be saying those words. She licked her lips and finally managed to answer. "I'm okay."

"Yeah. Sure." Slowly, as if he were afraid she was a fairy wisp who would vanish if startled, he knelt carefully beside her bed. "You're more than okay. You're damn near perfect."

Her mouth was dry, and her limbs trembled from a heady mixture of fear and excitement. She wanted this. She didn't want this. She was going to regret doing this. She was going to regret *not* doing this.

And then one thought grew clear in her mind: there was only one Clint Calloway, and he'd never come to her again if she sent him away now.

The realization seemed to loosen some silken knot deep within her. She forgot all her sane, rational reasons for not doing this, forgot that he was her partner and that they'd have to face each other across a desk for a long, long time. Forgot that he wanted her only in the sexual way, and that he was offering her nothing but a few hours of pleasure. Forgot that she had always intended to save herself for the man she would marry.

Clint was determined to marry no one.

He touched her—a light brush of his fingertips against the inside of her wrist. She caught her breath as delightful shivers trickled through her. How had she become so sensitive?

Gentle caresses, moving gradually up her arm to the inside of her elbow. She had been touched there a thousand times, yet had never realized what a touch in that spot had the power to do to her. Or perhaps it was only Clint's touch that had that power over her.

A sigh escaped her, a bare whisper of sound hardly indistinguishable from the gentle sound of the breeze. He heard it, though, and his hand grew bolder, slipping up her arm to her shoulder.

She caught her breath as anticipation replaced the last of her fear. Nothing existed any longer except the man who touched her and the exquisite sensations he aroused in her. Nothing else mattered.

His whisper was rough, a little ragged. "Easy, Dakota...easy. Just...let me..."

His fingers trailed downward from her shoulder, at once

confident yet strangely tentative. The brush of his fingers might have tickled, except that she was so enthralled. Each feather-light sensation seemed to arrow straight to her womb to join the growing ache there.

And every nerve in her body strained for more. Yes, she thought, touch me there.

He did. With warm strength he cupped her breast, at once possessing her and sheltering her. The sensation unleashed a tide of emotions along with a flood of passion. Helpless to prevent it, she writhed, lifting herself before him as she broke the spell of anticipation that had held her still. This was what she wanted, and she wanted more, much more. She needed to give all of herself to him.

Yearnings commingled with almost unbearable joy as his hand squeezed and kneaded her and finally began to play with her nipple, tugging and pinching without hurting. Spears of pleasure shot through her, pooling at her core with the heat and heaviness of magma.

She heard herself whisper his name brokenly, then do so again.

"Yes," he murmured roughly. "Yes..."

He rose up and yanked his jeans off impatiently. Another time she would fill her eyes with the sight of him, but right now she had other senses that needed him more. And suddenly he was there beside her, his leg thrown across hers, his hot skin pressed to hers....

Her universe blossomed in all the hues of physical sensation. Her own smooth legs were aware of the hair-textured roughness of his, of their power and muscular strength, of their warm weight. His hand now cupped her other breast, exciting it to aching fullness.

"Touch me," he whispered. "Anywhere...any way..."

She heard the air hiss through his teeth when she touched him tentatively on the chest. The sound of his pleasure emboldened her and she let her hand wander with delightful freedom along his side to his flanks. How incredible it was to feel him under her palm this way, to feel his muscles quiver with pleasure when she touched him, to hear his breath quicken in response. She was filled with a heady sense of power and awe.

His mouth found one of her aching nipples, taking her by surprise as he sucked strongly, drawing her into a compelling rhythm that soon filled her entire body. Helplessly caught in throbbing sensation, she tried to move closer, unconsciously opening her body in ancient invitation.

But still he teased her, nibbling now at her nipples, drawing her hand to his aroused flesh, placing his on hers. For an instant she froze, astonished by what she felt, but even astonishment couldn't last long before the force of the feelings he built in her.

She felt as if she were caught on the arc of a welder's torch, with sensations zinging dizzyingly throughout her entire body. The hand he slipped between her legs stroked her firmly, compelling her to climb a pinnacle she'd been only dimly aware of before. His soft whispers encouraged her as the night became a vast sea of sensations that swept her away.

By the time he moved between her legs, she felt as if her mind had whirled away, leaving her conscious of nothing but the aching, hurting hunger that pulsed throughout her being. She was past doing anything at all except responding.

There was a moment of sharp agony as he filled her, a moment of intense pain that somehow blended into the sea of pleasure as just another peak of intensity. The moment of transformation. And then she transformed in yet another way, exploding in sparkling ecstasy.

This was what she had been made for.

Twelve

"Last night was a hell of a big mistake."

The dry comment slammed into Dakota, dispelling the glow that had lingered throughout a night of beautiful lovemaking. She sat up, clutching the sheet to her breasts, and looked at Clint, who lounged fully dressed in the doorway. "Don't say that," she said, shoving her hair back from her face and trying to keep her voice from quivering. Tears prickled behind her eyelids.

"Why not? It's true. You're Montana royalty and I'm a guttersnipe. I'd never be good enough for you in a million years." He shrugged a shoulder as if he were indifferent, but the tightness around his eyes and mouth belied it. "Besides, we're partners. This will only mess things up."

She wanted to argue with him, but tears clogged her throat, making speech impossible. She could only shake her head and wonder why he wanted to hurt her. The man who had loved her in the dark last night was not the man who stood in her doorway now and criticized what they had shared.

He regretted what he had done. The understanding pierced her heart like a sword, leaving her feeling soiled. She had known this would only be a one-time occurrence, but the beauty of the passion they had shared had been worth it…until this moment. Somehow his regret tarnished what had happened, leaving her feeling used and cast aside.

"Go away," she said thickly, around the lump in her throat. "Just…g-go away…."

Twisting, clinging to the sheet as if it were a lifeline, she buried her face in a pillow and fought back the sobs she didn't want him to hear.

Oh, God, how could she have been so stupid? How could she have been dumb enough to give herself to that man? How was she ever going to face him again, pretending nothing had happened between them? How could she continue to work as his partner?

How could she ever again look herself in the eye?

She heard the front door slam, heard the roar of an engine and the squeal of tires as he drove away. Damn him! Damn, damn, damn him!

Dakota dissolved in helpless sobs, wondering how something so good could turn so sour.

When she arrived at work, Clint was seated at his desk playing with his matchsticks, as he had every morning since she'd started working with him. He even looked up and nodded, grunting the same "good morning" he always greeted her with.

As if nothing at all had happened.

Dakota hesitated in the doorway, wrestling with a nearly overwhelming urge to commit mayhem, but finally she was able to walk to her desk, answering politely as she did every morning.

"We have to do all those interviews today," he growled.

"Yes. I know." It was going to be a waste of time, though, and it would keep her in close proximity to Clint for hours. She wished she had given in to the impulse to call in sick. So what if he thought she was a coward?

"You're a son of a bitch, you know?" she said finally.

He looked straight at her. Pain flickered briefly over his face, the only indication that he wasn't immune. "I know."

The morning seemed to drag as they went from person to person, trying to discover whether anyone had heard a child cry, or even just cry out, and getting them to identify once again everyone who had been at the library that afternoon.

It proved to be about as useless as Dakota had anticipated. Nobody remembered hearing any of the children cry, other than a little boy who had skinned his knee, and not one name was added to the list of those who had been in the building. They were still facing a blank wall.

Dakota looked down at the picture of Jennifer clipped to the front of her notebook and found herself thinking that there was something terribly wrong with a world in which a small child could vanish without a trace. It was ridiculous, of course, to even entertain such thoughts. Bad things happened, often without rhyme or reason, and brooding about them would only hamper her effectiveness as a police officer.

As a police officer, she reminded herself, she was doing as much as was humanly possible to find the child.

Back at the station, they found Homer Gilmore waiting for them. He'd settled himself on the bench out front, looking quite content as he fed popcorn to some squirrels.

"Thought you'd never get here," he groused when he saw them. "Been up to visit my girls and Kane, and I remembered something."

Dakota, feeling a refreshing sense of excitement, sat down next to him. At once Homer passed her the popcorn. She tossed a few pieces to the squirrels, which had withdrawn a couple of feet to assess the situation. "What did you remember?"

"Perfume." He looked from her to Clint, who had squatted down beside them. "That dad-blasted alien was wearing perfume." He cackled. "That's why I thought it was a woman."

"That would sure make me think so," Clint agreed. "Did you recognize the perfume?"

"Well, you know, I did." He grinned. "Yep, the more I thought about it, the more I was sure I'd smelled it before." His head bobbed as he nodded to himself. "I smelled the spirit."

Clint sighed a little and looked at Dakota. "Homer, let's stay on the subject, huh?"

Homer's smile vanished. He looked a little confused, as if Clint had thrown him off track somehow. Dakota spoke.

"I think he *was* on the subject, Clint. Mr. Gilmore, about the perfume the alien wore. Where did you smell it before? At the dime store?"

Homer shook his head almost irritably. "No. I told you! On the spirit."

Clint leaned forward, his expression intent. "Which spirit, Homer?"

"The one at the sacred ground. The one where they found old Chuck."

Dakota's eyes met Clint's. "Charles Avery," they said simultaneously.

She turned to Homer. "Are you sure, Homer? Are you very, very sure?"

"Yup." He chuckled. "Like roses in a hot summer sun."

"And the alien wanted to know where the sapphires were, right?" Clint asked.

Homer nodded. "That's all it wanted to know, askin' over and over until my head ached." All of a sudden he looked perplexed, turning from Clint to Dakota and back.

"Why would an alien want sapphires? Maybe they've money on their planet?"

"I don't know, Homer," Clint answered patiently. "I don't know."

"They're moderately valuable here," Dakota said. "Maybe on another planet there are even less of them. Or none at all."

Homer seemed satisfied with that and rose to go. "Funny world, when aliens wear perfume."

"If you remember anything else," Clint called, "let us know?"

Homer lifted a hand in acknowledgment and kept walking.

"'Like roses in a hot summer sun,'" Dakota repeated. "How poetic."

"And probably useless. Perfume. Hell, that could be almost anything—shampoo, after-shave, soap—and just about anybody could wear it."

A car that had been standing in the far end of the parking lot suddenly pulled up to them, and Mary Jo Kincaid leaned out the window, smiling pleasantly. "What's that old coot been up to now?"

"Not much." Clint rose and sauntered over to the car, resting his elbow on the roof and leaning down. If blood could boil, Dakota's nearly did right then. Clint didn't like that woman, she reminded herself, but it didn't much help when he looked at her so attentively. "What have *you* been up to?" he asked Mary Jo.

"Waiting for a certain detective to show up so I could throw myself on his mercies."

Good God, Dakota thought, the woman actually bats her eyelashes! It was nauseating. Muttering something about work, she rose abruptly from the bench and went inside.

At her desk, she made notes about their brief talk with

Homer and tried not to think about her personal turmoil. Last night was branded vividly on her mind, long glorious hours of awakening to the wonder of being a woman.

Clint had been an incredible lover, sweeping her slowly and patiently to the outer reaches of sensation and then carrying her safely back. That spoke of a breadth of experience she didn't want to think about, because there was only one way he could have come by it.

And this morning... A pang squeezed her heart as she remembered how he had said their night together had been a mistake. That was going to hurt for a long, long time, and he probably knew it. Now he was out there smiling at Mary Jo as if he were trying to tell her that she hadn't been his first lover and she sure wasn't going to be the last. Did he really feel he had to remind her of that?

He probably thought so. Because of her inexperience, he'd probably been afraid that she would consider his lovemaking a declaration of love. He'd probably had visions of her traipsing after him like a lovesick puppy and wanted to prevent that from happening.

But that didn't excuse his brutality. Yes, she told herself, *brutality* was the only word for what he had said first thing this morning. He had made it plain that he couldn't forget she came from a wealthy family, and that he resented the hell out of that. Well, there wasn't a damn thing she could do about the family she'd been born into, any more than he could change his own background. Of all the unfair things to condemn someone for!

But after a moment she sighed and put her chin in her hand, letting go of her indignation. Clint had given her a glorious night of lovemaking, one beyond her wildest dreams. That was all he had intended to give her, and she had known that beforehand. He hadn't promised wedding vows and undying love. One way or another, she had to accept that and be grateful for the gifts he had given her.

Otherwise she wasn't going to be able to work with him any longer. There was no way she could endure feeling the way she had today for as long as they were partners. Something inside her felt raw and achy, as if something precious had been torn away. Anger danced at the edge of her every thought because he had been so callous this morning. It was damn near intolerable.

Either she had to wrestle her feelings into line or she had to move on. It was as simple as that.

Picking up another folder, she stared blindly at it. *Move on.* Maybe it was time to do just that. She knew for a fact she could have a job in Missoula if she really wanted it. The chief had told her so the last time she'd gone to visit her family. Maybe that's exactly what she needed to do— before everything got so messy she ruined her career.

Shortly after eight that evening, her phone rang. She picked it up, expecting it to be her mother, but instead heard Clint's gritty voice. "Dakota, could you come give me a lift? I've had an accident."

Her heart seemed to stand still. "Are you all right?"

"I'm fine. Really. I just need a ride back to town. Ethan Walker picked me up and I'm at his place."

"I'm on my way."

She shoved her feet into shoes, grabbed her purse and headed for the door, wondering what the hell had happened. It was odd that he would call her for a ride. If he'd had an accident, he'd need to talk to the deputy on duty, and that would be the easiest way to get a ride back.

Then it struck her that he obviously intended to continue staying with her. Why else would he ask her to come get him? For an instant she could hardly believe his gall, then she caught herself. Of course. It would look mighty strange for him to move into a motel two days after he'd moved in with her. So strange that everyone would be sure something had been going on between them. He was right; it was better this way—however tense.

The Walker place was some twenty-five miles out of town—past the turnoff to the Kincaid place. Damn. If Mary Jo was with him, Dakota was going to spit nails. There was absolutely, positively a limit to what she was willing to put up with, and having to rescue Clint and his date the night after he had made love to her was beyond comprehension. Dakota wouldn't be surprised if he had set it up precisely to make this happen. The man had more ways to drive a woman away than a magician had tricks!

But what she saw alongside the road just before the turn to the Kincaid ranch left her blood running cold. The burned-out hulk of a car sat nose down in the drainage ditch. The make was the same as Clint's car. It *was* Clint's car.

She jammed on the brakes so hard that she slammed against her shoulder harness. Good Lord, he could have been killed.

For several heartbeats she could only stare, but then she recalled that Clint was waiting for her at the Walker ranch and she'd be able to see with her own two eyes that he was okay.

He was standing out in front of the house, chatting with Ethan Walker. Dakota already had a nodding acquaintance with Ethan, since he often came to town to pick up his wife, Kate, who was a judge. Nearly every time Dakota had needed to testify in a case, she had run into Ethan. They now exchanged smiles and handshakes, then Dakota turned to Clint.

"What the dickens happened?"

He shrugged. "Engine fire. No big deal…except my car's a total loss. Come on, let's get back so I can do something about it. Thanks, Ethan."

"Any time."

She had the distinct feeling that Clint was hurrying her into the car and out of there, but she didn't say anything until they were out of sight of the house. Then she asked, "What's going on?"

"Someone tried to kill me."

"What are you talking about? How?"

"It was a pretty amateurish job. Somebody has seen too many movies. My gas line was tampered with."

"But you could have been killed!"

"Darlin', there wasn't a chance in hell. Cars don't explode that easily, Hollywood notwithstanding. What happened is exactly what should have happened. The gas burned, I couldn't put it out and now my car is a loss."

Dakota scowled down the road, thinking he was dismissing the danger too easily. "Clint, this makes the second time someone has tried to kill you."

"Believe me, I've noticed."

"But why? Who? We've got to do something about this!"

"I kind of agree. I'm thinking, Winston. I'm thinking."

"Have you put somebody away who might have just gotten out and came after you?"

"Naw. I think it has something to do with a current investigation. Could be any one of the cases we're working on. But it also made me remember Nick Dean. He's a private investigator Melissa Avery had hired to find out what happened to Charlie. Well, his car was blown up and a hitchhiker killed. We thought Ethan had done it, because he had some dynamite missing, but after his acquittal we couldn't get anywhere. Nick figured it had to do with one of his cases, but now I wonder…''

They drove by the hulk of his car, and he shook his head. "Trouble is, this was a real amateur job, and whoever got Nick's car was slicker. Listen, I was on my way out here to see Mary Jo Kincaid.''

Dakota felt her stomach knot. "I thought so.''

"Yeah, well, the damn woman is as insistent as a mosquito. I just *had* to come out here for dinner tonight. I'd rather wrestle with an alligator, to tell you the truth.''

The knot in Dakota's stomach transformed into a bubble of laughter, but she held it in. So he *wasn't* enamored of Mary Jo. Even though she'd been pretty much convinced that he was using Mary Jo to prevent things from getting any stickier between him and herself, a niggling doubt had remained. After all, Mary Jo was an attractive woman, albeit older than Clint. Dakota's relief was great, probably too great, but she ignored the little warning bell.

"I haven't called her to tell her I won't be making it tonight, and I'd like to leave it that way.''

"You want her to think you stood her up?''

"For the moment I don't want her to know I survived that fire.''

She braked again and looked at him. "Are you at that again?''

"Something about roses in summer sunshine, Dakota. Something about a woman dressed up like an alien. Yeah, it's bugging me. You don't have to agree with me, just keep your mouth shut for a few days, okay? You know, Ethan Walker was telling me that Charles Avery was real tight with this woman Lexine Baxter, who disappeared so long ago. Lexine was a small blonde. Ring any bells?''

"Oh, come on, Clint! Someone would have recognized her.''

"Unless she was so different she couldn't be recognized."

He shook his head. "Sometimes, Dakota, you flat out refuse to see what's plain as day."

"Sometimes you see too damn much, Calloway! Lexine vanished nearly thirty years ago. There's no reason to think she's come back!" She glared at him. "Even if she has, that doesn't mean she's a murderess. Or that she has anything to do with any of this other stuff."

He scowled. "I know. I'm working on it. Money keeps coming to mind."

"But Mary Jo has all that Kincaid money now."

"For the time being."

Dakota wanted to shout in frustration. This man could be absolutely impossible at times. Why didn't he just lay it all out for her? Why wouldn't he just tell her what he thought was going on?

Because you don't trust him. So he can't trust you.

The realization shocked her—especially because deep down inside she *did* trust him. All this stuff she kept telling herself—and him—had more to do with caution than with belief. By training, she was cautious in her assessment of the honesty and motives of others. A cop just couldn't afford to be too trusting, nor could the young, attractive daughter of a wealthy family.

But when it came to Clint Calloway, she trusted him. Her mind, trained to caution, kept throwing up objections, but her heart and soul trusted him implicitly. She'd trusted him enough to make love with him last night, and despite his nasty remark this morning, she still trusted him.

She must be crazy.

They were nearly back to town when she spoke again. "You need to report the accident."

"Not yet. I want to keep it quiet for now."

She let it pass. "What do we do first?"

"I think it's about time we looked into the whereabouts of Lexine Baxter."

"Because of the Avery case? You still think she murdered him?"

"Let's just say I think it could be real constructive to discover if she turned up anywhere else over the years. Maybe even got herself a rap sheet."

Dakota nodded. "Okay."

"The thing is, I want you to go in and request it. I'm going to lie low, at least for tonight."

"Clint, you're going to be reported missing! The department is going to look everywhere for you, because there sure as hell isn't a body in that car. Do you know the kind of trouble we could get into? I think we'd better at least talk to Judd!"

He was silent for a few seconds. "Okay, let's go talk to Judd. And Winston?"

"Yeah?"

"Sorry about what I said this morning." His voice was suddenly so rough it sounded gravelly. "I didn't mean it."

There didn't seem to be any way she could respond to that, so she let it go. And something inside her let go, too. Just a little. She didn't feel quite so bad about the night before.

Clint told Judd about the accident and explained that he wanted to lie low for a day or so, while he gathered some more information. That he hoped the shock of his survival would serve to shake the perp into a confession.

Judd looked a little doubtful. As well he should, Dakota thought sourly. There were enough holes in Clint's explanation to drive a truck through—especially since he refused to tell the sheriff just who he suspected and how he planned to surprise her.

Judd studied him doubtfully for a full minute before reaching his decision. "If it were anyone but you, Calloway, I'd tell you to stuff a sock in it. Okay, play your game. You have forty-eight hours."

"That's not a whole lot of time," Dakota commented as they drove to her place.

"If I need more, I'll get it. For now it's enough. Okay, I can't go to the station, so you'll have to do all the legwork, Winston."

She gave him a baleful look. "What's the magic word?"

"Magic word?"

"Yes, magic word. As in, 'Please won't you do this for me, Dakota?' Or, 'I'd really appreciate a favor, Dakota.'"

He turned to look at her. "Are you my partner or not?"

"I guess so, unfortunately. It would sure help if you learned some manners."

"They don't teach those in the gutter."

"Oh, come off it! You haven't been in the gutter your entire life, and you're not so stupid you haven't heard the word *please*. So get off the self-pity kick and act like the civilized human being you are."

She expected him to snap right back at her or make one of those disgusting comments males too often made when a woman was irritated. Much to her astonishment, he hesitated briefly, then said, "Okay. Will you do the legwork for me?"

"Sure. Be glad to." And now, as usual, she felt like a fool for getting snappish with him. Anytime she allowed her annoyance to show, she wound up feeling embarrassed, as if she had done something impermissible. Well, to hell with it this time! This man was keeping her in the dark and yet asking her to do his dirty work. He could at least be polite about it!

"I need you to check on Lexine Baxter, the way we discussed earlier."

"There could be a thousand Baxters with a record," she reminded him.

"Could be, but Lexine's an unusual name and I'm sure I can get specific details about her without any trouble. Hell, Winston, she grew up here. Just let me at a telephone while you head to the office and I'll have identifying information lickety-split."

Which was how she came to be at the station just before midnight, punching Lexine Baxter's name into the computer and waiting to see what the national crime-information system might have on her. Much to Dakota's surprise, the system coughed something back immediately.

A Lexine Baxter was wanted on an outstanding warrant for fraud in Denver along with an accomplice, Frank P. Travers. Travers had more than a dozen aliases listed, and checking them out, Dakota discovered he must be a pretty slimy con man.

But in the process of pursuing information about Travers, she discovered that the man was also wanted in Denver for aggravated battery. The victim's name was Lexine Baxter.

She called Clint. He must have been sitting right on top of the phone because he answered in the middle of the first ring. "Yeah?"

"It's Dakota," she announced. "I found some stuff on a Lexine Baxter, but until we know her date of birth—"

"It could be anyone," he completed. "I know. I did manage to find out her year of birth." He told her.

"It could be the same one, then. Okay, what I have is that she's wanted on a warrant out of Denver along with a guy called Travers. Apparently they were running some kind of scam. But here's something equally interesting— Travers is also wanted on an ag-bat charge. He apparently beat Lexine pretty severely.''

"In the morning we'd better call Denver and see if they can fill in some blanks for us. Anything else?"

"That's all on this end."

"It's a good start. Come on home, Dakota. I'll have a drink waiting for you."

It was as if something warm and fuzzy curled up in her heart as he spoke. He didn't mean it that way, of course, but it made her feel wanted just the same. The way she had felt long years ago when she had come home from school on a blustery winter day and her mother had had warm cocoa waiting.

It wasn't until Dakota got out to her car that she started telling herself not to be a brass-plated fool. The man had all but cut her to ribbons this morning. Yes, he'd apologized for it, but she'd be a fool to give him a chance to do it again.

Clint Calloway, she thought as she drove home, had one of the world's most caustic tongues. She ought to be used to it by now, and it shouldn't bother her as much as it did. But it *did* bother her, primarily because she often felt he wasn't the hard man he kept trying to convince others he was.

And wasn't that a dangerous train of thought! She shook her head, marveling at her own lunacy. The next thing she knew, she'd be telling herself he really didn't mean to do the things he did. But he *did* mean to. She was absolutely sure of that. And that's what kept persuading her he wasn't as gruff and tough as he made out. If he had been saying these things unconsciously, she'd have to admit he was a bastard. Instead, she got the feeling that each of his cutting remarks was purposeful, designed to keep distance between himself and others.

And why did people do that? Because they didn't want to get hurt.

This morning he'd shoved her away in the quickest way he knew how, to keep her from getting all goopy and emotional, and to prevent her from forming any notion about a long-lasting romance. But there had been something more in the way he had said, "Last night was a mistake." There had been something in his eyes at that moment that went beyond a desire to erect a barrier as swiftly as possible. Something that had given the words some other significance.

Damn, she wished he would talk to her! She was getting sick and tired of always being in the dark. He wouldn't tell her anything about himself—not really—and he wouldn't tell her how his thoughts were progressing on this damn mess, with all these cases he seemed to think were linked together. Oh, she knew he suspected Mary Jo Kincaid was involved, but damned if she could figure out how.

Something to do with the Kincaid land, he'd implied. With Mary Jo sending out feelers to sell it? Maybe Dugin Kincaid had been up to shady dealings of some kind. Everything Dakota had heard about the man since her arrival here led her to believe he was capable of underhandedness. Cowards usually were. And there was the suspicion that Dugin had been murdered, though nobody could really be sure. Yes, his skull had been smashed in a way that probably hadn't occurred in the fire, but how could anyone be absolutely positive? Freak accidents happened.

And he hadn't died in the fire anyway, but in intensive care. Which, according to Clint, shouldn't have happened, because he had been recovering. Although, as she well knew, someone in ICU could take a sudden turn in no time at all.

But suppose he *had* been murdered. Who were the suspects? Well, his widow, first of all. Statistically speaking, she was the likeliest one to want him dead. But a man in Kincaid's position probably had a lot of enemies. A lot of people who would gain by his death.

Then there was the Floyd Oakley case—the guy who was killed just before or during Mary Jo and Dugin's wedding a couple of years ago. Right about the time Jennifer Mc-Callum had been found on Dugin's doorstep.

Dakota sat up a little higher in her seat and hardly noticed that her tires squealed when she took a corner too fast. Now that was an interesting situation—a baby found just before the wedding, right on the bridegroom's front step. Why hadn't anyone wondered if Oakley were somehow connected to the baby? Maybe he'd been planning to blackmail Dugin or Jeremiah, and one of the Kincaids had taken him out.

She'd have to fly that one past Clint for sure.

And then there was Homer's alien, wearing what sounded like a motorcycle helmet that had been doctored somehow. Homer's remarks about roses in warm sunshine, and an alien who wanted sapphires. He'd been abducted on Kincaid land, hadn't he?

Good grief, she was beginning to think like Clint.

"Actually," Clint told her a few minutes later, "Homer was abducted on land that passed to the Kincaids only about thirty years ago. It was formerly the Baxter ranch."

Dakota, who had been slouching in the rocking chair, sat up straight. "Baxter, as in Lexine Baxter?"

"None other."

"How did the Kincaids get the land?"

"Bought it for a song when Cameron Baxter couldn't keep up with his mortgages. He gambled too much."

"Curiouser and curiouser." Although what was really curious was the feeling Dakota had that maybe Clint was right, and a bunch of things that appeared to be unconnected were, in reality, connected. He had started his matchstick thing on her coffee table, and she watched him organize his little piles of color-coded sticks.

"Curiouser yet," Clint continued, "is that the rumors about the old sapphire mine revolve mostly around the Baxter land."

"Ooh." She didn't need a map to see the connection. "Lexine Baxter maybe has an ax to grind?"

"Could be. But she'd have to get her hands on the land to see any profit from it."

"So maybe murder off enough Kincaids that the property goes on the market? Perhaps she made a fortune on her scam."

"Not very likely," Clint said dryly. "Let's stay within the realm of possibility here. Maybe she just wants to get even. Maybe she has a grudge against the Kincaids that goes beyond the land. Wouldn't surprise me. They managed to treat quite a few people like dirt."

Dakota thought about it some more. "Okay, say Lexine is getting even with Kincaids. That's possible. Especially if she was the one who killed Charlie Avery—after you've committed one murder, the second one must seem like a snap. But that still leaves Homer's abduction. She must think that she can get her hands on that mine somehow."

Clint nodded agreement. "That'd be my guess, too. I need to think about that some more."

"And then there's that darn Oakley murder. How does that fit?"

"Maybe he knew Lexine. Maybe he was going to warn

the Kincaids about her, but she got to him first. Tomorrow, why don't you call the Denver police and see what you can learn about Lexine, and maybe we can find a connection to Oakley.''

"But then we somehow have to find Lexine.''

It seemed to her that his mouth curved in an odd, almost invisible smile. "Yeah. There is that little problem.''

Thirteen

Dakota couldn't sleep. The breeze blew over her nude body, but instead of relaxing her, it reminded her of last night. Of the glorious hours she had spent in discovery with Clint. Tonight he slept on her couch again, as if nothing had ever happened between them.

But it *had* happened, and she couldn't forget it. Half of her yearned to climb out of bed and go to him. She wanted to slip under the sheet at his side, run her hands over his smooth, warm skin and open her body to his possession. She wanted to ride the whirlwind again and return safely in his arms.

But the price of that would probably be another painful confrontation in the morning. Clint didn't want anyone to get close to him. He reminded her of a prickly cactus, keeping people away with his thorns so they wouldn't touch his skin. Or his heart.

Had his mother's neglect done that to him? Probably not all by itself. There must have been numerous rejections for a guy to refer to himself as a guttersnipe. And who the devil had called him that? It wasn't a word you heard much anymore.

Sighing, Dakota rolled onto her side and watched the curtains stir gently in the breeze. Thunder rumbled distantly, a summery sound that she had always loved.

You're Montana royalty, and I'm a guttersnipe.

She heard the words as clearly as if he were speaking

them now, and they troubled her. She couldn't escape the feeling that he was reacting to something that had happened with someone else. That he was talking to someone besides her. Or that he was lumping her with someone else.

He hadn't been talking about the night they had shared. There was no way he could have been. What had happened between them had been too precious, too beautiful. There had been far too much sharing. No, it wasn't Dakota he was calling royalty in that scathing tone of voice.

Rolling onto her back, she stared at the faint patterns of light on her ceiling. Thunder rumbled again, and this time she saw the flicker of lightning.

She needed to talk to Clint. The question was how to manage it. That man had more electric fences strung up around him than the state penitentiary. He would discuss work and damn little else, and she seriously doubted if he was going to allow her to question him about what he had really meant. Nor was he going to sit still while she attempted to apologize for her suspicions of him. He wouldn't want to hear it and would undoubtedly make some scathing remark or other.

But the truth of the matter was she didn't think he was acting out of a desire to get his hands on the Kincaid money. She really believed he didn't want a dime of it. And the reason she believed that was because he was the first man she had ever known who had displayed absolutely no interest in her own wealth. Lord knew he had an opportunity to go for her, and by extension, her money, if he was mercenary. But he wasn't even a tiny bit interested.

That told her as clear as anything that money didn't motivate Clint Calloway. If he wouldn't romance a woman to get his hands on it, then he was hardly likely to frame a woman to get—

She sat up abruptly as she suddenly realized what Clint

believed. He believed that Mary Jo Kincaid was behind all this, not Lexine Baxter at all. He'd intimated it on earlier occasions, and she had been so quick to accuse him of base motives that he'd dropped it…leaving her to think he had discarded the idea. But that wasn't it at all.

He still thought Mary Jo was involved somehow. Certainly he thought she was involved in the attempts to kill him. Why else would he not want her to know he had survived the fire?

But why then had he sent her on this Lexine Baxter goose chase tonight? Because he believed Mary Jo wasn't working alone? That would make sense, if Lexine had met Mary Jo somewhere, told her about sapphires and God knew what else, and the two women had concocted a scheme to make themselves wealthy. Oh, yes, that would make a whole lot of sense.

It would also explain the disappearance of Jennifer McCallum and the attempts on Clint's life. Mary Jo and Lexine could believe that the little girl and Clint were a threat to the Kincaid inheritance.

There was no way Dakota could sleep now. Rising, she pulled on her silk robe and headed for the kitchen. She tried to tiptoe silently past Clint, but he was already awake.

"Can't sleep, Winston?"

"No. I've been thinking about the case."

"I've been thinking about you."

Her breath jammed in her throat, and her heart seemed to stop. "Me?"

"You." He sat up, little more than a powerful shadow in the dark room, and reached out, snagging her wrist. The next thing she knew, she was stretched out beside him on the sofa bed, and he was looming over her like a threat— or a promise.

"Clint?"

"Do you have any idea how a man's body aches when he thinks about a woman he wants to make love to?" His voice was low, hardly more than a rough whisper. "Do you have any idea how my body seems to remember sensations? Like the way your hair felt when it trailed across my skin. The way your hands felt when they stroked down my sides...."

He caught her hand and lifted it to his lips, kissing her palm. Sparkles of delight seemed to run up her arm. She wanted to give in, to reach for him and welcome him with all the yearning of her hungry soul, but the memory of that morning prevented her. "Clint..." Oh, heavens, how she hated to say what she had to. She had to force it past a throat that resisted. "Clint...I don't think... This morning..."

"I apologized for this morning," he reminded her. His hand smoothed down her side, over the silk of her robe, making her want to melt against him.

"You did, but I...don't think I can..." Oh, Lord, it was so hard to talk when all she wanted to do was forget reality and sink into the wonder and joy of his lovemaking. "I don't think I can handle it again."

"It won't happen again," he said firmly. "It won't."

And fool that she was, she let that simple statement persuade her to abandon her resistance.

All she wanted in the entire world was Clint Calloway. She wanted his rough murmurs and his gentle hands, wanted his passion unbridled, so that she could unbridle hers. She wanted to explore that exquisite world that only he could take her to.

"I've been thinking about you all day," he whispered roughly. "I've been thinking about touching you. Playing with you. Asking you to play with me. I've been hot and heavy and hard most of the day. Nobody's ever done that to me before, Winston. Nobody.''

The words deepened the growing throbbing in her womb, lifting her further from mundane concerns. "Dakota," she said breathlessly. "My name is Dakota...."

He gave a breathless laugh as he drew her closer. "Dakota. Hell of a name for a woman...."

"I was supposed to be a boy." She gasped and arched toward him as his hand found her breast through silk, squeezed with gentle possession.

"That explains it," he muttered, then deprived her of both breath and reason by lowering his head and taking her silk-covered breast into his hot, wet mouth.

The night became a sparkling, colorful web of sensations. In seemingly no time at all, he held her suspended in fire and air, every nerve ending alive with ecstasy. Her body moved with a will of its own, taking command in a search for pleasure and satisfaction as old as time.

She reached out and claimed him as he was claiming her. Moved far beyond shyness, she forgot that a man's body was still largely a mystery to her. Forgot that she was inexperienced and knew next to nothing about how a man liked to be touched and caressed.

She took her tutelage from the moans that escaped him, from the leap of his muscles beneath her hand, from the way he leaned into her touches as if asking for more. Pleasing him, she discovered, was just as wonderful, just as exciting, as anything he did to her.

When his hand slipped between her legs to stroke the hidden nub of her desire, she reached out and closed her hand around him, touching him as he touched her. The intimacy seemed to somehow perfect the moment, letting them share a connection that surmounted all barriers.

When he rose above her, she guided him to her, guided

him into her, telling him as no words could how she welcomed him.

When he sank into her, she knew she was his.

Afterward they cuddled under the blankets for a while, laughing quietly and talking at random about funny things they had seen on the job. She noticed that anytime she strayed from that subject to something more personal, he brought them back to safe ground. He didn't want to talk about his childhood, about his personal life, about anything that might expose him.

For a while she played the game his way, content just to be able to share these moments of bliss. It would have been so nice to let things stay at this easy level, but deep inside she knew that was a false security. If they never plumbed one another's emotional depths, they would never have anything but a casual affair—and she didn't want a casual affair. Not with anybody—but most especially not with Clint Calloway.

When there was a brief lull, she screwed up her courage and took the icy plunge. "You said I was royalty yesterday morning," she reminded him. "I had the feeling you were thinking of someone else. Who was it?"

He stiffened. Against her, beneath her hands, his muscles turned to unyielding steel. She braced herself, expecting him to push her away and rise, turning his back on the uncomfortable subject.

But Clint was tougher than that, and a great deal more honest. In the end, when faced with a direct question, he answered directly. "I was thinking of your cousin Carlene. I dated her when I was in college."

"*Dated?*" She barely breathed the words, feeling that she had been struck some kind of blow. Her cousin. She shouldn't feel betrayed, but she did. Good grief, she told herself, that happened years ago, when I was just a kid! But it hurt anyway. Hurt fiercely.

"Yeah." He sighed and stirred, but didn't pull away. "Sorry, Dakota, but your cousin is a bitch. Or at least she was then. It wasn't a good experience. She thought she was better than me, and I was young enough and unsure enough to put up with it. She treated me like dirt, and in the end she brushed me off as if I were a mosquito. I guess I was her rebellion. I don't know. I just know that yesterday morning I was…remembering, for some reason."

Dakota was breathing rapidly, trying to contain her pain, trying to understand his. She knew her cousin, knew she was capable of being a royal bitch.

Another thought occurred to her, one that caused an even deeper pang. "Is that why—is that why you keep making those remarks about my money and background?"

He sighed again, heavily. "Yeah. I guess so."

And now, she thought, he was using her in a fashion not so very different from the way he felt Carlene had used him all those years ago. The pain that squeezed her chest had become unbearable and was going to force tears from her eyes at any moment. She didn't want him to see them, so she sat up abruptly. *Used.* She had been used, for some twisted kind of revenge. That was the only reason Clint Calloway had made love to her.

"I—I need a drink," she mumbled, grabbing her robe up off the floor and rising.

"Dakota…"

She turned swiftly away from him, tugging it on as she stumbled toward the kitchen. She was overreacting. No, she wasn't. Clint Calloway had her tangled up with her cousin in his mind, and as long as that was the case she could only believe that he was getting even with her cousin through her.

God, she had to get away. Just as soon as she could she was going to find a job in some other county, a long way from Whitehorn and Clint. Maybe even in another state…

"Dakota?"

She stood at the sink, in the dark, and ignored him. With a shaking hand she reached out and turned on the faucet, wanting to drown him out with the rush of water. She didn't want to talk to him. She didn't want to listen to him. She just wanted him to leave her alone.

"Dakota—"

"Don't touch me!"

The words were torn from her the instant his hands brushed her shoulders. She could feel him hesitate and heard him take a step back. Reaching out, she turned off the water.

"Dakota, what's wrong?"

"Why the hell should anything be wrong? Other than discovering that I've been a stand-in for my cousin—"

"Now wait one minute!" he interrupted harshly. "I don't know where you're getting that cockamamie idea—"

"From you!" She whirled around, glaring at him. In the dark they were just two shadows, but the air crackled with their anger and tension. "From things you've said. Things you've done. If you want to get even with my cousin, get even with *her,* not with me."

She took flight then, pushing past him and running to her bedroom. She closed the door, remembering at the last minute not to slam it so she wouldn't disturb the people in the other apartments, and then leaned against it, lost in the whirlwind of anger and hurt that swept through her.

Minutes later—or maybe hours—there was a quiet knock on the door.

"Dakota? Dakota, you were never a stand-in. Never."

She didn't believe him.

* * *

In the morning she felt embarrassed by her behavior the night before. Not so much because she felt she was wrong in her interpretation, but because she hadn't behaved in a more sophisticated fashion. She should have been able to laugh it off or dismiss it as insignificant. After all, they were simply having a brief affair.

Instead she had made the classic virgin's mistake of becoming too involved with her first lover, which had led her to take the rest of it far too seriously. What did it matter, when all was said and done? Especially since there was no future for her and Clint.

Except that it hurt—a hurt she tucked firmly aside as she prepared to face yet another day. She had promised Clint she would do certain things for him this morning. They were still partners, and she wasn't going to do anything to jeopardize her record as a police officer. She could cry later, in private, but for now she had to restore things to a professional level between herself and Clint.

Easier said than done.

He was sitting at the dinette table in her kitchen, slumped over a mug of coffee, dressed in nothing but unsnapped jeans. The sight was enough to make any normal red-blooded woman want to reach out and touch. Dakota paused on the threshold, wishing there was a way to wear blinders.

He looked up with tired eyes. "I don't know what notion you took last night, Dakota, but you weren't standing in for anyone."

"Sure." She was proud of the steady, indifferent way she managed to toss that out, when she wanted to scream and shout and tell him what a low-life scum he was. No, she didn't believe him. How could she?

"Your cousin burned me pretty bad," he said. "And yeah, that had something to do with my remarks about your money. But it didn't have anything to do with making love to you.''

She forced a smile to her lips and made herself nod. ''Right. Listen, I need to get going on this stuff you wanted me to check into.'' Her knees felt like water, but she made herself walk across the kitchen and get a glass of orange juice. ''Lexine Baxter and Floyd Oakley, right?''

''Did you hear me?''

''I heard you,'' she snapped. ''Did you hear *me?*''

''Yeah,'' he growled. ''Oakley and Baxter. Get their rap sheets if you can. There's got to be a connection.''

''You think Mary Jo and Lexine are in this together, don't you?''

''It's beginning to feel that way, but keep it under your hat. I don't have a shred of evidence.''

''I know. Just good old intuition. Well, mine's telling me the same thing. So is Dugin's bashed-in head and your car fire last night. So they're up to something and we need to nail them somehow.''

''And get Sterling and Jessica's little girl back. Mostly, get the little girl back. If I don't manage to accomplish anything else, I want to do that.''

For once Dakota agreed with him.

Mary Jo Kincaid was parked at the curb when she went out to get into her car. As soon as she saw Dakota, the widow climbed out and waved. ''Can I talk with you a moment?''

Dakota smiled and nodded and crossed the grass to her, wondering what the hell the woman could possibly want at this hour of the morning.

''Have you heard?'' Mary Jo asked nervously. ''About Clint, I mean?''

''Clint?''

"His car was found burned up alongside the road and they can't find him."

Dakota nodded, hoping she looked appropriately concerned. "I heard. He's my partner."

"I know. That's why I'm here." She fluttered prettily, looking sad and worried at the same time. "I know that police partners are close...." She trailed off questioningly, waiting.

Dakota nodded, giving her the answer that was most likely to elicit more. "Very close. Like brother and sister."

Mary Jo nodded. "That's what I heard. So you must know that Clint and I...well, he must have told you."

What? Dakota wondered. What was Clint supposed to have told her? "Well, he mentioned..." She allowed her own voice to trail off significantly.

"I thought he must have." Mary Jo stepped closer, lowering her tone confidentially. "It's just that I was widowed so recently. People wouldn't understand. It's not that I wasn't happy with Dugin. He was a wonderful, wonderful man, but I just get so lonely...." She blinked back a tear.

Dakota nodded, feigning sympathy.

"Anyway, people just wouldn't understand why I'm seeing someone again so soon, so if you wouldn't mind, could we keep it a secret that Clint was on his way out to see me last night?"

"I don't see any reason to tell anyone where he was going."

Mary Jo smiled. "Thank you. I knew you'd understand. I just don't want to stir up any unnecessary scandal."

"Sure. I understand." What the hell, thought Dakota. Mary Jo just didn't want anyone to connect her in any way with the accident. Or to raise suspicions that she was anything less than a loving wife to Dugin, in case someone got the idea that she might have murdered him. Which, looking

at her now, Dakota was beginning to think might be a possibility, after all. "It's no problem."

Mary Jo's smile grew broader. "I think it was that terrible Homer man."

The change of subject threw Dakota, but she recovered
swiftly. "Homer Gilmore? What about him?"

"I think he set fire to Clint's car."

"Why would he do such a thing?" And how did Mary
Jo know the fire had been set? Dakota's heart began to
hammer.

"Because he's so crazy! Wandering in those hills, claiming aliens abducted him, seeing spirits. It's entirely possible
he's finally gone off the deep end completely."

"Could be." Her lips felt stiff with the effort to appear
to agree without really doing so. If Mary Jo knew the car
had been tampered with, something that Judd had agreed
would be kept absolutely secret for now, then Mary Jo
knew who had tampered with it—or had tampered with it
herself.

"Well," Dakota said, feeling as if her face was carved
out of wood, "I'll certainly give it some thought. It *does*
seem crazy that anyone would have wanted to set fire to
Clint's car."

Mary Jo smiled. "I think so, too! Heavens, what is the
world coming to?"

A good question, Dakota thought as she walked to her
sedan, aware that the woman was watching. What was the
world coming to? She wanted to run back into the house
and tell Clint what Mary Jo had just done, how she had
just slipped up, but the widow would wonder why she'd
turned around, so she climbed into her car, pulled out of
her space and headed toward the office. Only then did Mary
Jo start her car and head the other way.

Why would Mary Jo want to kill Clint—except to preserve her interest in the fortune from a possible challenge by him? And if the woman was prepared to do that, then she would certainly be prepared to kidnap a small child. The question was, would a woman who was prepared to burn a man to death also be capable of killing a small child? The answer was a chilling yes.

But Winona had said Jennifer was alive and well, and Dakota was willing to trust Winona's ESP, especially since she had been right about the fire at Clint's. Besides, what other hope did they have at the moment?

The minute she reached her desk, she called Clint. "There's no doubt that Mary Jo is involved somehow," she told him. "She knew someone had tampered with your car to cause the fire."

"Well, hot damn," he said. "How'd you find this out?"

"She wanted me to keep quiet about your date with her last night, and she tried to point the finger at Homer Gilmore. That's when she slipped up."

He laughed, a satisfied sound that rolled warmly over the wire. "Good show, Winston."

"Clint, you know what this means, don't you?"

"Yeah." His voice grew low, tight. "She probably had a hand in the kidnapping. She's afraid that kid or I might be able to get some of her money."

"If she's this money hungry, it's a bet that she had something to do with Dugin's accident."

"Very likely. Damn, it's a shame no one did an autopsy on old Jeremiah. It might be real interesting to discover why he fell in the shower."

"Well, I'll get to work on these rap sheets, see if I can come up with the Mary Jo-Lexine link."

"Maybe Lexine didn't have anything at all to do with any of this."

"Are you changing your mind?"

He was silent a moment, then said, "No, I guess not. My intuition is telling me there's a tie there somewhere. Go for it, Dakota."

She hung up, thinking it was really ironic that they finally seemed to be functioning as partners—just when she had decided the situation was untenable and that she was going to have to leave the department.

Couldn't life be fair just once in a while?

She sent off the requests for any available information on Floyd Oakley and Lexine Baxter, and then called the Denver police to see if there was any information on Lexine that might not be on her rap sheet.

"Ah...Detective Smitson is handling that," the officer in Denver told her. "She's out right now, but should be back before lunch. You want her to call?"

"If she has anything about the Baxter woman she thinks might be useful to me."

"You got it, Detective."

And now there was nothing more to do but wait for the information to start arriving. Dakota took the stack of folders containing all the unsolved cases from Clint's desk and put it on her own, determined to once again review each file, this time looking for connections between the cases rather than clues to the solution. If Mary Jo Kincaid and Lexine Baxter were capable of kidnapping and of the attempted murders of two other people, then they were capable of a great deal more than that. Capable, perhaps, of killing Floyd Oakley and even Charlie Avery. Maybe Lexine had all along been a murderess.

Maybe Blue Lake County would have always been an idyllic place except for that one woman.

Dakota caught herself and chuckled quietly. Yeah, Winston. Spread it on a little thicker! Idyllic indeed!

* * *

Floyd Oakley had a surprisingly long rap sheet. Evidently he was a penny-ante con man, a would-be big-time wheeler dealer who kept getting himself into trouble over relatively small amounts of money. He had a few convictions, but most of the time he had received probation. Apparently he had a good measure of charm.

So why had he been found dead in a grove of trees on the Kincaid ranch in Montana? It seemed like a rather out-of-the-way place for a con man with delusions of grandeur.

But then she found the link she had been looking for. Oakley had been arrested a few years back in the company of one Alexa Baxter, a.k.a. Lexine Baxter. Charges against the pair had been dismissed.

"Bingo!" Delighted, Dakota slapped her palm down on the paper and had to battle an urge to let out a *wahoo* of sheer pleasure. Oakley knew Lexine. Oakley had been found stabbed to death not too far from Lexine's birthplace.

That meant Lexine was back in Blue Lake County. Now where the hell was she hiding?

Dakota tried calling Clint to tell him the news, but there was no answer. To her great dismay, she was stuck at her desk, awaiting the call from Denver with regard to Lexine. It could well be important, and she didn't dare risk missing it, not just to pass on some news that could wait until Clint came back to the apartment anyway.

Assuming Lexine was involved in a scheme to obtain the Kincaid money—or even the missing sapphire mine—Oakley, Dakota surmised, must have somehow caught wind of her plans and come looking for her. Lexine had found this supremely inconvenient for one reason or another—perhaps Oakely had threatened her in some way?—and had removed him. There was hardly any other possible explanation.

"Dakota?"

She swiveled in her chair and gazed up at Sterling McCallum. Lord, the man looked awful. Worry about his daughter was eating him alive. "'Morning, Sterling. How are you and Jessica holding up?''

"Barely." His attempted a smile. "It doesn't get any easier. You found anything yet?''

She wanted to tell him that she had a strong suspicion about who had kidnapped his daughter, and that—if the child was still alive—she hoped to be able to recover her soon. If Sterling had just been another cop, she would have told him. But because he was Jennifer's father, she didn't dare raise hopes that might turn out to be false. Hope was nothing but torture if it proved to be unfounded. "We're working on some things, but nothing to get excited about yet.''

McCallum nodded. "I figured, but I had to ask anyway. If I ever get my hands on the son of a bitch who took her, I'll—'' He broke off abruptly and shook his head. "No, I won't. But I dream about it.''

"I bet you do.''

He flashed another crooked smile that didn't quite succeed. "Well, keep me posted.''

"I will, Sterling. I will.'' And Sterling wasn't the only one who wanted to wring someone's throat. Not by any means. There was one slender, pretty, pale neck she'd kind of like to get her own hands around.

Later. Later she'd deal with the anger she felt toward Mary Jo, knowing that the woman had tried to kill Clint. Knowing that if she'd succeeded—she and Lexine—Clint would have died a horrible, fiery death. Dakota might be furious with Clint for using her as a stand-in to get even with her cousin, but she couldn't bear the thought of anyone trying to hurt him.

God, she had it bad. She was crazy about the guy, and

all he saw in her was a slightly younger version of a woman he probably hated with a passion.

Thinking of her cousin, Dakota wondered why she had treated Clint that way. Carlene had always had a hard edge to her, but Dakota couldn't imagine her treating a boyfriend the way she must have treated Clint to have left him so bitter. But Carlene was older now. When she had known Clint, she had probably been young and heedless—and considerably more insensitive than she was now. Young people generally were.

And maybe Dakota was just making excuses. Her cousin could be a bitch at times. The years hadn't taken any of that out of her.

What did it matter, anyway? Clint would always see her cousin when he looked at her, and given what had happened in the distant past, it was unlikely he could ever feel a thing for Dakota except contempt for a "spoiled little rich girl."

Damn, that really hurt. For some stupid reason, his opinion mattered to her a whole lot. Too much. However falsely based it was, it still hurt her to know how he perceived her. Hurt her to know he would never be able to feel about her the way she had come to feel about him.

Oh, maybe she ought to just go find a good psychiatrist! There had to be something wrong with a woman who fell for a guy who had treated her the way Clint treated her. *Had* treated her. Except for the other morning, he hadn't been so bad lately. They'd been getting along pretty well, and she could handle his occasional sarcastic remark without any heartburn.

Clint was Clint, and somewhere inside him was that little boy who hadn't been wanted by anyone, and who had pulled himself out of the gutter without any help at all. Of course he had an attitude. Of course he built high fences to protect himself from hurt.

Of course he couldn't imagine that someone might actually be more inclined to hurt herself than hurt him. Someone like Dakota.

Sighing, she propped her chin in her hand and faced the fact that she'd gotten herself into a situation she'd always told herself to avoid. She'd fallen for her partner.

And what was making it even worse, was that her partner hadn't fallen for her.

Life was the pits sometimes.

Just then the phone rang, saving her from the well of gloomy reflection she was teetering over.

"Detective Winston, this is Detective Smitson in Denver. I understand you're inquiring about Lexine Baxter."

"Yes, I am. We think she's returned to Blue Lake County and may be engaging in some illegal activities. I understand she may have been involved in con jobs?"

"She certainly has been. We haven't been able to nail her yet, but we sure want to. She generally hooks up with some good-looking guy with a lot of charm and passes herself off as his sister. She does a wonderful job of playing sexy and helpless, I guess. She attracts the mark and keeps him befuddled—and she does a damn good job of it, from what I've been hearing."

"Can you fax me a recent photo of her?"

"Well, that's a bit of a problem. Our photos don't look anything like her. You see, her most recent lover beat her so severely that she had to have major plastic surgery. I understand her own mother wouldn't recognize her now."

Fourteen

Plastic surgery...her own mother wouldn't recognize her now.

"A woman with two faces..."

Damn it, Winona, how do you do it? Dakota wondered as she drove back to her apartment. And where the hell was Clint? He was supposed to be waiting for her so they could discuss whatever she had discovered. He was supposed to be hiding out so that they could spring a surprise on the person who had tried to kill him...which was probably Lexine Baxter, alias Mary Jo Kincaid.

Damn it! Dakota slapped her palm against the steering wheel in frustration as she got caught at the light. She couldn't quite shake the fear that something had happened to Clint. What if Mary Jo had managed to get to him at the apartment? What if Clint wasn't answering the phone because he was hurt or dying?

It was a stupid fear, she told herself as she waited an eternity for the light to change. A stupid fear. Clint could take care of himself, and it was highly unlikely that Mary Jo had managed to drug the orange juice in Dakota's refrigerator so that she could set another fire.

God, that woman was a real firebug. Given what had happened to Clint, Dakota no longer doubted that Dugin had been murdered. And when the fire hadn't managed to do the trick, Mary Jo had gone after Dugin in ICU, maybe smothering him with a pillow or something. Or adding something to his IV. There were probably several ways the woman could have done it.

What mattered was Dakota's gut certainty that Mary Jo *had* done it. That for whatever reason, Lexine Baxter had returned to Whitehorn with the intention of making herself a wealthy woman, and that anything that stood in her way was just an obstacle to be removed.

And if Lexine Baxter were capable of killing her husband and attempting to kill Clint, then she was capable of having killed her lover, Charlie Avery, and of kidnapping Jennifer McCallum, and of trying to kill Tracy Hensley....

Yes! That fit, too—the idea that Mary Jo had stolen the evidence bags that Tracy had been filling at the site of the murder.

The light changed and she zipped down the road, in a hurry to get to her apartment. She was undoubtedly speeding, but she didn't care. Something had happened to Clint; the certainty rested in her stomach as uneasily as a lead ball. Was this how Winona felt when she had one of her spells?

Dakota pulled into her parking place and slammed on the brakes, coming to a halt with a jerk. She barely paused to yank the keys out of the ignition, then ran up the walk to her door, hoping against hope that Clint had merely fallen asleep and failed to hear the phone. Hoping he was okay.

At the door she took a deep, steadying breath, trying to ready herself for anything. The problem was this was no routine police call, where the person on the other side of the door was a stranger. This time the person on the other side of the door was someone she loved.

Her hand on the knob, she stood frozen for a split second longer, not sure she was going to be able to go in. This wasn't ordinary anxiety. Someone had tried to kill Clint twice in just the last week. She had plenty of reason to be scared to death.

But she shoved the door inward anyway, holding her breath.

Everything looked just as it should. Nothing was out of place, except a shirt of Clint's tossed over the back of the rocker.

"Clint?"

"What's going on?"

The abrupt question from the doorway behind her nearly caused Dakota to have a heart attack. She whirled, then sagged with relief as she saw Rafe Rawlings. He was obviously on duty, in full uniform, and was looking at her from behind mirrored sunglasses.

"You came down that road like a bat out of hell so I followed you over here," he told her. "Is something wrong?"

"I'm not sure. I've been trying to reach Clint all morning and he hasn't been answering the phone."

"Clint? I thought he disappeared last night...." He shook his head and pulled off his sunglasses. "What the hell is going on?"

"Look, can I explain after I look around? Somebody's been trying to kill him and I'm worried!" She tried to keep her voice low, but her urgency made it all but impossible.

"Yeah, sure. Okay. Let's check it out." He unholstered his pistol. "I'll go first."

But Dakota was already moving into the living room, her own weapon drawn. Why, she wondered vaguely, did men always forget she was a cop, too?

Clint was nowhere to be found, nor was there any sign of a struggle that might indicate a problem.

"He must have just gone out for a while," Rafe said, holstering his gun. "Maybe to the convenience store."

Dakota shook her head. "I don't think so. Something is wrong. He's been gone too long. Besides, he was waiting for some information I was trying to get."

"Will you just tell me what's happening?"

It was then that she saw the piece of paper lying on the floor behind the front door, as if it had been shoved backward when the door opened. Her heart climbed into her throat as she bent to retrieve it.

"Dakota," Clint had written in his slashing backhand, "I've gone to confront MJ. Should have this tied up with a pretty ribbon by noon."

It was now nearly one. Dakota looked up at Rafe, who had read the note over her shoulder.

"*Now* will you fill me in?" he asked.

"I need to get out to the Kincaid place. Now."

"Trouble?"

"I'm afraid…" She shook her head. "I've got to get out there now."

"I'm going with you."

"You can't! You're on duty. It's off your beat."

"Like hell I can't. Just watch me."

They were three minutes down the road in her car when he got radio permission to go with her as backup. "Told you," he said. "So what's going on?"

She filled him in as best she could, making it perfectly clear just how much was pure speculation, but he kept right on nodding as she talked and drove.

"It fits," he said when she wound down. "It's circumstantial as all get out, but it fits. Especially the kidnapping. Who in the library was in a better position to walk off with the McCallum girl? Nobody. And she was the last person on earth anyone would suspect of such a thing. But my God, Dakota, how anyone could do that to a child…" He shook his head.

"It gets me, too," she agreed. "I don't know the woman well, and I don't particularly like what I *do* know of her, but it's hard to imagine her doing this."

"Maybe not so hard. She hides it well, but she does have a vicious streak. And she was spreading rumors and gossip when Ethan was on trial. Come to think of it, she was awfully interested in that case. In fact, Mary Jo has shown a lot of interest in Whitehorn's scandals."

It seemed to take forever to get to the Kincaid place. Dakota drove as fast as she dared, but that didn't seem fast enough. She hated to think of the trouble Clint might be in if Mary Jo had managed to take him unawares, rather than the other way around. What if she hadn't believed the story of his disappearance and had been lying in wait for him? What if she had managed to set some kind of trap?

All kinds of possibilities kept whirling through Dakota's brain, each of them equally distressing. One thing was perfectly clear to her: if Clint had succeeded in "tying things up with a pretty ribbon," he wouldn't be missing.

The drive up to the big house where Mary Jo lived was one of the eeriest Dakota had ever taken. A ranch this size, one that had made the Kincaids a power to be reckoned with, should not have appeared desolate. There should have been signs of activity around sheds and corrals, not this strange emptiness. Where were the people who took care of the livestock, the horses, the equipment, the overall management?

"Where *is* everybody?" Rafe muttered. "I didn't hear anything about her laying off all the hands."

"You'd have heard something, wouldn't you?"

"Hell, yes. A Kincaid can't sneeze in this county without everyone taking notice."

"Then they must be here somewhere." And for some

reason Mary Jo had gotten them out of the way. Why else was there no one in evidence by the main buildings? Dakota's scalp began to prickle. "Is there some legitimate excuse she could have used to get everyone away from here?"

"Plenty of 'em, I imagine. I don't like this at all, Dakota."

"Me, either." Without a moment's hesitation, she turned the car around and headed back the way they had come.

"What are you doing?"

"If I have to drive up to the front door and announce my presence, I'd rather have you on standby. As soon as we're concealed from the house, I'm going to stop and let you out. You can make it up there without being seen, can't you?"

"It'll be a snap." He nodded. "You wait until I get to the house, though, before you come back up the drive. Give me, say, ten minutes?"

"Okay."

To make the wait easier, she drove back out to the road after dropping Rafe off. God, she hoped Clint was all right!

But what was she going to do if Mary Jo denied her entry to the house? She didn't have a warrant, or—at this point—sufficient cause to get one. Clint might not be in the house, after all. He might have come out here to confront Mary Jo, missed her entirely and gone off to do something else until she turned up.

So what should she do if Mary Jo didn't invite her in? Break in?

Her stomach was knotted so tightly that it hurt with a sharp pain by the time Dakota parked in front of the Kincaid house. If Mary Jo didn't let her in, there was nothing legal that she could do. Not a damn thing.

So she'd have to throw away the rest of her career and

break in somehow. Damn you, Clint, why did you come out here without backup? she thought. Without *me?*

She was still trying to rustle up a good reason to use to persuade Mary Jo to let her in when the front door opened and the widow stood there, smiling at her.

"Why, Dakota! What brings you out this way? Looking for Clint?"

"Yes, I am. Have you seen him?"

Something flickered in Mary Jo's blue eyes, and Dakota had the distinct impression that this woman was not the softly feminine bit of fluff she pretended to be. "Now why would I have seen him? I sent everyone on the ranch out to hunt for him because he might have wandered this way, but no one's come to tell me he's been found. I gather you're still looking."

Dakota nodded, wracking her brains for a way to get invited inside. "Could I trouble you for a glass of water?" It was all she could think of, a ruse that was apt to fail because Mary Jo could just tell her to wait here on the porch.

The other woman's eyes narrowed slightly, but her smile never faltered. "Of course." She stepped back, opening the door wide. "Come in, Dakota."

She led the way across a spacious, comfortably furnished living room. Big enough, Dakota thought, to serve as the lobby in a small hotel. They went down a wide corridor lined with glass display cases full of Indian artifacts.

The place looked like a museum, she decided, then felt her heart slam into high gear. In one lighted case was a collection of ceremonial regalia, from a buffalo-hide mask to gourd rattles. The items came from an assortment of different cultures, as if someone had wanted to gather a sampling from each. There was not enough there to give a complete picture of any of the originators, but there was enough to make up a costume of one rather strange and scary spirit.

Dakota had to force herself to stop staring. This was it. This must be *it!*

"I want to sell those things," Mary Jo said offhandedly.

Dakota looked swiftly at her. "Why? They're absolutely beautiful."

"To some people, perhaps. Not to me. They give me the creeps." Her hands fluttered and she shivered prettily. "Sara Dean says they're worth quite a bit of money."

"Probably." Was money all this woman could think about?

"The kitchen is in here," Mary Jo said, leading her through a swinging door of natural pine.

Dakota let out a low whistle as she surveyed the kitchen. "This is great!"

Mary Jo laughed, but it was a brittle sound. "I don't spend any more time in here than I have to."

Dakota somehow figured that the woman didn't spend any time doing anything she didn't have to. *Clint, where are you?*

A glass of water, cool and sweet, gave her an excuse to dawdle for a few minutes, and she sipped it a little more slowly than she absolutely had to. "It's good of you to send all your hands to look for Clint."

Mary Jo continued to smile, but to Dakota it seemed as if there was a tightness around her eyes. "It's the least I can do. The poor man might be seriously hurt, and to think of him lost out there somewhere..." She trailed off and frowned prettily.

Dakota turned to place her glass in the sink, thinking that it was far more likely Mary Jo had sent her men out to help with the search so she would have a chance of getting to Clint first—probably to finish the job she had started with the fire. It must have been a real shock for her when he turned up at her door. If he had.

No, she thought, turning to Mary Jo, the woman looked as if she were under a strain of some kind. She hid it well, but with each passing minute it seemed to Dakota that the other woman grew more tense.

"Well, if that's all…" Mary Jo started to lead the way toward the door. With no alternative left, Dakota threw caution to the wind.

"Actually, Mary Jo, Clint is alive."

Mary Jo whirled, her hand flying to her breast. "What kind of game are you playing, Dakota?"

"No game. He's alive. What's more, he was coming up here to see you this morning."

"He never got here."

"I think he did. I think he got here, and that's exactly what the sheriff is going to think when Clint turns up missing."

"But he's already missing," Mary Jo pointed out. Something in her face was hardening, though, and the sight made Dakota uneasy. She wondered if she could get her hand nearer her gun without tipping Mary Jo off to what she was doing. Moving very slowly, she began to raise her hand.

"Clint isn't already missing, and the sheriff knows it. Everybody who matters knows it. They know he was coming up here to see you," she lied recklessly, "so guess where they're going to look first when he turns up *really* missing."

Mary Jo was perfectly still for a long moment, then she shrugged one shoulder. "Let them look. I have nothing to hide."

For an instant, Dakota almost believed her. Almost. Then, just as the other woman turned away, she saw something in Mary Jo's smile that chilled her. She plunged ahead.

"Nothing to hide? How about some bones that were found near an old Indian burial ground? Or what about a missing child? Do you know anything about what happened to Floyd Oakley? Or how about your husband's strange death in ICU?"

Mary Jo faced her again, her expression almost flat, as if something inside her had disconnected. "What *are* you talking about?"

"A little plastic surgery, perhaps?"

It was as if she had pushed a button. Mary Jo's face abruptly became a twisted mask of rage. She gave a minute flick of her wrist, and all of a sudden Dakota was staring down the barrel of a snub-nosed .38 Chief's Special.

"Floyd taught me that," Mary Jo said, indicating the gun. "It was about the only useful thing he ever did for me. Reach for your gun, Dakota. Slowly. Don't touch it with more than two fingers. This is a .38, and I'm a good shot."

Feeling like a fool, Dakota did as she was told. Right now, any resistance was apt to get her shot. The knowledge that Rafe was outside was reassuring. If she didn't emerge soon he would come after her—and he would come cautiously, not letting Mary Jo know he was there.

Doing as she was told, Dakota placed her weapon on the table and backed slowly away from it.

"I don't know where you got all that information," Mary Jo said, "but you couldn't prove a thing, anyway. No one can tie me to any of those murders. No one can tie me to the kidnapping. Not in any way that matters. There isn't any proof, Dakota."

Mary Jo was right, and Dakota knew it. They were a long way from having enough information to get an indictment, let alone a conviction. But now that they knew who the suspect was, there wasn't a shred of doubt in her mind that she and Clint could discover enough to make a good case on at least some of the murders.

She grasped at another straw and exaggerated a little. "Homer says you abducted him. He remembered."

"Who'll believe him?" Mary Jo laughed. "You know, a lawyer once told me that courts would be out of business if the accused persons would just shut up. I'm not going to admit anything."

"I haven't Mirandized you anyway," Dakota reminded her, although this wasn't exactly an interrogation while in custody, so reading Mary Jo her rights wouldn't matter. Not as long as Mary Jo held the gun. But maybe the other woman didn't know that. "Look, all this other stuff is water over the dam. What I really want to know is whether Jennifer McCallum is okay. I mean, her parents are so torn up, and the kid must be so scared...."

Mary Jo's eyes flickered briefly. "I'm not admitting anything. I told you that."

"But she's just a baby! And she couldn't inherit any of the Kincaid money anyway!"

"Of course she could—" Too late, Mary Jo broke off abruptly.

"No, she *can't* inherit," Dakota insisted. "Neither can Clint. The estate was already probated when their relationship with Jeremiah was discovered, and there's no legal way for either of them to touch that money." Which wasn't strictly true, but true enough.

Mary Jo blinked, looking a little uneasy. "That's not true."

"It *is* true. Did you ever bother to talk to a lawyer? You don't have to kill Clint or get rid of Jennifer to keep the damn money!"

"I haven't done anything!"

"Oh, come off it! Do you think we don't know you dressed up in those Indian clothes in that display case in the hallway to scare Tracy Hensley away from Charlie Avery's body, so you could steal the evidence she'd found? Of course we know it was you, Lexine. I'm willing to bet we'll find traces of dirt and plant life on the soles of those moccasins that will prove you were out there on the res." Now that was really stretching it—given the closeness of this ranch to the reservation, it was doubtful there'd be any significant difference between soil and plant life here and there—but from the wild look in her eyes, Mary Jo was buying it. "And who's going to believe you wanted to steal the evidence if you didn't kill Charlie Avery?"

"You can't prove anything!"

"And then there's the murder of Floyd Oakley at your wedding. Floyd Oakley who was once attached to Lexine Baxter—who is you with a little plastic surgery. A woman who is still wanted in Denver. Good God, Lexine, it's all falling down around your ears! It's only a matter of days before we have enough to put you in prison for a good long time!"

Mary Jo's eyes were shifting almost wildly, but the gun never wavered. "A couple of days? I'll be gone!" Her laugh was harsh. "And so will you. They might find your bones in twenty years, the way they found Charlie's. The bastard got what he deserved anyway, no matter what Melissa says about her sainted father!"

"I know he hurt you...."

"Hurt me? He knocked me up! He told me he was going to leave that insipid wife of his because he couldn't live without me, but when I got pregnant he didn't want anything more to do with me! I was just a kid! What was I supposed to do with a baby and no money?"

"So you killed him?"

Mary Jo's eyes suddenly became sharp. "I didn't say that. I wanted to get rid of the kid and he wouldn't let me.... God, it's so funny. The kid should have died, but that Rawlings woman found him and raised him...."

"Rafe Rawlings is your son?" Dakota felt a wave of shock. She wondered how Rafe would react to that.

Mary Jo didn't answer, however. She seemed to catch herself, and waved the gun toward the hallway. "Outside, Dakota. I don't want blood spattered all over the kitchen. It's too much trouble to clean up. No, I think I'll let them find your body out in the woods somewhere—in twenty years or so. Now move it!"

Dakota spared herself a split second of relief. As soon as they got outside, Rafe would come to her rescue. And now that Mary Jo had held her at gunpoint, they could nail the woman for assault with a deadly weapon and unlawful imprisonment. The rest would surely fall into place.

Holding her hands in plain sight so as not to startle Mary Jo, Dakota did as she was told. Her back prickled as she walked down the hall ahead of her, and she wondered how she was ever going to explain her own folly in letting this woman get the drop on her. Clint would probably roast her good over this...if Clint were still alive.

"Where's Clint?" she asked Mary Jo again, her heart hammering.

"I told you, I haven't seen him," the other woman snapped. "Just shut up. I've heard enough out of you."

"Damn it, Dakota," said a familiar voice, "you messed everything up."

Dakota whirled and found Clint standing in the living room, his nasty-looking 9 mm leveled straight at Mary Jo.

"Drop it," he ordered the woman. "Because I sure as hell wouldn't mind blowing your head off."

"Me, either," said Rafe shortly.

Dakota's gaze jumped past Mary Jo and found Rafe standing in the hallway behind the other woman. He must have come in through the kitchen door, she realized.

"You can't shoot us both, Mary Jo," Clint said. "You might as well just give up now."

"You can't prove anything against me, Calloway."

"Depends on what I want to prove. You've been holding my partner at gunpoint. That's two crimes I can think of, and we sure have enough witnesses to send you away. Just put the gun down before it gets any worse."

And much to Dakota's relief, Mary Jo did just that. Dakota reached for the pistol as Mary Jo lowered her hand, and Rafe stepped forward to cuff her wrists behind her back.

Then, almost before Dakota saw him moving, Clint leapt across the room, scooped her up in a tight bear hug and squeezed until she squeaked.

"Damn it, Dakota," he said roughly, "I ought to turn you over my knee. That was dumb. Stupid. Foolhardy…"

"And exactly what you were going to do," she argued. "Clint, you're hurting me…."

His arms slackened a little, but he didn't let go. Instead he covered her mouth with a kiss that left her dazed.

"Let's go," he said finally. "I swear, I'm never going to let you out of my sight again!"

Fifteen

For the first time in her career as a policwoman, Dakota Winston wanted to commit violence. She could have cheerfully wrung Mary Jo's neck in attempt to get the woman to tell them where little Jennifer McCallum was.

But Mary Jo wasn't talking, and there was no legal way they could get her to talk. At some time or other, she had learned her rights well, and knew that the hands of the police were tied from the moment she asked for an attorney.

To persist in questioning her once she had asked for a lawyer could result in the widow walking away scot-free from some or all of the charges against her. Neither Clint nor Dakota was prepared to allow that to happen; she had hurt far too many people to escape punishment.

Somehow they would find out what had happened to Jennifer. The prosecutor would probably reach a plea bargain of some kind to get the information as quickly as possible, but that was not something that Clint or Dakota could arrange.

Sterling McCallum was like a wild man when he heard what happened. He paced the corridor outside the interrogation room with his fists clenched and his expression as threatening as heavy storm clouds. Dakota didn't for a moment doubt that if he had been able to get his hands around Mary Jo's throat, the widow's life expectancy would have been short indeed.

"We need to wait until her attorney gets here," the prosecutor argued. "We might be able to work out something then."

"How long will it take?" Sterling demanded. "That woman knows where my little girl is. We can't wait indefinitely. Jenny's probably scared out of her mind—" He broke off abruptly and averted his face.

"But if we interrogate her illegally, nothing we discover can be used!"

"In court," Dakota said suddenly. "It can't be used against her. But we can use it to find Jennifer! What if that's all we ask her. Just to tell us where the child is? We won't be able to use it as an admission, so she won't be incriminating herself."

"But," the prosecutor said sharply, "any information we develop out of what she tells us will also be inadmissible. It'd be a nightmare, trying to prove that every item we want to use against her was developed independently of anything she tells us!"

"So what?" Clint growled. "So it makes it harder. There's another nightmare to consider here, Counselor, and what the McCallums are going through puts your petty courtroom nightmare to shame!"

"All right!" The man capitulated explosively. "All right! But make damn sure you don't ask anything except where the child is, and that you don't let her tell you one other thing or this whole case might just go up in smoke!"

"Videotape it," Judd said. "Just so there aren't any questions about what *was* discussed."

"Good idea."

"I want Dakota to question her," Clint said. "Just Dakota. It'll be less threatening."

He turned to her and, ignoring everyone else, took her gently by the shoulders. "I want you to talk to her, Dakota. Woman to woman. Play the sympathy for the baby and the parents angle and see if we can't get her to tell us where to look.''

Sitting in the interrogation room at the table across from Mary Jo, Dakota studied her for a few minutes, wondering where to begin. The woman was quiet, no longer quite so brash, but certainly not crushed.

"You know," Dakota said finally, "your attorney is on the way.''

"Yes.''

"We've informed you of your rights, and you don't have to say anything at all. In fact, now that you've asked for an attorney, if we question you and you answer before your lawyer is here to advise you, nothing you say can be used. It would be an illegal interrogation.''

Mary Jo nodded, looking bored.

"Which is why I'm here," Dakota said. "We want to know where the McCallum girl is, and you can tell us. We also know you aren't going to admit that if it can be used against you.''

"What kind of fool do you take me for?''

"No kind of fool," Dakota said flatly. "Like I said, we know you won't tell us if it can be used against you. So we're setting this up so it can't be used. Anything you tell me right now will be tossed out of court if we try to bring it in, unless you tell me you're waiving your rights.''

"I'm not going to do that.''

Dakota nodded. "I know that. Let me tell you a true story. Years back some little girl was kidnapped and killed. The cops picked up the suspect and read him his rights. The guy asked for an attorney, which means the cops should have stopped questioning him right then, until his attorney arrived. But on the way to the jail, one of the cops talked to him, pointing out that it was a cold night, that

that poor little kid was lying out there and if it snowed the body would be covered and they wouldn't be able to find it to give it a decent burial. The cop even told the guy not to say anything, to just think about it. The kidnapper broke down in tears and told them where the body was. You know what? The Supreme Court overturned the kidnapper's original conviction, because that information was used against him, making it an illegal interrogation. Even though the cop had told the guy not to say anything.

"That's what I'm doing now, Mary Jo. An illegal interrogation. Tell us where Jennifer is. Her parents are going out of their minds, and the little girl must be so afraid...."

Mary Jo compressed her lips and remained silent.

"You were a little girl once. You *must* remember how you felt when you missed your mother when you were little. How scary it was to be away from your parents...." Dakota kept on in that vein for a while, keeping her voice quiet and even gentle, trying to find the human being inside this woman. There had to be one somewhere. Mary Jo Lexine had once been a little girl who had had feelings, and life had probably been largely responsible for turning her into this kind of woman. Somewhere inside her that little girl still existed.

A half hour later, finally, Mary Jo spoke. "I'm not waiving my rights."

Dakota felt her heart leap. "No, I know you're not."

"The kid is in North Dakota. With some people who want to adopt her. She's okay."

"Will you give me the address?"

After another brief hesitation, Mary Jo nodded. "Okay."

It was a long day, but at last it was over. Driving home to her apartment with Clint, Dakota heard for the first time what had happened that morning.

"After you called and told me Mary Jo had slipped up by revealing that she knew the cause of my accident, I got to thinking about confronting her, seeing if I couldn't get her to talk. I was a bit optimistic in the note I left for you, though."

"I sort of panicked when I saw how late it was and you still weren't back. I was afraid she had managed to hurt you."

He nodded. "I can see that, but give me some credit, Winston. I'm a better cop than that." He shot her a wry smile that kept her from taking offense. "Anyway, I got to thinking I'd like to poke around and see if I could discover any evidence before I talked to her. I went to Kate Walker and got a warrant based on probable cause to believe that Mary Jo had set fire to my car. That's what slowed me up so much."

"A warrant? You had a warrant, and there I was running off at the mouth trying to find a way to get in the house without one...."

Clint laughed, that wonderful sound that Dakota felt deep inside like something warm and cuddly. "Try it my way sometime. It works better."

"What would have worked better was if you had told me what you were doing. I could have come along and helped."

"And missed the phone call that linked Lexine and Mary Jo. At that point, I didn't know whether I'd find anything at all, but you were on an important trail. I didn't leave you out, Dakota. I had you working on a different prong of the investigation."

He was right, of course, and she felt mollified. And at long last, she realized with deep pleasure, Clint was evidently seeing her as a full partner in the detecting business. Too bad she had just about decided to leave.

"Anyway, you didn't hear about this yet because we didn't have time, but I found a diary. I was reading it when you turned up. Mary Jo, like so many damn fool criminals, kept a diary of her misdeeds. Everything was in there except where she had placed Jennifer McCallum after she kidnapped her. Maybe someday I'll understand the psychology of it, but it sure as hell beats me why they so often write it all down. It's as if they need to keep some kind of memento. Like counting coup, or notching a gun, or keeping the severed heads…"

"A diary. You found her diary! That's fantastic! It admits to everything?"

"Yup. She murdered Jeremiah, Dugin, Fred Oakley and Charlie Avery—and Jennifer's birth mother when she blew up Nick Dean's car. She stole the evidence that Tracy Hensley found, caused Judd to break his leg, framed Ethan Walker, tried to block Elizabeth Bishop's investigation…and even kidnapped old Homer."

"Good heavens, she's been busy! Will the warrant cover the diary?" Finding things not explicitly listed on a warrant was chancey unless they were in plain sight.

"Oh, yeah. She must have been writing in it this morning because it was lying open on the desk in the back room. Plain sight." He flashed a grin. "Trust me, it's covered. We can use it to nail her."

"That means you'll inherit the ranch and all the money. You and Jennifer, I mean."

"Yeah." He paused to park the car in front of her apartment, then turned to look at her. "You won't mind if I give it all to charity, will you?"

Something about the way he was staring at her caused her heart to rise into her throat. "Uh…what does it matter what I think?"

"Plenty. Come on, let's get the hell inside. We need to

do some serious talking about things like money and your career.''

Yeah, she thought miserably. Her career. Probably something like, ''Dakota, how fast do you think you can move to the far end of the planet so you don't mess up my investigations in future?'' Or, ''Dakota, we're really not making it as partners, so I'm recommending you be transferred to Outer Mongolia.'' Something like that, no doubt. After all, she reminded him of her cousin.

Inside, he closed the door and leaned back against it. ''Sit down,'' he said. ''Please.''

She sat on the rocker, feeling very much like a condemned prisoner. Instead of waiting for the ax to fall, she decided to forestall it. ''I'm going to try to find a job in another police department.''

''You are?''

She nodded, not looking at him. ''Maybe Missoula. I have family there and it would be so nice to go back home. They've probably got a good opening or two. Heck, police departments always have a few openings.''

''I see.'' He looked at her sitting there, her hands clasped in her lap, her head bowed, like a young girl expecting to be chastised. That meant something important, but he couldn't for the life of him concentrate on interpreting her mood when his own had just plunged into the depths of hell. This afternoon, when Mary Jo had been pointing a gun at her, he had discovered just how important Dakota Winston had become to him. Hearing her say now that she was leaving left him staring at a future that was too barren and painful to tolerate. He cleared his throat. ''You don't like being my partner?''

''I didn't say that.''

''Then why do you want to leave?'' He braced for her answer, like a man facing a firing squad.

She looked up at him. "Because you hate having me for your partner."

"Did I say that?"

"Plenty of times! Good grief, Clint—"

"Okay, okay," he said, raising his hand. "Okay, I admit it. I said it when we started working together. Mainly because I never had a woman partner before."

"*And* because of my cousin."

"And because of your cousin. But I've changed my mind. You're a pretty damn good partner, Winston. A little impulsive, but that'll wear off in time."

It felt as if someone had poured warm syrup all over her heart. She wanted to reach out to him and curl up in his arms...tell him how delighted she was that he liked having her as a partner, except... "Thank you, but I'm leaving anyway. I have to."

"Why?" He sounded almost angry now, and she dared take a peek at his face, which turned out to resemble a lowering thunderhead.

"Because—because..." Oh, why the hell not? she asked herself. It'd scare him off, probably make him take to his heels in headlong flight and spare her any more painful explanations. "Because I'm involved with you. Because I can't work with you comfortably and have a casual affair with you at the same time. I'm just not built that way. It hurts too much to be with you when I know...when I..."

"When did I say we were having a casual affair?"

"You didn't have to! When you look at me you see my cousin, and you hate her. You only slept with me to get even with her!"

"I did not! Damn it, Dakota, I tried to tell you last night and you wouldn't listen. I don't make a habit of having casual affairs with my partners!"

"You've never had a female partner before!"

His patience snapped then, and he demanded, ''What the hell does that have to do with anything?''

''Everything!''

''Oh, for Pete's sake...''

Giving up all hope of a rational discussion with this frustrating woman, he scooped her up out of the rocking chair as if she weighed nothing and carried her back to the bedroom. There he put her carefully down on the bed, then stretched out on top of her, holding her still with his weight and kissing her into silence.

Not that she wanted to protest. Clint had a Neanderthal streak, but it was one of the things she loved about him. Besides, this was where she wanted to be, and where she would have stayed forever, if only he had wanted her. She needed these last moments with him, needed to store up every touch, every texture and taste. Needed to garner every little memory she could because all she was going to have would be the memories.

When Clint at last tore his mouth from hers, they were both breathless and looking at each other with glazed eyes. ''Now,'' he asked hoarsely, ''will you listen to me?''

She didn't want to listen to him. She didn't want to waste any of these precious minutes with arguing. What she wanted was for his mouth to cover hers again, and his body to take her to the places only he could take her.

''Dakota...Dakota, I wasn't taking advantage of you. I wasn't using you to get even with your cousin, I swear. I may have expected initially that you would be like her, but even then I wouldn't have made you a stand-in for her. Besides, that was a long time ago...''

He kissed her again, and rolled to one side so that they lay facing one another. His arms wrapped around her, holding her to him so snugly that she could feel every hard contour of his body. He smelled so good, like soap and man, and some indefinable scent that was Clint. Her throat tightened with anticipation of pain to come. She didn't want to give him up. She didn't know how she would be able to stand the anguish.

"Dakota...sweetheart...I've been so scared..."

For the first time what he was saying really penetrated the fog of impending loss and sorrow that engulfed her. She turned her face up and looked straight into his gray-green eyes. Her insides clenched in reaction when she saw that his eyes were moist. He was weeping! "Scared?" she repeated.

"Terrified." He tried to laugh, but failed miserably. "I wanted you so bad...it was beginning to feel as if nothing else in the world mattered. As if nothing else existed that was important. I wanted to see you smile and hear you laugh, and the whole damn world could go hang if I could just spend every minute of my days with you..." He was rambling, and didn't care. The words just kept tumbling past his lips as he breached a silence he'd kept for far too long.

"I was...I was... Oh God, Dakota, I never wanted to care about anyone so much they could hurt me and I was scared to death because I cared that much about you. Cared more than that much. The sun didn't rise in the morning until I saw your smile..."

She hardly dared to believe her ears, but the tears were still in his eyes, and his arms were so tight around her that it almost hurt.

"I can't let you go," he said. "I'll die if you go..."

And all of a sudden she was crying, too. Crying and laughing as her hands knotted into his shirtfront and tried to pull him even closer...

"Don't leave," he asked hoarsely. "Say you won't leave me...I love you... Please don't go..."

"I couldn't leave you! I can't!" She managed to wind her arms around his neck and at last pull his mouth to hers. "I love you," she said against his lips, sobbing with joy, tasting the salt of his tears. "I love you!"

A ray of sunlight found its way across the room, and touched the tears on their faces, making them sparkle like jewels.

"Marry me," he commanded huskily. "Say you'll be mine forever."

"You could ask," she suggested, even as her heart soared like a rocket heading for the moon. "You could say please…"

He laughed then, a ragged sound, and kissed her cheek. "Please."

It still sounded more like a command than a request, but she'd have been lying to herself if she pretended she cared. There was only one word she wanted to say now, and she said it.

"Yes! Oh, yes!"

Epilogue

Clint looked out across the yard behind the rebuilt bunkhouse, smiling as his friends and neighbors laughed and talked and ate, while their children darted around their legs and climbed in Martha Preston's apple trees. Martha herself sat in a lawn chair in the shade of one of those trees, nibbling on barbecue while she talked with Dakota.

Sawhorse tables had been covered with red-checked oilcloth on which sat huge bowls of potato salad and platters of barbecued ribs. Judd, Rafe and Sterling tended the barbecue pit while the other men tried to get up a softball game with an assortment of the kids. Rafe had long since resigned himself to "sharing Mary Jo's DNA." The part he liked best, he said, was having a half-sister in Melissa North.

Melissa was there, too, with her husband Wyatt. Travis and Lori Bains had their hands full with a toddler and their newest arrivals, twin girls. Kane and Moriah had showed up with Moriah's father, Homer Gilmore, and much to Clint's surprise, Homer seemed to be positively in his element among all the small children. They sure seemed to like him.

Sara Dean and Maris Rivers were comparing due dates while their husbands hovered protectively around them. Luke also kept an eye on his rambunctious son, Cody.

Jonas Bishop had managed to live down being a famous novelist, and his wife, Elizabeth was chasing him up the nonfiction bestseller charts with her own book. She decided to chart the legal injustices dealt to Native Americans and had cornered Maggie and Jackson Hawk.

And even Ethan Walker had overcome his shyness enough to show up. He kept one eye on his niece and the other on his wife, Kate, who was intently discussing a Supreme Court case with Raeanne Rawlings. The two women looked as if they'd forgotten there was anyone else on the planet.

Across the yard Winona Cobbs was trying to ignore Lily Mae Wheeler, as the other woman tried to figure out the ingredients in Winona's delicious pies. Clint shook his head ruefully. He pitied Winona because Lily Mae was always relentless in the pursuit of information.

Clint felt a tug on his pant leg and looked down to see Jennifer McCallum staring up at him with wide eyes. Nearly two years had passed since her kidnapping, and she appeared to have forgotten all about it. "Can I see?" she asked.

Clint squatted slowly, taking care not to lose his balance, and tugged the receiving blanket back from the sweet face of his six-week-old daughter. "Isn't she pretty, Jenny?"

Jennifer stared at the baby somewhat doubtfully. "I guess. What's her name?"

"Selena."

"She's kind of tiny."

"She'll grow. Someday she'll be as big as you."

"Mom says I'm her aunt."

"That's right."

"How come?"

"Because you're my sister. That means you get to be Selena's aunt."

Jenny nodded; then, losing interest, she trotted off to join a group of girls playing with dolls.

Clint wandered over to Martha and Dakota, but when

Dakota offered to hold the baby, he shook his head. "She's comfy right where she is."

Dakota's incredibly blue eyes smiled up at him. "I can sure understand that," she said softly, a hint of yearning in her tone. His blood pulsed heavily, as he thought about the night ahead. The doctor had said it was okay now, and he had sure missed making love to his wife.

Dakota pinkened a little and looked at Martha. "Tell Clint what you were telling me, Martha."

"I was just saying you two ought to buy this place from me," the old woman told him. "My kids will just sell it to some stranger after I die, and I'd rather see the two of you living here. It's your home."

"But what about you?" Clint asked.

"I'll just rent the bunkhouse from you."

Clint shook his head. "No. Absolutely not. But we could all live in the big house together…"

It was right, he thought, as he turned slowly and looked around at his friends, at the orchard, at the wide open spaces, at the mountains. It was perfect.

Dakota rose and stood beside him, smiling up at him as he wrapped his free arm around her shoulders.

"It's home," he said, looking down at her.

She nodded. "It's home. *Our* home."

*   *   *   *   *

Coming in January 2002 from Silhouette Books...

THE GREAT MONTANA COWBOY AUCTION

by
ANNE McALLISTER

With a neighbor's ranch at stake, Montana-cowboy-turned-Hollywood-heartthrob Sloan Gallagher agreed to take part in the Great Montana Cowboy Auction organized by Polly McMaster. Then, in order to avoid going home with an overly enthusiastic fan, he provided the money so that Polly could buy him and take him home for a weekend of playing house. But Polly had other ideas....

Also in the Code of the West

Available at your favorite retail outlet.

Where love comes alive™

Visit Silhouette at www.eHarlequin.com

PSGMCA

Silhouette Books invites you to cherish
a captivating keepsake collection by

DIANA PALMER

They're rugged and lean…and the best-looking, sweetest-talking men in the Lone Star State! CALHOUN, JUSTIN and TYLER—the three mesmerizing cowboys who started the legend. Now they're back by popular demand in one classic volume—ready to lasso your heart!

You won't want to miss this treasured collection from international bestselling author Diana Palmer!

LONG, TALL Texans

CALHOUN, JUSTIN & TYLER
(On sale March 2002)

Available at your favorite retail outlet.

Uncover the truth behind

CODE NAME: DANGER

in **Merline Lovelace's** thrilling duo

DANGEROUS TO HOLD

When tricky situations need a cool head, quick wits and a touch of ruthlessness, Adam Ridgeway, director of the top secret OMEGA agency, sends in his team. Lately, though, his agents have had romantic troubles of their own....

NIGHT OF THE JAGUAR
&
THE COWBOY AND THE COSSACK

And don't miss
HOT AS ICE (IM #1129, 2/02)
which features the newest OMEGA adventure!

DANGEROUS TO HOLD is available this February
at your local retail outlet!

Look for ***DANGEROUS TO KNOW***, the second set of
stories in this collection, in July 2002.

Where love comes alive™

Visit Silhouette at www.eHarlequin.com

PSDTH

When California's most talked about dynasty is threatened, only family, privilege and the power of love can protect them!

THE COLTONS

Coming in January 2002

TAKING ON TWINS

by

Carolyn Zane

With Wyatt Russell's reappearance in Wyoming, Annie Summers realized the safe life she'd built for herself and her twins had just been blown apart! She'd loved Wyatt once before—until he left her to pursue his ambitions. She couldn't open herself up to that kind of heartbreak again—could she?

Available at your favorite retail outlet.

Silhouette®

Where love comes alive™